SHE SHALL HAVE MURDER

"Deftly developed plot and smooth polish of humor."
—*Chicago Sunday Tribune*

"Engaging." —*Kirkus Review*

SHE SHALL HAVE
MURDER

DELANO AMES

PERENNIAL LIBRARY
Harper & Row, Publishers
New York, Cambridge, Philadelphia, San Francisco
London, Mexico City, São Paulo, Sydney

First PERENNIAL LIBRARY edition published 1983.

Library of Congress Cataloging in Publication Data

Ames, Delano, 1906-
    She shall have murder.

    (Perennial library ; P638)
    I. Title.
PR6001.M54S5 1983   813'.54   82-48240
ISBN 0-06-080638-9 (pbk.)

83   84   85   86   10   9   8   7   6   5   4   3   2

To Mother,

with my love.

SHE SHALL HAVE MURDER

1 ✳ The idea—not so much for the actual murder as for a book about it—struck me when Major Stewart said: "Somebody ought to bump off that woman." All he meant was that Mrs. Robjohn had kept him in the office with her old complaint—which has been driving us all crazy for months—for nearly ten minutes past the time when he inevitably announces, "We normally have one about now," and pushes off around the corner to the Carfax Arms.

But it started me brooding. Give the irritable phrase an undertone of suppressed hatred, let his grey eyes narrow slightly (two venomous slits would be overdoing it), and you've got the beginning of a book.

Of course it's bound to be a thriller, and originally I had had in mind something more psychological—about a girl called Scandal who painted, and her impact upon a shell-shocked Oxford Don whom she met in Aix-en-Provence. It was going to be called *Waking—No Such Matter*.

For years people have been saying to me, "It must be so interesting to work in a lawyer's office, you meet so many interesting people; you ought to write a book." Slowly I have been worn down by this sort of thing, and now every time Sarah's typewriter is free, I think, Now I'll do it. Sarah's typewriter is free now.

Actually Dagobert is responsible for the murder angle. Murder at the moment—late November—absorbs him. In between "seeing people" about jobs, he has been reading thrillers—about three a day.

I have nursed Dagobert through several such crises before: Gregorian Chant last year, followed by wild flowers and sixteenth-century French Poetry. My mind is a jumble of Mixolydian Modes, nipplewort and Joachim du Bellay—to which fingerprints and strangulation are now being added.

It has not occurred to Dagobert to write this himself—his style is to conceive great works rather than to execute them. He will inspire me, and correct my spelling. In any case his latest hobby is *my* writing a thriller.

I tapped out on Sarah's typewriter:

"For a long moment Major Stewart stared thoughtfully at the mahogany door through which Mrs. Robjohn had disappeared. Then, with a curiously furtive gesture, he removed the telephone receiver and swiftly dialled a Soho number."

I reread this without conviction. The number, actually, will have been a suburban number, a Purley number, and the conversation will have gone something like this:

"Hello—it's Jimmy."

"Oh, Jimmy, you shouldn't! Babs will have to get cross with her Jimmy!"

Babs is the one on the other end of the wire, the Fair Maid of Purley, the future Mrs. Stewart. Barbara Jennings is a nice girl (if somebody would only tell her about giggling) who can—I must in all fairness admit—wear her hair in a flat bun on top. Her father is Sir Ben Jennings, who owns the larger part of Glasgow. She is an only child, and she has this quaint—and apparently endearing—habit of referring to herself in the third person.

"I love you," says her Jimmy, who in these frequent con-

versations goes right to the crux of the matter. "I have loved
you continually ever since an hour ago, when I last telephoned."

"No, you haven't! You've been flirting with Jane and
Sarah and Rosemary." (The girl is not so dumb as she
sounds.) "You are *very naughty*, Jimmy, and Babs is *very
cross* with you." The italics are her own.

The conversation continues along these lines for some
time, not getting very far one way or the other. About eight
times a day they bill and coo over the 'phone, quarrel, make
it up again, go through the entire if limited emotional gamut
of young love. I get the details from Rosemary, in whose room
there is a telephone extension. Rosemary is our Chief Clerk.

Meanwhile I can hear Mrs. Robjohn padding along the
corridor making unconvincingly towards the front door. She
has been with Major Stewart for less than half an hour, and
not one of us really thinks he or she will get off as lightly as
this. A watchful silence reigns over the precincts of Daniel
Playfair & Son, Solicitors. We shall all breathe again when we
hear those padding footsteps descend the echoing wooden
stairs which lead down into Mandel Street.

She has reached our front door, the hinges creak. There is
an ominous pause. I type furiously, thinking in this way to
create an atmosphere of great busyness.

But no. Here it comes. A pause. She's changed her mind,
thought of something, perhaps a new codicil to her will.

"Miss—er, Miss Swinburne," I hear her say to Sarah,
"I wonder if you'd tell Mr. Playfair I'd like a word or two with
him. It's rather important."

"I'm sorry, Mrs. Robjohn. Mr. Playfair is still engaged."

Sarah has certain remarkable streaks of stubbornness in
her. One of them is the way she protects the sanctity of the

hour in which Mr. Playfair does his crossword puzzle from Mrs. Robjohn.

The two face each other. I don't dare open my door and peek out; but I can see the scene quite vividly enough to describe it: Sarah, her golden-red hair tumbling around her shoulders, a pencil stuck jauntily in one ear, her hands on her hips, literally barring the passage to Mr. Playfair's room at the end of the dark corridor. Mrs. Robjohn, peering at her with watery but surprisingly shrewd eyes, as though she were trying to place where she had met the girl before.

It was a contest of wills really, and the outcome was always uncertain. Sarah was more vital, energetic, blunt; but Mrs. Robjohn was more persistent. By Fabian tactics she not infrequently outwitted Sarah.

"How tiring!" Mrs. Robjohn spoke as though to herself rather than to Sarah. "It's most important—and I *may* have no further opportunity."

"Could I take a message into him?"

"No, thank you so much. The matter is private."

"Couldn't you telephone and make an appointment in the usual way?"

"I have no telephone." She spoke sadly, as though other luckier people in this world have telephones, but not Mrs. Robjohn. "And—" she lowered her voice so that I had to strain my ears to hear her words—"and *you* know what public call boxes are . . ."

Between Sarah and Mrs. Robjohn a curious antagonism exists. Antagonism is too strong—a lack of sympathy would describe it better. Mrs. Robjohn is a bore—every legal firm has such clients. But when we are not cursing her we feel a little sorry for her. Sarah doesn't. Sarah thinks she's a self-centered old harridan, who blatantly plays for our sympathy.

And yet Sarah can always be depended upon to give sixpence to an obviously bogus beggar.

Mrs. Robjohn for her part does not help to smooth the situation. She treats Sarah as though Sarah were beneath her notice. With Rosemary it is always "that nice Miss Proctor" or even "that dear Rosemary Proctor." Rosemary's father was an Indian-Army officer, and "these things, whether you like it or not, do make a difference." She is equally gracious to me, though luckily she knows less about my private life and antecedents.

She delights in referring to Sarah as "your little typist" in front of Rosemary and me, which embarrasses us much more than it does Sarah.

There was a long pause in the corridor. Mrs. Robjohn and Sarah were still facing each other, neither willing to give ground.

"It's about my will," Mrs. Robjohn said finally. "If anything . . . well, if anything *happened* . . . I'm sure Mr. Playfair would be very annoyed if he thought I was being *kept* from him."

"I'll tell him that you called."

"Perhaps I could see Miss Hamish?"

I typed furiously. I am Miss Hamish.

"Miss Hamish is busy with the Hartley Estate."

"Then I'll just have a word with Miss Proctor. You see, I don't want to go out into the street—*just yet.*"

I heard a door open—not the front door—and I knew that Mrs. Robjohn had not been utterly defeated. Sarah a second later poked her head into my room.

"Poor old Rosemary's for it!" she said. "The Robjohn nabbed her before I could fling myself into the breach. Where are those sardines?"

"Under the pile of Templeton's deeds."

"I thought we could toast up these rolls on Jimmy's fire. He's 'having one' about now."

Neither Jimmy nor Rosemary awfully like Sarah's calling them by their first names, but I've long since given up trying tactfully to tell her so.

"Hello," she said, peering over my shoulder. "Started the book at last? Am I in it?"

"I'm just making some rough notes. You'll probably turn out to be the murderess."

"I could be—easily. I'll give you a shout when the kettle's boiling." And she was gone, whistling, as though one whistler of "the latest" (Oates, the office boy) were not enough.

2 ✳   A few minutes later my door opened and I saw Mrs. Robjohn.

"They're out there again, Miss Hamish," she announced without preamble.

"Who are out there?" I'd tried this question before, but I couldn't think of any other one.

"That's just the trouble. I only wish I knew." She slipped down uninvited into the shabby leather armchair beside my desk, removing a crumpled bag of boiled sweets from her string bag.

"There were three of them." She carefully counted out exactly half of the boiled sweets and put them on my desk. "I brought these for you, Miss Hamish," she said.

They were half her week's ration and of course I im-

mediately felt like a beast. In recompense I tried to be sooth-
ing or at least sound interested.

"But what did they look like? Were they men?"

"Yes. This morning all three were men—they almost
always are."

"Are they always the same people?" I asked.

She shook her head; the point clearly baffled her as much
as me. "That's just the trouble. They keep changing. That's
so that I can't get their descriptions and report them to the
police."

"But what makes you think they are watching you?"

"That's rather obvious, Miss Hamish, isn't it?"

"No, it isn't at all obvious!"

I get a kind of carefully restrained heartiness into my
manner during these eternal colloquies with Mrs. Robjohn,
the hopefully cheerful tone of voice you use with small children whom you suspect are about to be difficult. Unfortunately Mrs. Robjohn sees through me at once.

"You know you're imagining the whole thing! Now have
a cigarette and in a minute Sarah will have the kettle boiling
and we can all have a nice cup of tea."

She gathered up her gloves at this, her string handbag and
three or four of the small unidentified parcels she always
carries around with her. "I don't want to be a nuisance," she
said, pretending to rise. "I realise you're all very busy."

This was a familiar twist in the conversation and called
for no comment beyond vague conciliatory throat noises. I
gave her a cigarette and continued along the lines I knew
she hoped I would.

"But where were these men, Mrs. Robjohn?"

"Just across the street. They knew I was coming here and
they were waiting. One of them wore a grey felt hat, turned

down at the brim to hide his face. He was pretending to light a cigarette. The other two had their backs to me. I didn't look at them carefully but I think they were shabbily dressed—like workmen, you know—and they were pretending to carry something between them, a crate or something."

"They weren't *pretending*, Mrs. Robjohn," I said, still gaily, but a little strained by the effort. "They *were* carrying crates. They're unloading things at Derry and Toms' goods entrance."

She smiled wanly at my wrongheadedness. "What about the one in the grey felt hat?" she asked cunningly. "Why do they do this to me, Miss Hamish? Why do they?"

Her watery eyes sought mine wonderingly, and her voice quavered. Her fear was real even if the three men weren't, and her bewilderment was unbearably pathetic. I didn't want to feel sorry for her, so I began to feel angry.

"What have I done, Miss Hamish?" she appealed. "What have I done?"

"Nothing, of course."

But as I spoke it occurred to me that I know almost nothing of her past, though Mr. Playfair had known her vaguely for years. Her files with us go back to 1914.

"Then *why*, Miss Hamish?"

That quavering, perplexed "Why?" still makes me feel shaky when I recall it.

I rose abruptly and went to the window. Below there was the usual traffic jumble—vans, lorries and private cars parked under the impression that Mandel Street—of which our office is Number 11—is a quiet little backwater off Kensington High Street. By pressing my face to the windowpane I could distinguish the now gaunt plane trees which mark Mandel Square and catch a glimpse of the stone steps leading up to the door of Number 17, the apartment house where Mrs. Robjohn lives.

"I don't see anyone who looks in the least suspicious," I said to Mrs. Robjohn.

But oddly enough, I found myself suddenly frowning and thinking I *did* see someone who looked as though he were loitering, and who also looked vaguely familiar. He was standing on the corner of Mandel Street and the High Street where he had probably paused to buy a newspaper. A young man wearing a mackintosh turned up at the collar and a dilapidated felt hat. I gained an impression of sunburned features. He seemed to be gazing intently in the direction of Number 11 Mandel Street, towards me, in fact.

At this point I took hold of myself. I was beginning to catch it too!

"Come here," I said to Mrs. Robjohn, "and point out your men to me."

She made a little fluttering sound in her throat. "I wouldn't go near that window for anything," she said, and I knew from the way she said it that she wouldn't. "I wouldn't give them the chance."

"The chance? What do you imagine they're going to do?"

"I don't know what they're going to do," she whispered. "That's almost the worst part of it. The uncertainty."

Instead of exploding in exasperation I played along with her for a while. If you take "they" seriously, she calms down and becomes almost human. If you tell her the truth: that she is a self-centered old woman with a persecution mania, who is making up the whole farrago in order to attract attention to herself, she merely smiles, sadly and tolerantly, like one who has seen things hidden from lesser men.

"The uncertainty—yes, I see that," I said.

She looked grateful, almost cheered up. "I've been bolting my door every night as you suggested, Miss Hamish," she said conversationally. "And I also see that the windows are securely latched. You know I've kept the black-out curtains up ever since the war, and that's been such a comfort. At least they don't know when I go to bed."

I tried not to imagine the atmosphere in that hermetically sealed, over-furnished room. I am not a fresh air fiend myself, but I do like to let the cigarette smoke out.

"What does Dr. Forsyte say?"

"Dr. Forsyte gave me some pills last time he got me there," she said darkly.

"And did they do you any good?"

"Naturally I didn't take them, Miss Hamish." She lowered her voice confidentially. "I took them to a little chemist in Mill Hill and had them analysed."

In spite of myself I was getting interested.

"And what were they?"

"They were aspirin. . . . At least that's what the chemist *said* they were." Her fingers seemed to flex and writhe as though they led a separate tortured existence of their own.

Watching them I suddenly felt a little like screaming. Instead I continued to watch them, thus at least avoiding her eyes, while she said:

"*He* couldn't be in it too, could he, Miss Hamish?"

"No, I'm sure he couldn't."

Her hands had been lovely once. Though the flesh on them was wasted and almost transparent and the joints were twisted with arthritis, there was still agility and strength in those fingers. They seemed to be executing rapid scales and arpeggios in an endless, intolerable fugue. I remembered Mr.

Playfair's saying that Blanche Robjohn had once been a promising concert pianist.

Blanche. It struck me as peculiar somehow that she should have a first name, that anybody could ever have called her Blanche.

And yet Mr. Robjohn—whoever he was, or for that matter is, for he seems to have faded out of the picture long before my day and whether he is living or not I do not know —must have called her that. And I suspect that Mr. Playfair may have too; although their manner together is always strictly that of family solicitor and client.

In fact how very little I know about Mrs. Robjohn's background. Relations? Half a dozen distant cousins of her own generation somewhere in Somerset.

And then there is her son.

Almost all I know is that his name is Douglas, and he lives in Ceylon. She brought him into the office once just before the war was over. That was in the days before Major Stewart and Rosemary and Oates. In those days Sarah and I, impeded by Mr. Playfair, used to guide the destinies of Daniel Playfair & Son alone, and do a very efficient job of it, too.

Douglas Robjohn had just been invalided out of the Services. He was a captain in the Commandos and covered with ribbons. I retain an impression of an agreeable young man of the strong silent type, very tongue-tied. He helped Sarah make the tea for us, and broke the spout of the teapot. We still use the same teapot, and the spout is still broken.

Otherwise Douglas left little impression on the office. He went off to Ceylon shortly afterwards, I believe, and has remained there ever since. Mrs. Robjohn told me the other day that he is coming home for a visit just before Christmas this year.

It is almost the only reference she has made to him since that day many years ago. He is her sole heir, but she never mentions him. This fact is remarkable, for reticence is not her strong point.

For a moment I watched the fingers continue their noise-less fugue. The fugue simile struck me, for her mind must have been like that: a medley of voices with the single theme constantly reiterated—varied, inverted, altered, transposed, but always the same: *"they are after me."*

Suddenly she gathered her belongings together and stood up. She smiled quite normally and held out her hand.

"Thank you so very much, Miss Hamish," she said cheer-fully. "I've enjoyed our little chat. I think they've gone now. You've been such a comfort. I'll see myself out. I know the way." And she was gone.

This time she walked briskly down the corridor, paus-ing only to call out good-bye to Rosemary. I was left won-dering how on earth I had possibly been any comfort to her, and wishing I could return the compliment. . . .

3 ✳   I brightened immensely when Sarah appeared making a schoolgirl grimace of distaste to in-dicate that the coast was clear. Oates had gone off with a packet of deeds to the Land Registry in Somerset House; we wouldn't see *him* again until about tea-time. Neither of the partners, Junior or Senior, was in the habit of bolting his midday meal. This meant that we had nearly an hour and a half alone for girlish chatter and such important questions

as whether sloping shoulders and the lower waistline were here to stay.

This was the part of the day we all enjoyed most. Major Stewart was under the manly but false impression that it was dull for us—three women—to hold the fort alone. That was why—before Babs had taken over—he had often invited one of us out to luncheon himself. I was the first thus honoured; then, for about a week, Sarah was singled out, and finally Rosemary. We can still embarrass him if, when the three of us are together and he enters the room unexpectedly, we all abruptly stop talking. He thinks we are comparing notes.

He hates being laughed at. I kept myself under control for a month or two, largely because I was having a prolonged emotional crisis about Dagobert at the time and had totally lost my sense of humour, even about men who told me I was "different."

Sarah only lasted two or three luncheons, the last of about half an hour's duration.

Rosemary, who has far too much sense ever to laugh at any man unless he's telling a story clearly labelled "joke," stayed the course the longest of any of us. It was only with the formal engagement to Babs that the relationship between Junior Partner and Chief Clerk became more regularised.

Rosemary Proctor tells us she is twenty-nine (my age) and for lack of documentary evidence we do not contradict her. She has been very pretty; in fact she is still very pretty, when the light is right. She dresses well, if a shade youthfully, and she knows how to make up. She is very kind to animals, and spends hours in queues to provide for the Pekinese and white Persian cat with whom she shares a small flat in Knightsbridge. She is immensely efficient and knows what to do when fuses go wrong. Mr. Playfair thinks highly of her.

She worked for the firm before the war which she spent, knitting a great number of khaki garments, in a safe area.

She had a sad war; both the men she was engaged to—one an American, the other Canadian—were killed. At least, that's the assumption; for neither was heard of after the liberation of Paris.

I seem to have got off on the wrong foot in attempting to describe Rosemary Proctor; I have somehow missed her charm. Dagobert, who has read the above three paragraphs says I haven't so much described Rosemary as I have myself—whatever that means.

Actually I'm very fond of Rosemary; but since it is unlikely that anybody will believe me I'd better jot down the hard facts I know about her.

She lives with her pets in Oratory Street, off the Brompton Road, in something called a "flatlet" which means there's a bookcase built round the divan bed. There is a small upright piano, always brilliantly polished, which she never plays. In the kitchenette, neat, shining and immaculate, there are two plates on the floor, one pale pink, labelled CAT, the other blue, labelled DOG. Her clothes are tidily arranged in the built-in cupboard, each frock on its own hanger with a tiny sachet of lavender dangling inside. Her shoes are all on trees and stand neatly in a compartment of their own labelled SHOES.

"Jane," Sarah announced as we entered Rosemary's room, "is writing a novel. We're all in it."

"I'm delighted. I've always said Miss Hamish is so clever."

Sarah missed the gentle correction, the "Miss Hamish" part that is, while I thought over the "so clever."

When Sarah had run out for a can-opener Rosemary

said thoughtfully: "I've often thought that no novelist has really ever done justice to women like ourselves—business girls who live alone like me and—" she stared ingenuously at me with her pale violet eyes—"like me," she repeated, "and you. The life we try to make for ourselves outside of office hours. Our special problems."

"You mean men?"

"Yes, if you must put it bluntly. After all, one is no longer eighteen and it's sheer hypocrisy to pretend that— er . . ."

"Oh sheer!" I agreed hastily.

For some reason—and this is not sheer hypocrisy—I never like to get involved in this sort of conversation with Rosemary. It was too apt to work round to the subject of those men—apparently numerous—whose intentions towards her were obvious.

Her attitude was: "You must have had similar situations to deal with, Jane. How do you handle them?" I wasn't quite sure whether her object was to probe the mysteries of my private life or to dilate on her own. Probably both.

"It's all right for Sarah!" she said a little bitterly. "*That* kind plays at a job for a year or two, and then runs off with some pimply faced bank clerk and starts raising families. But slightly more intelligent women, I mean women of our own sort, what do *we* do?"

"What indeed?" I echoed.

This line of conversation was beginning to depress and I was relieved when Sarah returned with the can-opener.

"Sorry," she apologised for being so long, "somehow it had got itself into Jimmy's In-Basket. That reminds me," she added: "What did Jimmy and Babs have to say today?"

Rosemary glanced at me significantly. The glance signified, "Isn't it a little *infra dig* to discuss these things in front of the typist?"

I said: "Yes, what had they to say?"

"Didn't you listen in?" prompted Sarah with the bluntness of youth. She was blissfully unaware of the finer points, such as whether it was altogether honourable to listen in to other people's telephone conversations, and whether—if you had—you wanted to admit it.

"Well, I happened to remove the receiver to make a call of my own," Rosemary confessed reluctantly, "and I did just happen to overhear a little of it."

"I bet you did!" Sarah laughed.

I kicked her gently; nothing will ever teach her common diplomacy. Rosemary flushed, but I could see she was dying to spill something. Personally I was dying to hear it.

"The usual billing and cooing?" I suggested.

"Well, no. Apparently not. Very much *au contraire*."

"Good!" Sarah exclaimed heartlessly. "A row."

"The row of the century," Rosemary nodded.

All three of us, I'm afraid, leaned forward eagerly. Not that we were jealous of Barbara Jennings—the male reader who concludes this will be guilty of a common fallacy—but there was something not entirely displeasing in the thought that Babs and her Jimmy were in emotional difficulties.

It seems that that imaginary conversation I have given between Babs and Jimmy was wildly inaccurate. The voice on the Purley end of the phone was not all gentle, whimsical reproof of her "naughty Jimmy."

She had rung him, not from Purley, but from a call box around the corner, to announce that "this was the end."

"We, it seems, are the villains," Rosemary explained.

"We?" Sarah said. "What fun."

"But she's always on about us," I pointed out. "She thinks any unattached female has only to take one look at her Jimmy to join the scramble."

"But this time she says she's got proof," Rosemary said. "And she's not going to marry a man who keeps a harem and she's just posted back the engagement ring. Apparently she's got names and dates and everything, and as far as I could make out her facts are not far wrong. That day you came back from lunching with him, Sarah, in a taxi by yourself—"

"I should dam' well think so!" Sarah interrupted indignantly.

"I made a shorthand note somewhere," Rosemary consulted a pad on her desk. "Here it is. It was on the fifth of August, according to Babs's information. Is that right?"

Sarah shrugged. "Search me."

"Well, she's got dates and places," Rosemary continued, again consulting her pad. "You, Jane. July the eleventh, twelfth *and* thirteenth; the Savoy, and, according to Babs, God knows where afterwards!"

"What a filthy mind she has!" I snapped. "If she wants to know we walked interminably while he talked interminably and I got blisters on my heels. But what business is it of hers? She didn't even know him in July."

"You're just thrown in for background, to show what kind of man he is."

"I like that way of putting it," I nodded.

Babs, it seems, was generously willing to overlook me. A man of the world like her Jimmy was permitted an early indiscretion or two, an occasional disreputable ex-acquaintance like myself. What stuck in her gullet, apparently, was what I can only describe as the attempted pass at Sarah and more especially the continued liaison with Rosemary herself. These had both taken place in Babs's heyday.

"You did rather overlap, didn't you," I said.

"The worst part of it is," Rosemary said, "she says she knows he emerged from my flat last Tuesday well—rather late. Past midnight."

"Did he?"

"Well, yes, as a matter of fact. We'd both worked late here at the office. We walked along together to the bus stop and then suddenly decided to go to the films. Afterwards he more or less had to feed me—"

"And you more or less had to have him in for a cup of cocoa."

"Yes. Then we talked a bit . . ."

"I know how he talks."

". . . about the office and legal work generally, and when he finally went it was later than either of us realised."

"Ummm," I rumbled, "these things happen."

Sarah asked the only interesting question.

"How on earth did Babs get all these details?"

"That's the rather worrying part," Rosemary said thoughtfully. "An anonymous letter."

"Good Lord!" Sarah exclaimed. "Do you mean to say someone's taken the trouble to write down all that rot and post it to the poor sap?"

"Apparently. She got the letter in this morning's post."

"But who in the world . . . ?" Sarah broke off suddenly.

The implication of her question had struck us all simultaneously. The only person in the world who could have known all these things was someone in our own office. In fact one of ourselves.

4 ✻   I may have given the impression that no work ever goes on in our office and that we spend all our time chattering about men. This is false. We generally work like beavers.

Our sardines were scarcely swallowed before the telephones began to ring: irate executives demanded Major Stewart, Estate Agents begged for appointments with Mr. Playfair and people started to swarm in to swear to affidavits. Rosemary remembered that the accountants were coming tomorrow, which meant spending all afternoon and probably most of this evening deep in her ledgers. Sarah recovered her typewriter and began to bang away furiously at a draft conveyance.

I sat in Major Stewart's room, which is the first one on the left as you enter the office, kept clients at bay, answered 'phone calls and did the our-Miss-Hamish act for the benefit of elderly Kensington ladies. ("Mr. Playfair will be so upset he missed you; he had to go down to the Law Courts this afternoon. . . ." "Major Stewart may be a little late today; an important business luncheon. But can't I help you? Let me just find your lease. . . . Yes, the landlord is responsible for the drains. I'll get on to the builders at once and see that they're put right. I'm so sorry there was any inconvenience. . . . No, please never hesitate to bother me. It's no bother at all. After all, that's what I'm here for, isn't it?") That sort of thing.

In such pursuits I was rushed off my feet until nearly four when Major Stewart turned up. He had been having luncheon with Babs and obviously he hadn't been enjoying it much. He looked strained and his grey eyes were haggard. I was dying to ask him what had happened, but as I officially knew nothing about it I couldn't.

He glanced at me and remembered that he was a Junior Partner.

"Any messages, Miss Hamish?" he said.

"Nothing of any importance. I've made a note or two on your pad of a couple of people who want you to call them. Sampson and Sons is the only one there's any hurry about."

"Thank you, Miss Hamish."

We were all very formal suddenly; I took the hint and began quietly to withdraw, every inch the unobtrusive secretary. I had reached the door when he stammered:

"Oh, Miss Hamish, there *was* one little matter. It's not really important, but well—would you mind closing the door? —it's rather private."

I came back, all agape. He rose, forced a smile and held out his cigarette case. "Cigarette, Jane?"

I took one. I noticed that his hand was shaking as he lit it for me.

"By the way," he said, as though he had just thought of it, "do you remember those rather jolly evenings last summer when we went to the Savoy?"

"They are a continual source of consolation to me," I admitted.

He laughed, a little heartily. "That's what I like about you, Jane, you've got such a good sense of humour. You're different from some of the others."

"It takes all kinds to make a world," I said airily.

He agreed. I thought for an awful moment he was going to suggest that we go Savoying together again. But no such luck.

"Not that it makes the slightest difference," he began again, working round to the point, "the whole thing was quite open and aboveboard, but I was wondering if by any chance you might ever have mentioned our little . . . er, our little . . ."

"Jaunts?" I suggested.

"Yes. If you ever mentioned them to anyone."

I saw what he was driving at and considered my answer, trying to be truthful.

"Probably. You know what women are. We chatter among ourselves."

He flushed slightly at my admission; he'd suspected something of this sort. I could see him making an inward resolution to confine his future jaunts to women outside the office. Even primitive man—Dagobert points out—had this much common sense. They chose their women outside the tribe, a custom called exogamy.

"Quite," he said. "Naturally. . . . Er, would you also have mentioned the matter to Mrs. Robjohn?"

I tried not to let him see that this question had suddenly gone home. For until this moment I hadn't even thought of it myself. Of course I'd told Mrs. Robjohn all about my flights into high society! She was always most interested in the romantic life of Sarah, Rosemary and myself. It was one of the few subjects—horse-racing, oddly enough, was another—which could distract her from "they." Naturally I had not deprived her of the simple pleasure of any of the publishable details.

"Yes, I think so," I nodded.

"I see." He sat down abruptly in his swivel chair. "It doesn't make the slightest difference," he said.

I might have felt sorry for him if it had not been so plain that he was sorry for himself. Of course he was passionately keen on Babs; he was one of those men who are always passionately keen on someone. Babs was also the only child of a very rich man. All right—he was suffering. So what? He'd asked for it.

"By the way, Jane," he said, "my engagement is off."

"I am sorry."

"The only thing," he rumbled on, brave, patient and long-suffering now, "is it seems sort of a pity after the formal announcement in *The Times* and all our plans. Still . . ." He shrugged philosophically. He was furious.

"Babs is off to stay with some relations in Scotland," he continued. "I saw her off at King's Cross."

"Did you?"

"Yes. So that's that." He snapped the point of the pencil with which he was doodling on the blotting paper. Jimmy is not used to having women walk out on him.

I heard Mr. Playfair's stealthy footsteps pass the door on the way to the sanctuary of his office. I would give him time to disrobe and settle himself at his desk in the attitude of a man who has been there all the afternoon; then there were a couple of urgent matters for him to attend to.

I began to withdraw again, leaving Jimmy to face this thing alone. He looked up from his blotting pad.

"I've got a couple of seats for the new Firth Shephard show," he said. "If you're not doing anything tonight, Jane . . ." He'd already forgotten about exogamy.

"This is where I came in—six months ago," I said.

"I only thought you might . . ."

"I'm the world's worst holder of hands," I shook my head firmly. "My shoulder is rotten for weeping on. Besides I must get on with my mending. Sorry."

The next hour was full of violent activity. I got Mr. Playfair to sign half a dozen letters and to placate Pirbright Watkins & Co. by telephone. We had no return visit that afternoon from Mrs. Robjohn.

Oates looked in from his pleasure excursion to the Land Registry with a copy of the evening paper containing the racing results. As usual he had won heavily, thanks to the tips he gets from some "blokes he knows." Laughing Boy in the 2:30 at Newbury had come in at twenty to one. Our office boy has some very shady—if useful—acquaintances.

Shortly after five Sarah dashed off to Lillie Road where she lives with her father and invalid mother. She seemed in an especial hurry. Major Stewart had already vanished without saying goodnight to anyone. Mr. Playfair had suddenly become very conscientious and hardworking—he always does this about five when we're supposed to close shop—and it wasn't until nearly ten to six that he left. I like to see him off the premises, but I don't waste much time after he's gone. I locked up the strong room, dabbed powder over my face and poked my head into Rosemary's room, where she was still at her ledgers.

"Can I help?" I asked tremulously.

But I need have had no fear. Rosemary was not a great admirer of my ledger technique.

"No thanks, Jane. It's very sweet of you, but I'll manage. I'll have to come back again this evening. But as it so happens I've nothing else on."

I drew a breath of relief.

"I've left everything reasonably in order," I said. "Did you mention anything about last Tuesday to Mrs. Robjohn?"

"Last Tuesday?"

"The night Jimmy had that cup of cocoa with you."

She went on totting up her column of figures. "I may have. I don't know." She finished her column and made a neat check mark beside it. "Probably," she said after she had given my query fuller consideration. "I usually chat pretty freely with the poor old thing. It distracts her."

"It does. Goodnight. See you in the morning."

"Cheery-bye," said Rosemary.

5 ✳   I met Dagobert in the Nag's Head in the Earls Court Road. We see a lot of the country by this method of foregathering in different pubs, though we sometimes miss each other which leads to mutual recriminations.

Dagobert was already there, having a game of darts with one of the natives. I'll say that for Dagobert: he's never late if you arrange to meet him in a pub.

"Just a minute," he said. "I only need ninety-one. A treble seventeen and a double top."

He weighed his dart delicately, flipped it. It went into the treble seventeen. Concealing his surprise, he poised his second dart. It landed bang into the double twenty.

"For a moment I was afraid I wasn't going to do it," he said with a smugness which destroyed the instinctive pride I had felt in his achievement. Actually he was just as startled and pleased as I was; for he insisted on buying his opponent a drink.

"There's no doubt about it," I said, "you *are* good at pub games. Of course you get more practice than most people. Any luck today with your job?"

"No, but I've been doing a lot of thinking."

There were almost too many replies to that, so I restrained myself. After a trying day at the office it is always a mistake to start an argument before you've had at least one drink. Besides I was genuinely delighted to see Dagobert. I always am.

We all had beer—because that was what Dagobert's defeated opponent wanted and Dagobert thinks women ought to learn to drink pints on these social occasions—and after a few words about the weather, which was remarkable for the time of year, we went.

The next port of call was The Swan in Lillie Road, a modest establishment which we had never before visited. I was vaguely aware that we were in the Sarah territory, in fact her house is diagonally opposite The Swan, but I had no idea that Dagobert had guided me there for a purpose. I keep forgetting his one-track mind.

"I've been thinking," he said as we settled down in a corner with our usual tipple, gin and sherry, at a glass-topped table behind a potted fern. "I've been thinking about that book of yours. Have you got on with it today?"

"Not very far. Little things like my job keep interfering."

"Good," he said, missing—or ignoring—the sarcasm. "Because I've got a theory."

"Seriously, Dagobert, why don't you write the thing?"

"We've been into all that." He swept the suggestion aside. "You want to write a story about a murder in your office. The whole thing starts when people begin to receive anonymous letters."

I gulped suddenly. "How's that?" I echoed feebly.

"You know. Poison-pen letters. Giving the low-down on the seamier side of all your lives—well, not yours, maybe. But Rosemary's, say, and that tame Adonis, what's his name, Stewart. There must be a lot of nasty details in his private life. So this Mrs. Robjohn, say, starts spilling the beans about him. She's in and out of the office at all hours and knows all about everyone. One day the first of these anonymous letters arrives. You walk into Stewart's office and find him in a state, pale, haggard . . ."

"Do you mind if I have another drink?" I said.

Later, of course, I would tell Dagobert accurately what had taken place in Major Stewart's office this afternoon, even though it meant dragging up the Savoy excursions again, but at the moment I felt the need for peace and tranquillity, and another subject of conversation.

"Tell me what you did today," I suggested when he returned from the bar.

"I told you. I've been thinking. I also went to the movies," he added as an afterthought.

"What did you see?"

"Nothing any good. Do you know why we came here tonight?"

"Presumably for a drink."

"Yes, of course. But why the Lillie Road?"

"I give up. Because you liked the name?"

"Because Sarah lives around here somewhere, doesn't she? I thought we'd look in on her."

"Well, think again," I said.

I have never introduced Dagobert to any of my office colleagues. The office is out of bounds to him. I am not one of those women who brings her office worries home with her; or vice versa.

"I want to become more closely acquainted with the characters involved," he explained. "I thought I'd start with Sarah because she's the youngest."

"Oates is the youngest."

"Is he? . . . Since we're here we might as well start with Sarah."

"She is, of course," I admitted, "the prettiest."

"Is she? I wouldn't know."

"And you're not going to find out!"

He separated his long legs from the legs of the glass-topped table and rose. "The landlord probably knows where she lives," he said. "Sarah Swinburne, isn't it?"

"Don't shout names," I warned. "Sit down and modulate your voice. The man who's just come in and ordered a mild and bitter is Mr. Swinburne, Sarah's father."

I indicated the short stout man in a shiny serge suit and a bowler hat, who was exchanging greetings with the proprietor behind the bar.

I should have known better than to take Dagobert into my confidence. I'd no sooner pointed out Mr. Swinburne than he strode across the room and clapped him on the shoulder.

"You're Mr. Swinburne, aren't you? Sarah's father," I heard him say. I couldn't hear what followed, but he and Mr. Swinburne seemed to be hitting it off like old buddies. They had a pint together and when finally Mr. Swinburne left Dagobert rejoined me.

"He's an awfully interesting chap," he said. "Drives a train on the Underground. By the way, we've drawn a blank about Sarah."

"How do you mean?"

"She's not home. She's stepping out with her young man. In fact, she's already stepped, about half an hour ago."

"Are you sure?"

"Unless she's grossly deceiving her father."

"Sarah hasn't even got a young man—at least that I've ever heard of."

For some reason I was a little annoyed with Sarah. Nipping off like that without so much as breathing a word about it to me. It didn't seem fair. Sly, that's what it was. Then I laughed at myself. I was delighted to think that Sarah was enjoying herself. She'd tell me all about it tomorrow, anyway.

We found a taxi and went to Ciccio's in Church Street for dinner: delicious Italian things. We sat over coffee and cigarettes until nearly nine-thirty, both in the mellow and friendly mood engendered by civilised dining. We discussed North Africa and Ella Wheeler Wilcox.

Afterwards we walked to the bottom of Church Street and turned right into Kensington High Street. It was a raw evening, but we both felt warm and energetic. A white haze, which might later turn into fog, softened the familiar outlines of the High Street.

We passed Mandel Street, at this hour silent and deserted and curiously foreign to me. I slipped an arm sentimentally through Dagobert's. He was not at all foreign. The occasion seemed vaguely symbolic: on my left my office, my legal career; on my right, Dagobert.

I was rudely torn from these reflections. Indubitably

starry-eyed I had not recognised, as we passed the post office, the bundled-up figure stooping cautiously over the letterbox as though to slip something surreptitiously inside.

But the bundled-up figure *had* recognised me.

"Oh, Miss Hamish," Mrs. Robjohn called after me, "how very lucky!"

6 ✳   I had been miles away from Mrs. Robjohn and all that she represented. I should have known you cannot prowl around the neighbourhood of Mandel Street at any hour of the day or night without running the very real risk of encountering her. But it was too late to do anything about it. I withdrew my arm from Dagobert's and returned.

"Hello, Mrs. Robjohn. Isn't it a bit chilly for you to be out?" For it struck me for the first time that it was chilly.

She ignored my silly question. She had more important things to think about. "Just on the corner over there," she whispered. "Across the street. Do you see them?"

I looked, and smiled reassuringly. "I see two people waiting at the bus-stop, that's all."

"They're pretending to wait," she said significantly. Then to clinch the thing she added: "A bus just went past. *They didn't take it.*"

"Obviously it was the wrong number bus," I pointed out, forgetting what a small part reason played in her mental processes.

"They saw me post that letter."

"Does it matter?"

"Yes, it does matter, terribly. The letter was private and confidential. It was addressed to Mr. Playfair and marked Private and Confidential."

In order to post this letter Mrs. Robjohn had walked the length of Mandel Street, from the Square to the High Street; she had passed our office door where she could have slipped it through the letterbox, thus saving herself the extra walk and a two-penny ha'penny stamp. But her mind doesn't work like that.

"Good evening, Mrs. Robjohn," Dagobert said cheerfully, joining us. "I'm Dagobert Brown, Jane's lover. I've heard so much about you."

She perked up at once, extending an almost skittish hand to him. She appreciated Dagobert's old-fashioned use of the word lover.

"I hope you don't believe half Jane says about me!" she smiled back at him in a flirtatious way I can only describe as outrageous. "I'm not half such a scandalous old woman as people say."

Dagobert shook his head. "I can see at a glance that you are. A very dangerous woman and a bad influence on impressionable young creatures like Jane."

Mrs. Robjohn was delighted with the accusation. She laughed gaily. Her down-trodden, harassed manner vanished at once. She looked twenty years younger suddenly. I stared at her aghast. I'd never seen her like this. I actually believe the old fool was trying to get off with Dagobert.

"I was just trying to persuade Jane to walk home with me," she lied. "I live in the Square at the bottom of the street. Why don't you both come?"

"We'd love to," said Dagobert enthusiastically.

"We'll just walk along to your door with you," I said. Then, to show Dagobert the sort of thing I'd often told him about, I added: "Mrs. Robjohn believes those two men by the bus-stop are following her."

"Of course they are!" Dagobert agreed. "I'd be following her myself if I weren't a respectable, engaged man."

Mrs. Robjohn burbled happily. "I think your Dagobert Brown is a thoroughly wicked man, Jane," she said, taking possession of his arm. "I don't approve of him at all!"

We crossed the road and walked together down Mandel Street to the Square. Mrs. Robjohn was getting on with Dagobert like a house on fire. No one could have been saner. She was really most exasperating.

When we entered Mrs. Robjohn's room I waited for its effect upon Dagobert.

It was a large room, but the immense patterned carpet was turned in at the ends, for it had originally covered the floor of an even larger room. On top of this there were Oriental rugs, Persian, Bokhara, Chinese, all overlapping each other. Then came a layer of occasional tables, nests of them, brass platters on carved ebony stands, pedestals for vases and bits of statuary, chairs, Chippendale and Hepplewhite, chairs stuffed with horsehair, chairs covered with tapestry and brocade. Around the walls lay the more solid pieces, massive sideboards with carved cupidons, monstrous tallboys inlaid with rare woods and mother-of-pearl, a four-poster bed with red velvet hangings. There were collections of majolica ware and snuffboxes in glass cases, not to mention a stuffed bird or two.

For all I know there may have been some valuable pieces among this heap of rubbish. But it always filled me with an acute sense of claustrophobia.

"It's cosy," said Dagobert. "It has character. I like it."

We lighted the gas fire and Mrs. Robjohn produced a bottle of South African port.

At the end of ten minutes Dagobert had her producing photograph albums. We looked at pictures of herself in the fashions of 1919. She'd been strikingly lovely as a young woman, with intelligent eager eyes and a full voluptuous mouth.

There were group pictures which suddenly interested me when in one, taken in 1920, I unmistakably recognised Mr. Playfair in a boater and flannel blazer.

Dagobert had picked out another man in the same photograph, a man with heavy, dominant features and a fierce black moustache.

"Who's that?" he said, pointing. "He's been featured several times."

"That? Oh, no one in particular."

She dismissed the query too rapidly, I thought. She flicked over the pages of the album quickly, and for some reason I was seized with the unreasoning conviction that the man in the black moustache had been—or still was—Mr. Robjohn.

Finally we came to a revolting photograph of a nude infant labelled "Douglas—age eleven months."

"The son and heir?" asked Dagobert.

She nodded. "They're adorable—*at that age*," she said, emphasising the phrase "at that age."

I left Dagobert and Mrs. Robjohn engrossed in albums and wandered aimlessly around the room. Thanks to the tightly fastened windows and the black-out curtains, the single gas fire had made the room almost too warm. I was feeling sleepy. The port could have contributed to this.

Mrs. Robjohn was showing Dagobert a diploma she had

received back in 1913 from the Royal College of Music. A scrapbook was reluctantly produced which contained photographs of her at the piano and notices of several public performances she had given. Very good notices, Dagobert told me later.

"What made you stop playing?" I heard him ask her.

"There were so many other things to do," she said. Did she speak in bitterness? I could only just hear what she added: "I suppose I didn't have the stuff of real greatness in me."

My own attention had suddenly been fixed elsewhere. I had wandered over to her Chinese lacquer writing desk to get a better view of the "Yorkshire Sheepfold" which hung in a gilt frame over it. On the desk I saw a pile of new one-pound notes, twenty-five or thirty of them, I estimated. But what fixed my attention was an open address book. Pencilled in it in Mrs. Robjohn's spidery handwriting I read: "Barbara Jennings, The Turrets, Purley."

Babs's address.

When I rejoined the other two around the fire Dagobert had just poured out the remainder of the port and the conversation had switched to horses. It seemed that Mrs. Robjohn had cleaned up a tidy sum on the 2:30 this afternoon at Newbury: Laughing Boy. This was the same horse that Oates had done so well with. Either they were in touch with the "same blokes" which seemed on the surface unlikely, or with each other, which was quite possible, though unexpected, or it was a coincidence, a twenty to one coincidence.

I gave it up. Clues were getting entirely too thick. And clues, incidentally, to what? To nothing, nothing yet.

Yet? What on earth was I expecting?

I was delighted when about half a dozen clocks in that

one-room antique shop suddenly began to wheeze, thump or tinkle eleven o'clock. With that hourly uproar no wonder Mrs. Robjohn complained of sleeplessness.

Dagobert rose. "I'd better take Jane home," he said. "She works, you know."

To my relief Mrs. Robjohn did not try to detain us. She thanked us warmly for "taking pity on a lonely old woman." She said it so sincerely that I felt touched and wished I'd been more entertaining. But she'd loved having Dagobert there. I had to admit he'd behaved very well and I patted his hand approvingly as he helped me on with my coat.

I had, of course, forgotten my gloves. I left Dagobert on the front steps while I went back for them. I tapped on Mrs. Robjohn's door and opened it. I apologised and recovered my gloves.

She was still smiling as she had been smiling all evening, and the port had given a touch of colour to her usually pallid chee¹ · But something had gone out of her eyes. I knew that blank, haunted expression only too well. Tonight's attack of sanity had passed, an hour's oasis in the desolate tracts through which her mind roamed.

"They're going to get me, Miss Hamish," she said dully, with intolerable patience. "They are, you know. . . ."

It was impossible to mutter the usual words of comfort which sufficed in the office. I said: "Would you like Dagobert and me to stay for a while?"

"No, Jane. You two run along. He's charming, your Dagobert."

She seemed all right again, or at least I persuaded myself she was. I murmured a hasty final goodnight and joined Dagobert on the steps. It seemed bitterly cold after the warmth inside.

"I don't think we ought to have left her," I said after we had walked back nearly to Kensington High Street.

"Good lord, why?"

I couldn't think of any very adequate reason so I didn't answer him.

"I don't know why you're always on about her," he remarked a few minutes later. "That woman is as sane as you or I."

"In fact I've been making it all up!" This is the kind of remark you make when you want to start a quarrel. I don't know why I made it, possibly because to quarrel with Dagobert would be one way of forgetting that look in Mrs. Robjohn's eyes. "In fact you think," I pursued, "that the mysterious people who are 'after her' and are 'going to get her' are real."

"I didn't hear her mention any mysterious people."

"I made them up too!"

"Did you?" he shrugged.

We walked on for a while in silence. Whether Dagobert was thinking, or whether he was merely paying me out for my unreasonable attack of snippiness, I couldn't tell. I am always snippy, cross and ill-tempered when I'm frightened, a most unfortunate reaction, totally depriving me of sympathy.

"I got several good points for your book tonight," he said finally.

"Shall we discuss it tomorrow?"

"Point one," he said, "Mrs. Robjohn is not our victim. She isn't the type to get murdered. Too obvious."

"Will you *please* be quiet!"

It was a totally unsatisfactory walk home. I was in a filthy humour by the time I arrived.

And to cap it all the gas fire wouldn't work. Apparently there had been another gas strike. I went to bed without a hot-water bottle.

7 * My impressions of the first few hours of the next morning, the thirtieth of November, are sketchy. I put them down as faithfully as I can in case they have any bearing on what occurred afterwards. Naturally I have edited them since and shall inevitably misplace the emphasis, making that which seemed trivial to me at the time sound important and vice versa. I can only try to recapture what I did, thought and felt at the time; I'm bound to be affected by what's happened since.

For instance that Private and Confidential letter which Mrs. Robjohn had addressed and posted last night to Mr. Playfair. The truth probably is I had forgotten all about it. And yet subconsciously I may have been looking out for it. For I remember clearly what private letters Mr. Playfair received that morning—one from his tailor, one from his bank and a Hobbies & Fretwork Ltd. catalogue.

Another point, vivid now, dim at the time: I *think* I noticed a charred piece of paper in Mr. Playfair's grate which *might* have been a letter recently burned. It might also have been left by the charwoman from the day before, and of course it might not have been there at all. It wasn't, the next day when I had special reason to look.

Except for Mr. Playfair himself, I was an easy last to reach the office that morning. I removed my things, sent

Oates out to the post office to get some postal orders and got down to the Hartley Estate. I had said a perfunctory good morning to the others. Again, any impression they made on me is largely an imaginative reconstruction.

Major Stewart was cold and smug, the big business executive who has it all at his finger tips. I think he had a hangover. There was an open bottle of aspirin on his desk. "Oh Miss Hamish," he greeted me, "I shall want you in about an hour to take some shorthand." He anticipated my protest by adding: "Miss Swinburne is already behind with her typing."

Rosemary, cool and collected and looking as though she had spent a leisurely hour dressing instead of scrambling into things thrown the night before over a chair as I had done, was with the chartered accountants. Last night she had come back to the office after a lettuce sandwich and a raw cabbage salad, and her ledgers were a model of clarity. "It is a pleasure," as one of the accountants put it, "to do Miss Proctor's books."

Sarah, as Major Stewart had already said, was behind with the typing. She was hard at it catching up when I stuck my head in to say good morning. I thought she was looking flushed and excited as though she were simply bursting to have a moment alone with me to tell me all about it. This, too, may be a preconceived notion of mine; for that's what I was expecting her to want to do.

As I said, I got down to the Hartley Estate. I drafted out a letter in reply to a long series of tricky questions Sir John Hartley had put to us. It meant digging into a couple of volumes of Forms and Precedents and consulting the Rents Restrictions Acts.

My ambition was to have it ready for Mr. Playfair's

approval and signature before he went out to luncheon. By about eleven o'clock I was beginning to feel fairly pleased with myself, when I came across a point dealing with Company Law which floored me. It was humiliating, but it meant running to Mr. Playfair for help.

I tapped at his door hesitantly and went in. He got up as I entered. Unless he is deep in work he always rises when Rosemary, Sarah or I come in, and begs us to sit down. I don't think he is to this day really reconciled to having women work in offices. He always treats us as though we were something halfway between clients and friends of the family. It may not lead to efficiency, but I must say it makes working for him agreeable.

Mr. Playfair is nearly seventy and has been talking for years about retiring. He will not, I am convinced, retire until he is no longer able to climb the stairs which lead up from Mandel Street.

His wife died in childbirth. It is a pity there is no son to go with the Daniel Playfair & Son of the firm's name. That son never actually worked in the office. He was killed at the age of eighteen in the second battle of the Marne. He had just published a first volume of poetry and would probably not have become a solicitor anyway, so perhaps I am being sentimental about his carrying on his father's profession.

Mr. Playfair looks very young for his age and we all think him extremely handsome. He is tall, emaciatedly thin and dresses smartly, in the fashion of a generation ago. He has fine eyes, which can twinkle engagingly over the top of his spectacles, and a noble brow. His voice is gentle and I've never heard it raised in anger.

He said as he rose: "And what can I do for you, Miss Hamish? Do sit down."

"It's the Hartley matter, Mr. Playfair," I said, sitting on the edge of the chair he indicated. "That letter from Sir John."

"I'm sure you're dealing with it perfectly," he smiled. "There's no great hurry, is there?"

That, of course, was the weakness I had to fight against, the one flaw in his character. No hurry. There was never any hurry.

"I thought, if we could clear up this one point," I made a pencil mark beside the query on Company Law which had stumped me and pushed Sir John's letter in front of him, "I thought we might get off the reply today."

"Umm, let's see." He glanced over the relevant paragraph. "Umm, quite, er, quite . . . May I offer you a cigarette?"

I took one and he leaned forward to light it, reluctantly eying Sir John Hartley's letter.

"I had an interesting bridge hand at the Club last night," he said. "I didn't quite know what to do about it."

"You promised me you'd see the film at the Academy last night!" I said severely. The film was about Switzerland, which he is passionately interested in, and this was the last week.

"Oh yes. The hand must have been the night before."

"Did you see the film, then?"

"I did. Excellent, very excellent indeed. The snow scenes and the Alps." He adjusted his spectacles on the high bridge of his nose. "I had six hearts to the queen-knave—I'd opened the bidding with them, you know—my partner supported me so, having three outside aces, I went four. Game." He kept glancing at Sir John's letter as though its presence on his desk was distasteful to him. "Umm, that would be clause seventeen . . ." he murmured. "The trouble is we made a small slam and old Alistair argued that I ought to have bid something called the four-five no trump convention. I don't care for all these conventions. How would you have bid my hand, Miss Hamish?"

"Exactly as you did, Mr. Playfair," I said promptly.

"Good. I'll tell old Alistair that. He's an argumentative old codger. Now where were we?"

"Sir John's query," I suggested hopefully.

"Of course." He glanced down through his glasses, mumbling something to himself, something about the Act of 1937, then up over the top of them at me. "Have you looked over *The Times* crossword this morning, Miss Hamish?"

I said I hadn't, not yet having had time as I was most desirous of *finishing the letter to Sir John Hartley*.

He opened the top drawer of his desk, the drawer in which in American films all normal businessmen keep a loaded revolver. Mr. Playfair instead kept it full of Hobbies & Fretwork catalogues, a few odd nails, a fretwork saw which he had bought and forgotten to take home, private letters, bits of string and sealing wax and an old pack of playing cards. I thought for a moment he was proposing to deal out the hand which had caused old Alistair such pain, but he only removed *The Times*, open and folded back at the cross-word puzzle. I suspect he had thrust it hastily into this drawer when I tapped at the door.

"I'll have a shot at it later," I said, trying to ward off the inevitable session, "when *we've* got this letter off."

"Yes, do, Miss Hamish," he agreed. " 'She was disguised as Fidelio,' " he pursued, peering down through his glasses. "I suppose it's an anagram, it's the same number of letters."

"Wasn't there someone in the opera," I said, getting

interested in the thing in spite of myself, "who dresses herself up as a man?" My memory of the opera was vague; in fact I'd never heard it.

"Leonora, of course!" he said, fumbling for a pencil. "That's seven letters too. And the 'L' fits in. I haven't seen 'Fidelio' since before the war, the first war, I mean." He half closed his eyes and sat back in his chair reminiscently. "I remember the night vividly, more vividly than I remember things which happened last week. They say that's a sign of getting on, Miss Hamish. Dear, oh dear." And he sighed, not at all unhappily.

I flicked my cigarette ash in the ashtray and tried to squint at the crossword. I could already see the Hartley matter being deferred until tomorrow.

"I used to go to Covent Garden frequently in those days. I grew very fond of music—especially piano playing." He smiled gently, privately, obviously miles away. "It's a very fine sight, a woman's fingers on the ivory keys of a pianoforte. D'you know in the eighteenth century, Miss Hamish, they used to make black keyboards just to show off the artiste's fingers."

I found myself wondering, in my incurably imaginative way, if he could be thinking of that Blanche Robjohn who had once played the piano so beautifully. The charming Blanche Robjohn of the wide floppy hat and the diaphanous muslin dress I had seen in the group photograph last night, the photograph in which I had also recognised Mr. Playfair himself.

"I never seem to listen to music these days," he mused aloud. "I don't know why. Now, where were we?"

"Sir John," I began, taking advantage of the opening.

"Yes, of course. Leonora," he said, and he filled in the

seven letters carefully. "That will help immensely, Miss Hamish. Thank you."

He smiled across at me graciously as though to suggest that the interview was finished. He glanced wistfully at the clues, and then with reluctance refolded the paper and replaced it in the drawer.

"Hello," he murmured to himself. He scrabbled for a moment in the bottom of the drawer as though looking for something. "Hello," he repeated, "I'd have sworn I left those . . ." He broke off as he looked at me. He seemed surprised to find me still there. "Or did we take them down to the strong room?" he said.

"Something missing?" I asked.

By this time he had begun to open other drawers, rummaging through them in perplexity.

"It's those coins Mrs. Wolf-Heatherington brought in for safe custody," he explained. "I was showing them to old Billings of the bank the other day, he knows a lot about old coins, you know. I thought he might be interested."

I remembered the coins he meant. Clients are always bringing in bits and pieces for us to keep in the strong room, boxes of broken jewellery, bundles of old letters, keepsakes and the like. Mrs. Wolf-Heatherington's handful of old coins was typical of the kind of thing.

"Were they valuable?" I asked.

He shook his head. "No. According to Billings the lot was not worth more than a pound. One William the Fourth shilling in mint condition, the rest the sort of small change travellers bring back from the Continent. But it's vexing to have mislaid them. I was nearly sure I left them in this drawer."

"I'll have a look in Mrs. Wolf-Heatherington's box in the strong room," I promised.

"Do, please Miss Hamish. Meanwhile I'll turn out these drawers. They could do with it, in any case," he admitted with a twinkle.

Mrs. Wolf-Heatherington's William the Fourth shilling and the rest of her coin collection did not seem to me nearly as important as the matter of a certain outstanding letter to Sir John Hartley. I stuck stubbornly to my chair.

"Shall we look now," I said, "or shall we first finish the point raised in . . ."

He was saved by the telephone. I tried to look patient as he reached out for the receiver.

"Are you there," he said. "Yes, I'm speaking. No? You don't say? Dear, oh dear."

He didn't raise his voice, nor was there any particular emotion in it, but for some reason I found myself edging forward on my chair.

"Just a moment," I heard him say. Then he covered over the mouthpiece and glanced at me. "In answer to Sir John's inquiry, Miss Hamish," he said, "quote to him paragraph twelve of the Companies Act of 1929. You'll find it in the fifth volume on the left there on the top shelf, page 116. It will tell him exactly what he wants to know."

This time I had no excuse for lingering. I whispered thank you, took down the volume indicated and tiptoed to the door. As I closed it behind me I heard Mr. Playfair saying into the 'phone:

"But of course. I'll come round immediately."

He left the office almost at once. From my room, where I had found the page which did give me precisely what I—

and Sir John—wanted to know, I heard his departing foot-steps. They seemed more hurried than usual.

I finished my draft and made a fair copy of it on the machine in Rosemary's room, ready for Mr. Playfair's signature when he returned.

He did not return that morning. About an hour later he telephoned Major Stewart. Major Stewart came into my room.

"Mr. Playfair has just telephoned," he said. "He wants us to look out the draft of Mrs. Robjohn's will."

The brief remainder of that morning was a rush. But at the first opportunity I slipped outside for a moment, to catch a breath of air partly. I went into a public call box and 'phoned Dagobert. I needed badly the sound of his voice.

"It's Jane," I said to him when he answered. "You were wrong about Mrs. Robjohn not being the type to get killed. She's just been found dead."

8 ✳ Nearly a week has passed since the events which culminated in my telephoning Dagobert from the public call box. During this week life in the office has returned to normal. We miss Mrs. Robjohn's continual visits; it isn't quite the same without her, but most of our clients are elderly, and inevitably in the course of time they die. We grow used to running down to the strong room in search of suddenly needed Last Wills and Testaments.

Among the tasks I have performed during the past week, the chief has been writing the above narrative. I have done it at the express behest (for "behest" read "perpetual bullying") of Dagobert, who wants my impressions while they are fresh in my mind.

He has read over the MS. three times, emitting occasional grunts and provocative "Ahs" and wandering around the room kicking things. He has just come, he says, to the inescapable conviction that Mrs. Robjohn was murdered.

Nothing will shake his conviction.

Before dealing with the vagaries of Dagobert's imagination, I'd better put down the unvarnished facts. They can be varnished afterwards. The facts—which are good enough for the police, the Coroner, the deceased's solicitor, her doctor —but not, of course, for Dagobert—are as follows:

Shortly after eleven o'clock on the morning of the thirtieth of November Mrs. Hawthorne, the landlady of Number 17 Mandel Square, observing that the curtains of the ground-floor front room were still undrawn, knocked at the door to inquire whether her lodger, Mrs. Blanche Robjohn, might be ill. There was no answer. Mrs. Hawthorne knocked repeatedly and becoming worried unlocked the door with a spare key she had. (The door was therefore not bolted on the inside.)

An overpowering smell of gas greeted her and instantly she grasped what had happened. The unlighted gas fire was still hissing faintly and the room was filled with gas. She dashed across and turned off the fire, threw back the curtains and flung open the windows. Then she ran to the four-poster bed in which Mrs. Robjohn was lying. Mrs. Robjohn was apparently dead.

Mrs. Hawthorne escaped from the still gas-filled room and ran to the telephone in the hall outside. There she telephoned Dr. Forsyte, whom she knew to be her lodger's medical adviser. Dr. Forsyte arrived shortly afterwards—the room was by this time free of gas—and his preliminary examination confirmed Mrs. Hawthorne's first conclusion that Mrs. Robjohn was dead. Later he certified that her death had been caused by gas poisoning. Meanwhile, leaving the dead woman in the four-poster bed in which she had apparently slept as usual, Dr. Forsyte telephoned her solicitor and the police. Mr. Playfair went to Number 17 Mandel Square immediately and identified the body. The body was then removed to the mortuary for post-mortem examination and Mr. Playfair locked up the room.

When this was done Mr. Playfair telephoned Major Stewart and gave instructions that the draft of the deceased's Last Will and Testament be found.

Barclays Bank were Mrs. Robjohn's executors and they asked us to act on their behalf. We immediately sent off a cable to Ceylon to inform Douglas Robjohn of his mother's death and to ask him to call on us as soon as he reached London. In the event of his now deciding to cancel his proposed visit to England—Mrs. Robjohn had told us she was expecting him a week or two before Christmas—we added that a copy of the will would be immediately dispatched. We instructed our Valuer to make an inventory and valuation of the contents of Mrs. Robjohn's room for the purpose of Probate. The bank supplied us with a list of her holdings and securities. We placed a brief notice of the death in *The Times*.

Meanwhile the inquest had taken place. It did little but establish the facts recorded above. Mr. Playfair attended it on behalf of the firm. Before he went I told him of my visit to Number 17 the night before the tragedy. It was his opinion that I had no relevant information to give the Coroner and he advised me not to attend. (He always shields Rosemary, Sarah and me from the grimmer sides of legal practice.)

At the inquest a representative of the West London Gas Company stated that the gas had failed at about five minutes past eleven p.m. on November the twenty-ninth, and had come on again at about one-thirty a.m. on the thirtieth. The public had been warned by both press and radio of varying pressure.

From this, a clear picture of what had happened was easily arrived at. Mrs. Robjohn's fire had gone out at five past eleven. Since the fire was already out, she had neglected to turn off the tap. When the pressure had come on again two and a half hours later, she was asleep and unconscious of the fact that the tightly sealed room was filling with gas.

The Coroner recorded a verdict of "Accidental Death."

That is the whole story and the more I look at it the more flawless it seems. A hint of mystery here and there would, admittedly, improve it; but I can't see one.

Dagobert can, but he has a little difficulty in putting his finger directly on the point.

"Where was Stewart on the night of the murder? And why does he call himself 'Major' anyway—he's not in the Army!"

"How should I know? And it wasn't a murder. It was accidental death. . . . He had two tickets for the Firth Shephard show."

"Did he use them?"

"I don't know."

"You're a hell of a detective."

I explain that I'm not supposed to be a detective. I'm a simple law clerk, earning six pounds ten a week. He, Dagobert, is apparently the detective.

"What about the Private and Confidential letter she posted that night which Mr. Playfair never received?"

There was that. And there was also the anonymous letter which had caused such havoc in the Babs-Jimmy romance. They didn't exactly mean that Mrs. Robjohn was murdered, but they were loose ends.

"What about the charred remains of a letter you saw in Mr. Playfair's grate that morning?"

"I'm not at all sure I did see them."

"The thing is lousy with clues. They stick out a mile." He measured out another whisky in the best amateur detective fashion. "I wish I could see them."

Over food that evening I brought him up to date on what had gone on in the office. Not much, in fact, had gone on which could possibly interest him. We had had a reply to the cable sent to Douglas Robjohn, stating that Douglas had already sailed for England.

"Did they mention the name of the ship?"

"Yes. It was the S.S. *Van Dam.*"

Dagobert immediately jotted down the name in a notebook. But I plunged him into gloom with my next remark.

"It arrived in Southampton late this afternoon," I said. "Mr. Playfair checked up on its time of arrival as soon as we received the cable."

Dagobert was disconsolate. "If the S.S. *Van Dam* had only arrived in Southampton a week ago, the day of the murder, think of the possibilities. It would have meant that Douglas, the sole heir to the Robjohn millions . . ."

"Thousands," I corrected.

". . . would have been here to do it himself. Do you remember that mysterious man you saw on the corner of Mandel Street and the High Street from your office window that morning when Mrs. Robjohn thought the three men were watching her? The one that you fancied looked vaguely familiar?"

"Yes."

"You said you gained an impression of sunburned features."

"So I did."

"What are men doing with sunburned features in London in November? Obviously they come from Ceylon. Obviously they're Douglas. I was counting on that."

"Well, here's one to think about instead," I said. "Do you remember the morning of the thirtieth when Sarah was catching up with her back typing? Do you remember I thought she looked as though she were bursting to tell me all about her party of the night before? Well, she wasn't bursting."

I was holding my audience, so I enlarged. Far from bursting with girlish confidences, Sarah has not to this day told me a word about that evening. There is a limit to human endurance and finally I had asked her outright what she did on the evening of the twenty-ninth.

"Let's see," she hesitated, searching her memory. "I cooked some cod for Mother and Father's supper. Then I darned Father's socks and helped Mother with her knitting pattern. Afterwards we listened to the wireless till bedtime. My usual sort of evening, really."

All this she had told me so casually and convincingly that I couldn't possibly call her a liar to her face.

Dagobert was delighted with the incident.

"It would be fascinating," he said, "if we found that that second ticket which Stewart had for the Firth Shephard show had been used by Sarah."

That would, indeed, be fascinating and, if I know anything about human nature, most unlikely.

"Find that out tomorrow," he urged, apparently unaware of the fact that I have to work with these people into whose private affairs he wants me to poke my nose. "Check up on everyone's movements that night—and don't forget Oates. Do that the first thing tomorrow . . . Tomorrow," he repeated. "Oh Lord!" He broke off with a sigh to look at his wrist watch. "I've got to get up at some ungodly hour."

"Do you mean before nine?"

He nodded sadly. "There's something I've been keeping back from you, Jane. I've got a job."

"No!" No wonder he'd been in such a depressed mood. "What sort of job, Dagobert?"

"With the West London Gas Company," he said.

9 *

I think Mrs. Robjohn's death upset me more than I've admitted. For some reason she did not merge into the "Robjohn Estate" quite so smoothly as usual when elderly clients die. Though the office routine was scarcely ruffled, you felt that Mrs. Robjohn was still a personality, invisible but none the less real. We rarely discussed her—except in connection with the administration of her estate—but I think all of us were aware of her. Mr. Playfair was frequently thoughtful—I almost said moody. For three or four days he hadn't the heart to do *The Times* crossword. Even Rosemary and Jimmy Stewart and Oates seemed affected.

And now a development has taken place that has entirely changed the complexion of her death: Dagobert has just *proved* to me that Mrs. Robjohn was indeed murdered!

I'd better tell it the way he told it to me at luncheon on the day he went to work with the West London Gas Company.

I had arrived at the office at about my usual time, half past nine, and the morning had been uneventful. Douglas Robjohn had telephoned to say he'd arrived in Southampton the previous day, and to fix an appointment with Mr. Playfair for that afternoon.

I had not followed Dagobert's instructions to check up on everyone's movements on the night of what he called the "crime." At that time I didn't believe there'd been any crime.

I was wrong.

Rosemary, Sarah and I had already opened fish paste and started brewing tea when Dagobert telephoned. He almost never telephones the office—I discourage this—and I was a little terse. He said he *had* to see me at once.

"Meet me at the corner of Church Street in three minutes," he said. And he rang off to avoid argument.

I was at the corner of Church Street in three minutes.

He said hello briefly and tucked my arm through his. He strode along so quickly I had to take two steps to his one, and he didn't say anything. We entered Kensington Gardens. We had them to ourselves, for it was a grim day. We found a deserted bench and for the first time Dagobert spoke.

"Jane," he said quietly and without a trace of his usual enthusiasm, "I'm afraid Mrs. Robjohn was murdered after all."

Though he had said something very like this a dozen times during the past week, I felt the skin around the corners of my mouth tighten. There was an empty feeling in my stomach.

"Go on."

"Jane, there's something that wasn't mentioned at the inquest and which you didn't tell me about. Mrs. Robjohn had one of those shilling-in-the-slot gas meters."

The empty feeling in my stomach became more acute, though I still could not see what difference the type of gas meter made.

"Yes, that's true," I confirmed. "It's in the little alcove where you hang up coats. Does it matter?"

"I'm afraid it does."

He was silent for a moment; as though he wasn't at all enjoying this conversation which, as I realised a few minutes afterwards, confirmed the belief he had held from the beginning. It is a curious fact, but I believe Dagobert hated proving himself right.

"I have just examined the gas fire which heated Mrs. Robjohn's room and checked up on how long it would burn for one shilling. One shilling would have lasted three hours and ten minutes."

I wetted my lips. "I see," I said. I didn't yet, but that was partly because I didn't want to see it all at once. I was, as it were, averting my mental eyes.

"On the morning of November the thirtieth the gas went on again at one thirty-three a.m."

"Yes, I know."

"Mrs. Hawthorne found Mrs. Robjohn's unlighted fire still hissing at eleven o'clock that morning—about nine and a half hours later."

"Yes."

"Nine and a half hours would have consumed at least three shillings."

"Yes." I spoke with an effort, for my throat was dry. I listened to my own words impersonally as though someone else were saying them. "That means there were at least three unconsumed shillings in the meter."

"It does. . . ."

Again he was silent. I wished he'd go on, quickly, get it over and done with. I contributed what I hoped was a breath of common sense, but I had suddenly lost confidence in common sense.

"In other words," I said, "it means that Mrs. Robjohn had put three shillings—I mean *at least* three shillings—in the slot."

Again silence. I wondered afterwards if my voice cracked slightly as I filled in the intolerable void of those silences. Dagobert tells me that I sounded quite normal.

"Go on," I said. Surely my voice rose. "Go on—go on! Mrs. Robjohn *didn't* put in those shillings! They were put in by somebody else! Purposely! Somebody who was trying to murder her! Who succeeded! Who in fact did murder her! Go on! Is that it?"

"I'm afraid that's it, Jane," he nodded.

His quietness, instead of grating further on my nerves, was ultimately comforting. Now that the truth was stated in so many words my incipient attack of hysteria abated.

"But how do you know, how can you be certain she didn't put the shillings in herself?" I said. He was going entirely too fast, I told myself.

"I *am* certain, however," he said. "Cigarette?" I shook my head. "Mind if I have one?" I shook my head again. "I

went around to Number 17 Mandel Square this morning," he
said.

"How did you get in?" I asked. "We have all the keys
at the office."

"I didn't go into Mrs. Robjohn's room. It was, as you
say, locked and there seemed to be too many people around
for me to enter via the window. No. I merely had a talk with
Mrs. Hawthorne."

I waited.

"We talked for a long time. We touched on the weather,
the Government and of course her late lodger. She told me
how peaceful Mrs. Robjohn had looked that morning when
she found her lying there in the four-poster bed, as though she
were asleep. She thought that it was best, perhaps, that the
poor creature should have gone like that, in her sleep, peacefully."

I nodded. "We all feel that in the office," I said. "It was
best, Dagobert. Believe me, it was. She was lonely, unhappy,
wandering and tortured in her mind. If anyone ever had a
right to cease living it was Mrs. Robjohn."

"I don't question her *own* right to take her own life," he
said coldly. "I question the right of somebody else to do it."

"Mrs. Hawthorne was telling you . . ." I prompted.

"We worked round to the last occasion on which Mrs.
Hawthorne had seen Mrs. Robjohn alive. This was at about
a quarter past nine that evening we met her. She was just
going out to post a letter. Mrs. Hawthorne 'chanced' to catch
a glimpse of that letter. It was addressed to Mr. Playfair and
marked Private and Confidential."

"Was it addressed in her ordinary handwriting?"

"I asked Mrs. Hawthorne that. Luckily her powers of observation were acute that evening. She 'chanced' to notice that the address on the letter was printed."

"So it could have been an anonymous letter."

"It *could* have been. But she told you she'd posted it when we met her at the post office."

"True."

"I discussed this letter with Mrs. Hawthorne rather particularly because I don't think it is of any especial importance and I wanted her to believe that the letter was the thing I was interested in. But what she had already told me—casually, completely overlooking its significance, I believe—was a small detail which I am convinced will hang someone."

I had twisted my gloves into a small tight ball. I now deliberately unfolded them, smoothing out the creases carefully.

"This small detail was . . . ?"

"As Mrs. Robjohn met Mrs. Hawthorne in the hall she came up to her and said: 'How fortunate! I was coming down to look for you. I wonder if you could possibly let me have a shilling for two sixpences?' That's all, Jane. Just that. '*I wonder if you could possibly let me have a shilling for two sixpences?*'"

For a long moment I said nothing. I didn't exactly think the thing out logically step by step. I think it came to me in a rush, like a word in a foreign language which you have totally forgotten and which suddenly presents itself from nowhere when needed. Mrs. Robjohn was murdered.

I said inadequately: "Did she let her have a shilling for two sixpences?"

"Yes. One. It was the only shilling between them. Before going out Mrs. Robjohn returned to her own room where she put this shilling into the gas meter. Then she came to the post office where she met us. Unless she met someone in the street during that three minutes' walk from whom she borrowed at least three more shillings she did not possess sufficient shillings to supply her fire with gas from one-thirty a.m. until eleven o'clock. I think we can dismiss the unlikely theory that she stopped a stranger in the street for those extra shillings."

I nodded.

"We are therefore left with the only alternative," he continued. "Someone else supplied them. Someone who visited her after we left. Someone who probably himself—or herself—inserted them into the slot, *after* the gas had failed. For it failed at five minutes past eleven, practically at the time we left. That much we can be certain of—and it's enough."

He threw away his cigarette, relaxing slightly. "From this point onwards we're dealing with conjecture," he admitted, and I could see he felt happier suddenly. Dagobert always enjoys theory more than brute fact. "I personally believe," he went on, "that when the gas failed, she did remember to turn off the tap. She was not scatterbrained about that sort of thing. She'd remembered to turn it off before going out to the post office, because we had to light it again when we arrived. I also believe she bolted the door after you left—she was having another attack of fright, you remember. I believe someone visitd her after we left, someone she knew well enough to let in. This someone was told—or knew—that the gas had failed. He—or she—*may* have suddenly been seized by the idea, or he *may* have arrived with the idea already in mind. At any rate he turned the gas tap on again when Mrs. Robjohn's attention was elsewhere, knowing that the pressure would come on later—the public, you may recall, was warned by press and radio of varying pressure, and in any case last week wasn't the first time the gas has behaved in this way. He knew the pressure would come on later and he hoped that Mrs. Robjohn would be asleep by that time. Then he suddenly remembered (or had thought it out in advance?) that to be sure of sufficient gas to do the trick there must be enough shillings in the slot. We know he put in at least three. That was a precaution he *had* to take, and that was the flaw in an otherwise unprovable murder. There's always supposed to be one flaw in every perfect murder," he added digressively. "I wonder if that's true."

I still made an objection or two, but I knew that Dagobert was right.

"But what if the pressure hadn't come on again at one-thirty a.m.?" I suggested. "It might have remained off until the next morning."

"In that case there would have been, quite simply, no murder. Well tried, sir—or madam—but no murder." He added inexorably: "But the pressure *did* come on."

"Yes. Wouldn't she have heard those shillings going into the meter?"

"I don't know. . . . Shall we have something to eat?"

"I'm not very hungry."

"A glass of beer then."

We walked to the Castle, a public house we normally avoid as it is usually crowded at lunch time with neighbouring bank clerks etc., etc., who might be startled to find our Miss Hamish with one foot on the brass rail. But I was in no mood to observe the proprieties. I had a small glass of mild ale and, as my appetite came back, several large sandwiches.

Suddenly Dagobert stared at the clock in horror, grabbed his hat—a very odd-looking bowler I observed for the first time—and made for the door.

"Nearly two o'clock!" he exclaimed, shouldering a bag

apparently full of tools. "My mate'll be expecting me back on the job."

As he disappeared I realised that I had been in very intimate converse with a man who from his appearance was a local workman. The interested glances of Mr. Smith of the bank and Mr. Williams of the Estate Agents followed me as I retreated with dignity into the High Street.

10 ✳

I can't say that my brain was exactly reeling as I made my way up Mandel Street towards the office. It was not doing anything so constructive.

I began to wonder what Dagobert was doing in that peculiar outfit. In a shabby bowler, a shiny blue overcoat, a stringy necktie of floral design, with grubby fingers, a cursory shave and a bag of tools over his shoulder, he looked—to put it mildly—most unusual. I thought about this to prevent myself from thinking about Mrs. Robjohn. But it was no good. . . .

The real problem was, what did I do next? What action did I take? Did I go straight to Mr. Playfair and lay all the facts I had on the table? Did I go to the police? You can't go round all by yourself carrying the knowledge that someone has been murdered.

I tried to avoid it in another way. I said that Mrs. Robjohn's death had been a blessing to her, a quietus. I said that the verdict of accidental death had been good enough for all the authorities who uphold the law of the land. I said that I could only bring fresh pain to all concerned by raking up what had been buried for ever.

It didn't work. Mrs. Robjohn had been murdered. Spilt blood cried aloud for vengeance.

I made the feeble last-ditch stand which works well enough for the minor sins of our neighbours: I said it was none of my business. It was still no good. Mrs. Robjohn's murder *was* my business.

As I reached the street door of the office I encountered Oates. He was just coming back from luncheon, a meal which he ate at oddly assorted places, generally a coffee stall on the corner, sometimes Barkers' Cafeteria and, occasionally, the Plantation, which is a restaurant which even Mr. Playfair and Major Stewart find too expensive.

Oates's wages are three pounds five shillings a week and I must say he does remarkably well on them. I always feel a little embarrassed calling him our office boy; for he is a very self-possessed young man, slightly over six feet tall and terrifyingly sophisticated. He came to us two years ago when he was sixteen, and during the last two years he has grown up amazingly in all senses of the word.

He has a fascinating accent—very Oxford with just a redeeming hint of the East End. He leads, I imagine, a double life at least. I've seen him slouching along with his hands in his pockets in aggressive conversation with men in checked waistcoats who look as though they might suddenly shout: "Six to one, bar one." I've also seen him talking earnestly to youths of his own age who need hair cuts and gesticulate airily and wear sandals.

Oates's reading matter shows the same dichotomy: he takes *The Greyhound Standard* and *Horizon*. I once caught him deep in *Ulysses* though by the haste with which he closed the volume I imagine he had found one of the pornographic passages.

In appearance he is equally remarkable. He has a long thin face, big ears, a mop of fair hair combed straight back and a rather small, heart-shaped mouth. In time he may be good looking in a Modigliani sort of way; at the moment there is still something unformed about his features, as though he had sprouted up too quickly.

He has an extensive wardrobe which he acquires in a shop in Shaftesbury Avenue called Hollywood Haberdashery Ltd. They specialise in American fashions, stressing such lines as Robert Taylor shirts, Ray Milland hats and Charles Boyer ties.

As we met outside the office he languidly touched his wide-brimmed pearl-grey felt hat and inquired: "Nice lunch, Miss Hamish?"

I said I'd just had a snack and asked him if he'd posted those letters.

"Sure," he reassured me easily.

I was suddenly conscious that he was eying me, measuring me from head to foot with a kind of studied insolence borrowed from Stewart Grainger, his favourite film star. He kept his hands in his pockets. I was too astonished to do anything but stare at him. He grinned at me lazily.

"I like your shoes, Miss Hamish," he volunteered outrageously. "I bet you walked the length of Oxford Street to find them."

I gasped. As a matter of fact I had walked the length of Oxford Street—and also Regent Street and Bond Street—but that I should be standing outside Number 11 Mandel Street discussing my shoe problems with Oates struck me as the final stage of fantasy.

"I could put you on to a place where you'd find just what you want," he continued. "And no coupons."

The situation was grotesque. This was our office boy, the eccentric but heretofore quite manageable Oates, and we were getting into a huddle about Black Market shoe shops. I am not unduly haughty, but I draw the line somewhere. I flushed and groped for something simple, cutting and dignified to say. I got as far as: "Thank you, Oates, but—"

"That's okay, Miss Hamish," he put me at my ease. "Anything for a pal."

Now I was his pal. I hoped fervently that he was drunk.

"Thank you," I murmured again, my voice as I hoped an icicle, "but I must really go up to the office."

He stepped aside gallantly. For a perfectly awful moment I had wondered what to do if he tried to prevent me.

Then I got a slight clue. "I saw you in the Castle, Miss Hamish," he said, grinning. "But you know me. I never talk."

I suddenly remembered that Dagobert as he left the Castle had absent-mindedly pushed back his bowler and kissed me. That's when I'd noticed his inadequate shave.

Now there was nothing exactly criminal in having been kissed in the local pub by a shabbier member of the proletariat, but I felt it lessened the dignity I attempted to maintain at Number 11 Mandel Street. Unfortunately I let Oates see this, not that he wasn't quite quick enough on the uptake to know it anyway.

I made the further mistake of prolonging the conversation. "Talk as much as you like!"

"I believe in people leading their own lives," he drawled.

"What you and I do out of office hours is nobody's business, eh Miss Hamish?"

This time I did what I should have done some time ago. I swept with marked hauteur up the stairs, refusing to bandy further words. He had the impudence to run after me.

"There was just one thing, Miss Hamish," he said. "I've got something rather important on this afternoon. Can I say you gave me the afternoon off?"

"You cannot."

"Okay, okay, Miss Hamish," he said soothingly. "I'll ask the Major."

I didn't look round, but I fancied he sounded a little chastened. I marched past the outer office, where Sarah glanced up inquiringly, and into my own room without even saying hello. I was inwardly boiling.

I sat down to cool off. My first impulse was to go at once to Mr. Playfair; but Mr. Playfair wasn't in yet and I had time to think again.

I was glad at least that I'd had the final sense to refuse Oates the afternoon off. To have done so would have put me in an unthinkable position. From then on we should have been "pals" indeed! It would have been yielding to a kind of blackmail.

I paused to reflect upon the word blackmail and upon Oates's swiftness to cash in on what he had seen, were it only to the extent of demanding an afternoon off.

As I cooled off I reflected further. I considered Oates's recherché wardrobe, his occasional luncheons at the Plantation and his three pounds five shillings per week. The general theory was that he got the extra money by judicious investments with bookmakers. Perhaps he did. Perhaps he also eked out expenses by the trade he had let me have a glimpse of;

perhaps he observed other people besides myself out of office hours. Thinking it over I didn't altogether like the way he'd said: "Okay, I'll ask the Major."

I heard Mr. Playfair come in, pass my door and retire to his own room. I rose to follow him. It would be best to get the Oates business settled once and for all.

But as I stepped into the corridor I changed my mind. I decided to try an experiment. I wanted to find out just what it was like to be slightly blackmailed.

I found Oates with his feet up on a desk, scanning the *Greyhound Standard*. I asked him to step into my room.

He came docilely and when he reached my room I sat down and told him to close the door. He remained standing and I am glad to say he looked gauche and awkward.

"You don't wish to lose your job here at the office, do you?" I said coolly.

He looked worried. "No, Miss Hamish."

"I thought not."

And yet, I could not help wondering, why not? Three pounds five shillings a week must be small-time stuff for the intimate of bookmakers and Black-Market shoemakers. Was it loyalty to the firm of Daniel Playfair & Son that made him pale at the suggestion of losing his job? Or was a solicitor's office a useful base for operations?

"I'm ever so sorry, Miss Hamish, if—"

I cut him short. "We'll say nothing more about it."

But this wasn't at all the way I'd intended the interview to go. I wanted him to blackmail me, not for me to scare the wits out of him. I decided I was being entirely too self-possessed.

"Oates," I said hesitantly, as though approaching a delicate subject, "sit down, won't you, please."

This unexpected mark of esteem puzzled him and slowly —as I had hoped—reassured him.

"I—I don't quite know what you saw just now in the Castle," I went on, by this time a picture of maidenly confusion, "but, but, well, you see . . ." I floundered helplessly.

He swallowed it like a fish. I could almost see him inwardly relaxing. The pale blue eyes came to life again and he even thrust his hands into his pockets.

"Who was the bloke?" he inquired conversationally.

"A friend of mine." I corrected myself hastily. "Well—an acquaintance, that is . . ."

"Sure," he grinned. "I understand."

"I'm so glad. You see, I have a *special* reason why I don't want people to, well, to talk about Bill and me. You know how people talk."

"Sure. I know. His name's Bill, eh?"

I nodded. "Bill Perkins. But you won't say any more about it, will you?"

"The whole thing's a secret between you and me, Miss Hamish," he said magnanimously. "The only thing is I can't somehow picture you—well, you and a bloke like Bill Perkins."

I conquered an impulse to giggle. Dagobert would enjoy this. Then Oates added a remark which really left me gasping.

"I guess it's another of those things like *Lady Chatterley's Lover*," he decided.

My mind reeled before the picture in Oates's mind of Dagobert in the rôle of the elemental gamekeeper and me, the effete aristocrat swept away by earthy passion. Things like this make you wonder about universal education.

"Not exactly," I murmured hastily. "But if you don't mind I'd be very grateful if you'd forget all about it. And, Oates, if you really want the afternoon off do take it."

"Thanks, Miss Hamish. I always said you were a sport."

I didn't ask him to whom he always expressed this opinion; I thought the interview had gone far enough for the first day. He would come back again. He was convinced he had something on me and he wasn't the sort to pass a good thing by.

His manner was vaguely patronising as he prepared to go. He paused to choose a cigarette from an expensive looking silver case.

"That offer about the shoes still holds," he said generously. He lit his cigarette and regarded me with the eye of a connoisseur. "I might take you down there myself one day if you ever feel like having an afternoon off," he suggested, blowing a perfect smoke ring.

"It's very kind of you," I said feebly.

"If people do favours for me, I do favours for them," he said handsomely.

"Is that why you used to give Mrs. Robjohn racing tips?"

I regretted the question as soon as I asked it. It might have ruined all the good work I had done. I saw his face go a shade paler and there was a nasty pout to his too small mouth.

"Did she tell you that?"

"She mentioned that you'd recommended Laughing Boy for the two-thirty at Newbury," I lied. "I think it was rather sweet of you. Betting on races was almost her only amusement."

He seemed to breathe again. "I'm soft-hearted," he said. "That's my trouble. Well, so long, Miss Hamish."

And he went, looking, I thought, a little preoccupied.

11 ✳   I was still trying to sort out my thoughts about Oates when Rosemary came in. She was wearing a navy woollen frock with a demure high neck and the suggestion of a vestigial bustle at the back which was the envy of my soul. She greeted me in practically the same words Oates had used. "Nice luncheon, Jane?"

"Not bad."

"You must bring him round to the office one day."

"And let you and Sarah compete?" I shook my head. "Free enterprise may be fine in a young and expanding country; but in the present case I believe in planning."

Rosemary sighed. "I have quite enough on my hands already," she said, showing off. Then very casually: "I don't suppose you saw Jimmy? He hasn't come in yet and Mr. Playfair wante him to run round to 17 Mandel Square."

I shook my head.

"I suppose it's his own business," she went on, "but two hours for luncheon seems to be overdoing it. And anyway," she added with sudden bitterness, "why can't he wait until evening for that kind of thing?"

"That kind of thing?" I queried innocently. "Food?"

"Don't be stupid, Jane!"

She sounded so angry that I regretted my mild pleasantry. I knew quite well the "kind of thing" referred to. Our Jimmy was at it again. Babs was no sooner safely in Scotland—writing I understood to her naughty Jimmy by practically every post—than the gallant Major had found consolation with, rumour had it, a wide-eyed blonde who worked around the corner in the bank.

"I'll say one thing for our Major Stewart," I admitted. "He keeps trying. Have you seen the new Firth Shephard show?"

She nodded. "It's quite good in patches."

"Did Jimmy like it?"

"I've no idea," she said. "Has he seen it?"

"He had two tickets the day Babs fled to Scotland. I know because he asked me to go with him instead."

"Did he?" For a brief instant she looked daggers at me. Then disconcertingly her large violet eyes filled with tears. She turned away and when she spoke again she was quite under control. "He's at perfect liberty to ask whom he wants to ask."

"Quite," I agreed dryly.

I had started a line of thought in her mind, for she frowned speculatively. "I wonder who he did take that night?" she mused.

"Perhaps he didn't take anyone," I suggested.

"He'd been out with some woman," she stated. "I know because he came up here to the office shortly after eleven o'clock that night in tails, a gardenia in his buttonhole and smothered in face powder.

"After eleven!" I exclaimed. "The things that go on in this office! But I remember now. You were doing the ledgers for the accountants."

"Yes. I was horrified when he suddenly turned up."

"What did he do?" I asked, fascinated and scenting scandal.

"He was tight and in a vicious mood. He kept muttering: 'I'll fix 'em. I'll teach 'em.' Then he locked himself in his room and tried to put through a trunk call to Scotland. It was really rather awful, Jane. It was a relief when he went about ten minutes later. I suppose I ought to have seen him home, but he probably found a taxi. I got one quite easily when I went. To tell the truth I was really a little frightened of him in that mood."

"I don't blame you," I said. "A spoiled man when frustrated can be dangerous. But he seems to have regained his poise and equanimity."

Rosemary had also regained hers. "I'm completely forgetting what I came in for," she said. "Mrs. Hawthorne has just rung up for us to come round with the key to Number 17. Mr. Playfair suggested if Jimmy weren't back yet that I go. To tell the truth I'd rather not."

"Sensitive?"

She turned away again, nodding. "I suppose so. . . . Poor Mrs. Robjohn. I grew very fond of her, Jane, in a way. But it *was* best the way she died, wasn't it, Jane? It was, wasn't it?"

I agreed mechanically.

"And you'll go round with the key?" she said. "Here it is."

"What's it wanted for?" I asked.

"Apparently two men from the West London Gas Company want to go in."

"In that case," I said firmly, taking the key, "I shall certainly go."

12 ✳ The two men from the West London Gas Company were, needless to say, Dagobert and his mate. They were having a nice cup of tea in Mrs. Hawthorne's kitchen in the basement when I arrived. Dagobert, Mrs. Haw-

thorne told me, had kept her so entertained with his many strange experiences as a gas inspector that she had not been able to get on with her housework. "Mr. Brown," she said, "is really a most extraordinary man." She was telling me! "And well-spoken, too," she added. "I think he may have come down in the world. He says he hasn't *always* been used to this kind of work."

"He means: used to work. Period." But I didn't say this out loud. Out loud I said: "What exactly do they want?"

"To collect the shillings from the meter, I believe," she answered. "They usually only come once a quarter and they last came only a day or two before—before the accident. But I suppose, in these exceptional circumstances . . ."

The awful thought occurred to me that Dagobert wasn't working for the West London Gas Company at all, that his intention was quite simply to rob the meter! But there was the matter of keys and probably of cards he had to show. The simpler explanation was that he'd probably talked someone at the Gas Company into letting him collect the shillings.

Dagobert and his mate rose when I followed Mrs. Hawthorne into the kitchen. She introduced me as the young lady from Daniel Playfair & Son.

Dagobert touched his forelock. "Pleased to meetcha, Miss," he said. "And I do hope it's no inconvenience."

"I haven't a great deal of time to spare," I said coldly.

We went upstairs again and I unlocked the door. It was the first time I'd been in Mrs. Robjohn's room since that night. Although our Valuers had been through it and made an inventory of its contents nothing appeared to have been moved. In the grey daylight, and with the accumulation of a week's dust, it looked more like a second-hand furniture shop than ever. The clocks had run down and stopped at different times.

Dagobert closed the door carefully behind me and his mate, letting the Yale lock click to. He ran an eager but inexperienced eye round the room. No small, tell-tale detail rewarded his inspection. He knelt down and examined the tap beside the gas fire. He was thinking of fingerprints; but the last person who had touched that tap was Mrs. Hawthorne when she turned the gas out.

I strolled over to the Chinese lacquer desk where I had seen the address book with Babs' name and the pile of crisp new pound notes. The address book, now closed, was still there. There was no sign of the pound notes. What had happened to them? They were certainly not mentioned in the inventory and Mr. Playfair had not said anything about finding them when he brought back, for safe keeping in our strong room, Mrs. Robjohn's gold wrist watch, her rings and her handbag containing about three pounds in change—but no shillings!

Where had that not despicable sum of money gone? Could it have been sufficient as a motive for murder? And had Mrs. Robjohn actually written that anonymous letter to Babs? Was an anonymous letter a sufficient motive for murder? Since my talk with Dagobert on the park bench these questions could no longer be ignored.

"Got a bob anybody?" Dagobert asked. His mate produced a shilling which Dagobert pocketed. "Back in a second," he said.

And he disappeared into the alcove built into the corner of the room opposite the foot of the four-poster bed. The alcove, which was really a small boxroom or a huge hanging cupboard, contained shelves packed with old suitcases, hat boxes, cardboard boxes and stacks of ancient clothes. Even the Valuers had boggled at the contents of this alcove, describing them airily as "sundry articles of wearing apparel."

Dagobert's mate glanced significantly after him and then to me, shrugging tolerantly.

"He's a rum one," he summed up, mildly I thought. "Cigarette, Miss?"

I shook my head tensely. For though aimlessness was a condition of the experiment I knew Dagobert was about to perform, I couldn't help listening for the plunk of that shilling which I knew he was about to insert into the slot. I heard it quite clearly.

Dagobert emerged a moment later and looked at me expectantly. I nodded sadly.

"Did you hear it?" he asked anxiously.

"Yes."

The experiment had been a failure. Dagobert looked so downcast that I felt sorry for him. But the fact remained that *normally* Mrs. Robjohn must have heard those shillings drop.

The next item on the programme was to empty the meter. Dagobert's mate produced the necessary key and got the coin box out. There was only a handful of shillings, less than a dozen. As Mrs. Hawthorne had told us the meter was emptied only a few days before Mrs. Robjohn's death.

Dagobert, with an eye trained by a month of violent numismatics, immediately picked out the shilling which he had borrowed from his mate and returned it. I saw him weighing the remaining coins in the palm of his hand, possibly counting them, for he said, "Nine."

His mate filled in the sum on a sheet he kept for the purpose and opened his little black bag to receive the money. Dagobert pocketed the nine shillings.

"Remind me that I owe nine bob to the kitty," he said.

Then he began prowling round the room, looking thoughtful and lynx-eyed. I watched admiringly, expecting at every moment to see him produce a pair of pocket lenses to examine a rouge-tipped cigarette butt or a bit of cigar ash. As a matter of fact, he did discover a rouge-tipped cigarette end which brought him to a triumphant halt in the best sleuth manner.

"It's mine," I said before he got too excited.

Dagobert winked broadly at his mate who accurately interpreted this as a signal to hop it. I thought Dagobert seemed uncommonly cheerful in view of the failure of his experiment.

When we were alone he made for the tallboy where Mrs. Robjohn kept her photograph albums. He picked out the one he was looking for and slipped it into his toolbag.

"You can't do that," I said. "It's in the Inventory."

"Is it?" he said. "Bad luck."

He strolled over to the four-poster bed, which had been neatly remade by Mrs. Hawthorne. He prodded it critically and then stretched out luxuriously upon the counterpane, black boots, bowler hat and all.

"I could very comfortably spend the rest of the afternoon here," he said, "thinking."

"I'm sorry to be unco-operative, but I have to spend the rest of the afternoon in the office."

"Shush," he warned.

We both listened for a moment. I identified the sound a second later; it was a key turning in the Yale lock of the hall door behind me. I realised suddenly what a state my nerves

were in today, for my heart was thudding. I heard the door
pushed open. I spun round and stared at the intruder.

"Oh," I said. "Major Stewart."

13 ✳   I was aware that the tableau presented to our
Junior Partner's eyes needed a little explana-
tion. Miss Hamish, a picture of respectable legal efficiency in
her neat tailored suit, black gloves and restrained hat, made a
reasonably conventional figure in the foreground. What did
not fit into the scene so well was the unshaven workman
sprawled on the bed beside me, flicking cigarette ash over the
rich red velvet counterpane in the vague direction of his
muddy boots.

I couldn't think of any very convincing explanation of
this, so I said nothing.

Dagobert who would, I hoped, have at least scrambled
with decent embarrassment to his feet and removed his hat,
but who on the contrary merely raised his head slightly on one
elbow, gave neither of us a chance to speak.

"So you're Major Stewart, eh?" he grunted, eying Jimmy
with suspicion.

Jimmy glanced from the spectacle on the bed to me. To
say that there was a note of inquiry in his eye would be under-
statement.

"The gas man," I explained briefly.

Dagobert adjusted his bowler hat at an angle more con-
venient to his recumbent position. He continued to fix Jimmy
with a fishy stare.

"I've been wanting to have a little talk with you," he said portentously.

Jimmy made an effort to regain his dignity. It was uphill work with Dagobert lying there in oriental ease.

"If you have any inquiries to make will you kindly address them to my firm at Number eleven—"

"What are you doing here?" Dagobert interrupted him sharply. "Why did you creep in here stealthily, using a private latchkey?"

I thought Jimmy was going to choke. "This is outrageous," he said. "Will you—"

"Don't stall!" Dagobert said. "Answer my question."

"Since you must know," Jimmy began, trying sarcasm, "I happen to be a partner in the firm of solicitors who is administering the late Mrs. Robjohn's estate, and I would be very much obliged if you—"

Dagobert cut him short. "We know all that. Where did you get that second key?"

"We happen to have possession of all our late client's keys."

"*Happen!*" Dagobert echoed derisively. "And how did you *happen* to be sneaking in here?"

"I will not be questioned, sir!" the Major exploded.

"I see. No adequate explanation. Very interesting."

"And will you be so good as to get off that bed at once!"

"Don't bluster," Dagobert said. "Blustering will get you nowhere. I want you to keep quite calm and consider your answers. Sit down, *Major* Stewart."

By this time there was a kind of wild light in poor Jimmy's eye. Somebody had gone stark raving mad, he felt, but he could not make out whether it was himself or the gas man. He looked at me beseechingly.

"Shall I fetch a policeman?" I asked.

The question roused his manliness. "No," he said. "I'll handle this." And striding towards the recumbent Dagobert he boomed authoritatively: "Were you in the Army, my good man?"

"I was," Dagobert confessed. "Were you?"

Jimmy ignored this. "Then perhaps you will recall it is the custom to stand up when you address a field-grade officer," he snapped. "And when you speak to me say, sir!"

Dagobert lit another cigarette from the butt of the one he'd been smoking and glanced up at the towering figure of Major Stewart with wide-eyed interest.

"Why?" he asked.

Jimmy turned to me. "Perhaps you'd better go, Miss Hamish," he said. "The man is obviously drunk and I may have a little difficulty with him."

"I prefer Miss What's-her-name to stay," Dagobert said mysteriously. "A witness to these conversations is sometimes useful—afterwards."

"What on earth are you talking about, man?" Jimmy was plainly getting rattled, and I cannot say I blame him. "Are you mad or drunk? Must I call a policeman or throw you out myself?"

"You'll have to figure that one out yourself," Dagobert said, making himself more comfortable on the bed.

Though the field-grade-officer approach had clearly been played out, Major Stewart nevertheless returned to it in desperation.

"And what branch of the Army were you in?" he demanded, possibly hoping that he might know the name of one of the gas man's superior officers.

"M.I. 26 (b)," Dagobert answered promptly.

"There is no such thing," Jimmy said, letting himself be drawn into the argument.

"We didn't advertise ourselves widely," Dagobert drawled. "And for a very good reason. However I don't think I shall be betraying military secrets when I tell you that the (b) part refers to that section which dealt with anonymous letters. The C.G.I.S. had a lot of trouble with that kind of thing."

I think the phrase "anonymous letter" went home, for Jimmy visibly started. He was never a man who concealed his emotions very well and the scene of the past few minutes had not exactly put him at his ease.

"Who is this man?" he murmured to me.

"He told me he was the gas man," I said.

"Ever seen him before?"

"Never."

"Don't whisper, you two!" Dagobert said. "My name is Brown—whether it's an assumed name or not I leave to your judgment." He adjusted some pillows behind his back, removed his bowler and replaced it more comfortably on his head.

"You were telling me," he said to Major Stewart, "about anonymous letters."

"No," I pointed out in the interests of fair play, "you were telling him."

"Was I? So I was. Now, Major Stewart. Perhaps you will realise that it is for your own good to answer a few straight-forward questions. On the 29th of November your ex-fiancée, Miss Barbara Jennings, received an anonymous letter giving certain details—doubtless unsavoury—of your private life."

This time Jimmy was clean bowled. Up to this point he

had believed he was dealing with a madman. He stared at Dagobert again, badly shaken.

"Who are you?" he demanded.

"Brown of the Gas Company. We've already gone into all that. Did you see that letter?"

"No."

"What happened to it?"

"Miss Jennings burnt it."

"Did she describe the handwriting? Or was it typewritten? Or perhaps hand printed?"

"Hand printed, I think. But you have no right to ask me these questions. If you have any official status you will approach me in the normal way. I will not be—"

"Don't digress. So she burnt it, eh?" Dagobert blew a thoughtful column of smoke up his nostrils and with unexpected delicacy tapped the ash of his cigarette neatly into the turn-ups of his trousers. "Burnt it," he repeated sadly, "just as the private and confidential letter on Mr. Playfair's desk the next morning was burnt. Why did you burn that letter, Major Stewart?"

Jimmy hit the ceiling. During this interview I must confess all my sympathy was with him. There must be laws against the way Dagobert was behaving.

"How dare you suggest that I burned that letter!" he shouted.

"So you *did* see the letter?" Dagobert nodded gently.

"I've said nothing about seeing it. I may have seen it. I may not have seen it. Sometimes I do see the unopened letters which go into Mr. Playfair's office, sometimes I don't. I really don't remember what post he had that morning. Possibly there was an anonymous, I mean a private and confidential letter, probably there wasn't."

Dagobert smiled. As a rule I dislike that smug smile of Dagobert's, especially when I am its recipient, but this time I knew how he felt.

"You are rattled, Major Stewart. You can talk yourself into a lot of trouble that way." He sighed. "Yes, you burned that letter all right. By the way, did you read it first? Or were you in too much of a hurry?"

"I've told you I know nothing about it! What's more I'll damn well not be questioned without . . ."

Dagobert clicked his tongue reprovingly and jerked a thumb towards me. "Ladies present, Major," he murmured.

I think Major Stewart had nearly forgotten about me, for he flushed a deeper red as he turned towards me.

"Do please go, Miss Hamish," he said sharply, glad to change the subject. "I'll lock up here before I leave. I came round to remove some of the more valuable pieces of silverware."

"So you've finally thought up an excuse for why you came round," Dagobert said. "The silverware. Feeble, but let it pass. The trouble, Major Stewart, with destroying anonymous letters is that the author of them can write them over again. The only efficient thing to do is to destroy the author himself—or, in this case, herself." He glanced up at Jimmy ingenuously. "Don't you find?" he added conversationally.

I thought for a second that Jimmy was going to strike Dagobert. Afterwards Dagobert confessed that the same thought had terrified him. But Jimmy didn't punch him.

"I shall get in touch with the West London Gas Company immediately, Mr. Brown," he said with dignity, "and lodge a very serious complaint."

"Do that," Dagobert nodded absently.

With a sigh of reluctance he crawled from the bed and

to his feet. He would have been as tall as Jimmy had he stood up straight, but nothing I can say will cure Dagobert of slouching.

"I don't think there are any further questions at the moment, Major Stewart," he said, gathering up his toolbag. "Naturally I'll be seeing you again. Before then I should get things straight in your mind if I were you."

He shouldered his toolbag and strolled towards the door, pausing for a final scrutiny of the room and to touch his hat deferentially.

"I will say good-day. And thank you, Miss Hamilton."

"Hamish," I corrected.

"Hamish," he repeated, without interest. "Don't forget the silverware, Stewart. It would look odd if you returned to the office without it. And I hope you can give a convincing account of your movements on the night of November 29th–30th. *If* you used those two tickets you had to the Firth Shephard show it might be a good idea to have your guest on that evening available to back up your story. No, no, no. Don't thank me. Just a suggestion. You can take it or leave it."

And he was gone, having had, as usual, the last word. Not, I imagine, that poor Jimmy Stewart had anything in particular to say. Probably he felt he had let himself talk too much; certainly he had betrayed a knowledge of that letter Mrs. Robjohn had written to Mr. Playfair. Dagobert, I knew, was convinced that Stewart himself had destroyed it, and I was now inclined to agree with him. But to destroy a poison-pen letter was not the same thing as destroying the author of the letter!

I found myself glancing cautiously at James Stewart and trying not to think of the implications of Dagobert's remarks. Could I be looking at a murderer? I thought I knew every line of Jimmy's clean-cut handsome face, but now I kept seeing little features of it I hadn't noticed before, a hint of cruelty about the self-indulgent mouth, a gleam of passion in the frank grey eyes, a suggestion of menace in the throbbing network of tiny veins above his temple.

All this was my imagination, of course. I said with a casualness which must have sounded horribly false:

"It was strange his knowing about those seats you had for the Firth Shephard show. Do you remember, you very nicely asked me to go with you?"

"Yes."

"I wonder how he knew about them."

"I got them from Keith Prowse round the corner," he murmured. "He may have seen me."

Though the explanation was highly improbable we both left it at that.

We collected the silver—a collection of snuffboxes—and walked back to Number 11 Mandel Street together. There was no light conversation; we both had things to think about.

I carried the snuffboxes down to the strong room where I put them into a box labelled MRS. B. ROBJOHN DECD. I paused to rummage for a while among Mrs. Wolf-Heatherington's possessions, remembering that I had never found the old coins which were missing from Mr. Playfair's desk. There was no sign of them. Luckily they were without value and Mr. Playfair had not mentioned them since. I returned to my own room.

But I paused for a moment in the corridor outside Rosemary's room. I am becoming a terrible snooper. I heard Rosemary laugh. She sounded very pleased about something. "I'd love to," I heard her say.

Then her door opened and I retreated guiltily into my

own room. But I caught a glimpse of Major Stewart coming out and I heard him say in his most winning manner: "Seven o'clock, then. At the Normandy."

Putting two and two together, it appeared that there was a Jimmy-Rosemary *rapprochement*. I was glad for Rosemary's sake, since that's the kind of thing she liked. But with the suspicious attitude of mind I was rapidly developing I couldn't help wondering about Jimmy's motives. Was he, perhaps, desirous of persuading Rosemary not to mention that little scene on the night of the twenty-ninth when he'd appeared so unexpectedly in the office?

14 ✳

I tried to whip up a flagging interest in the Hartley Estate, but gave it up after ten or fifteen minutes. What with one thing and another I had not had the kind of day conducive to concentration. More as an excuse to abandon the affairs of Sir John Hartley, than from any urgency to report on Mrs. Wolf-Heatherington's coin collection, I tapped on Mr. Playfair's door; and hearing an indistinct murmur, which I took for an invitation to come in, I opened it.

He was not alone and I immediately began to withdraw. But he had already spotted me.

"Come in, Miss Hamish," he said. "I can't remember whether you two have met each other or not."

Mr. Playfair's companion had risen. He was a rugged-looking young man who wore tweeds and looked as though he would be masterful with dogs and horses. His hair was dark and crinkled off a low forehead. But the dark eyes were intelligent. Grave, as they met mine, they immediately smiled, transforming a bronzed face, serious in repose, into a cheerful countenance which was both youthful and likeable.

"I don't think I've had the pleasure," he began, holding forth a powerful hand.

I took it diffidently. As I had feared he nearly crushed my fingers.

"Mr. Douglas Robjohn," I said. "You see I do remember you. You came into the office one day in uniform, before you went to Ceylon."

"Of course," he said. "I remember perfectly, Miss, er . . ."

"I'm sorry you had to come home to find such sad news awaiting you," I said.

The smile faded from his face. "Mr. Playfair has just been telling me details," he said. "And also some other things I didn't know." He turned with a certain confusion to the older man. "I don't know how much of our conversation was confidential, sir," he said.

"That's entirely up to you, Douglas," Mr. Playfair said quietly. "It's all very unimportant, isn't it. I suggest that Miss Hamish gives you a cup of tea and, if you can bear the company of an elderly family solicitor for an entire evening, I shall be delighted if you'll dine with me in Hampstead this evening."

"Thank you, sir. I'll be there." He hesitated, not sure whether or not the interview was finished and still obviously feeling that there was more he wanted to get off his chest. "I was a rotten son," he rumbled on to no one in particular. "I never liked my mother, you know."

"You never knew her, did you?" Mr. Playfair said gently.

"No."

"She was very fond of you, Douglas, and women have an infinite capacity for forgiving those they are fond of."

"God knows I hope so," Douglas almost whispered.

"When you give Douglas that cup of tea, Miss Hamish," Mr. Playfair smiled at me, "don't forget to bring me in a cup."

It was a courteous way of dismissing us both and at the same time cutting short a painful conversation.

"The last time you had tea with us," I said to Douglas, "you broke the spout of the teapot. You may find the price of a new teapot on our bill of costs. Meanwhile we still use the broken one."

"That's bad," he said, himself again. "We'll have to do something about that."

He followed me into my room. Sarah was already there, sorting out the curious collection of cracked crockery which comprised our office tea set.

"This is Mr. Douglas Robjohn," I introduced them. "Miss Sarah Swinburne. You may remember each other."

"Rather," said Douglas, clasping Sarah's hand warmly. Sarah did not, I observe, wince at that mighty handshake. In fact I thought she smiled up into his eyes with downright boldness. "Miss Swinburne and I made the tea last time, four years ago. She jerked my elbow. That's why I broke the spout."

"Your hand was shaking because you were afraid of being alone with me!" Sarah accused him.

He appealed to me: "She's become very forward in these last four years, hasn't she, Miss Hamish?"

Personally I had been thinking that she had become very forward in these last four minutes. I had never seen Sarah react so strikingly. Her colour had heightened, her eyes were sparkling and even her golden-red hair seemed brighter. It is generally painful for one woman to observe this effect in another, but I felt suddenly tolerant and big-sisterly towards Sarah. Love at First Sight, I decided.

It was plainly mutual. Douglas's reactions were no less apparent. Boy was meeting Girl. It took the outward form of banter, fascinating doubtless to each other, if a little trying to the outsider.

"She looks more like Rita Hayworth than ever. Do you ever manage to get any work out of her, Miss Hamish?"

"We probably shan't this afternoon," I said with marked dryness.

"He looked much better in his uniform, didn't he, Jane?" Sarah said.

"Maybe if I went, you'd be able to address each other directly," I suggested.

"Good idea!" Douglas choked as he realised what he'd said. "I don't mean about your going, Miss Hamish," he corrected himself hastily. "I mean, about addressing each other directly. Here goes: Sarah."

"The name is Swinburne." She tossed back the mop of her hair. "You Colonials are so go-ahead . . . Well, go ahead."

"What are you doing tonight? Let's go out and dance."

"Tonight?" Sarah mused, as though she would have to consult her engagement book on the matter.

"She's not doing anything," I put in. "But you are. You're dining with Mr. Playfair."

"Gosh! So I am."

"Oddly enough, I'm engaged myself," said Sarah. "Meanwhile the others are waiting for their tea." She had poured out cups for Mr. Playfair, Rosemary and Major Stewart with which she swept towards the door.

I relieved her of the tray. "I'll take them, if you two can spare me for a minute."

I left them in my office for what seemed a reasonable length of time, reporting on the business to Rosemary.

"I think we have a bad case of love at first sight on our hands," I said, as I handed Rosemary her tea.

Rosemary spilled the tea into the saucer. "What do you mean?" she said quickly.

"Sarah and young Robjohn."

"Oh." She appeared to breathe again. "That."

"You don't seem surprised. It struck me as being rather precipitous."

"They met each other years ago, didn't they? Before he went to Ceylon."

"For about ten minutes. Here in the office." I thought for a moment and then added: "Well, maybe for half an hour or so."

"Lots can happen in half an hour," Rosemary murmured significantly. She was in one of her mysterious moods. "That would account for a certain coldness between Sarah and the young man's mother, wouldn't it?"

"I fail to follow."

"Mrs. Robjohn once told me she'd cut Douglas completely out of her will if he married a member of the lower orders. She didn't specifically mention Sarah, but she said it in this room in front of Sarah and she stared at Sarah while she said it. What's he look like? I haven't seen him since before the war. He was a leggy youth who stammered. I used to wonder if he'd ever grow up."

"He has," I said, remembering his very determined approach towards Sarah.

"She did her best to prevent him. They lived together in a house in Highgate. She wouldn't even let him go to school. He had tutors. He was supposed not to be strong."

"When I first saw him at the end of the war he was a Commando," I said.

She nodded. "The war was his opportunity to escape and he grabbed it. Poor Mrs. Robjohn."

"I should have thought poor Douglas."

Douglas stared at me when I entered my own room. "Oh hello, Miss Hamish!" he exclaimed.

"Hello, Jane," Sarah echoed.

"There's no need for the enthusiastic welcome," I said. "I was in here with you just a few minutes ago. Remember?"

"We, we, er, were pouring out your tea." Sarah was blushing furiously.

"Yes, let me, let me hand it to you." And Douglas made a lunge for my teacup, thus managing to remove himself from the corner, where Sarah now had more space to move in.

He dropped my cup and broke it, but as I had more or less expected something of the sort I remained unperturbed. I helped myself to Sarah's cup which had not, of course, been touched, and regarded the pair of them unemotionally.

"I see," I said to Douglas, "that you've been taking Sarah's advice; you've gone ahead."

"Gosh! Is it so obvious?" he grinned sheepishly.

I nodded. "Even to my inexperienced eye."

"Jane, you know it isn't really so sudden," Sarah put in defensively. "We used to write to each other, you know. Practically every week. We don't feel at all like strangers."

"Yes, I gathered that. Mr. Playfair would probably excuse Douglas from tonight's engagement."

"Do you think he would!" both exclaimed.

"I'll speak to him," I sighed patiently, "since this is the first time you've seen each other for four years."

I thought they looked slightly embarrassed suddenly.

"It *is* the first evening you'll have had together in four years, isn't it?" I added, glancing deliberately from one to the other.

I got no reaction from Sarah, but Douglas swallowed heavily a couple of times. "Er, well, er . . . as a matter of fact . . ."

"As a matter of fact," I supplied, "you *have* seen each other before. Why the modest confusion?"

"He came round to see me last night," Sarah came to the rescue. "As soon as the boat train from Southampton arrived."

"I see."

But I didn't altogether see why they had made such a thing about it.

15 * By some oversight Dagobert and I had not arranged where to meet that night. I went directly home. He was there in my sitting room with volume three of the telephone directory, diligently dialling everybody in it named Robjohn. He had just ticked off the last one, Zachariah W. He'd had some fascinating conversations—including one invitation to dinner—but none of them seemed

to be even related—much less married—to the late Blanche Robjohn of Number 17 Mandel Square.

I could have told him that, but Dagobert was not fully launched on his career of amateur detective, and he had to make his own mistakes in his own way.

He said hello and pushed a photograph in front of me of a face which seemed vaguely familiar. It was a man's face with a square-jutting jaw and crisping black hair growing low on the forehead. He looked about fifty and I was certain I had seen him somewhere before.

"Got it?" Dagobert asked.

I shook my head. He produced another photograph. It was the one he'd stolen this afternoon from Mrs. Robjohn's album. It was of a group which contained the gentleman with the fierce black moustache whom we had both independently decided might be Mr. Robjohn.

"A friend of mine made an enlargement," Dagobert explained, "scratched off the moustache from the negative, shaded in a few lines to represent the ravages of age and here we have a picture of what Mr. Robjohn probably looks like if he's still knocking around."

I confessed that it was very ingenious. And I was impressed by the resemblance between Dagobert's hypothetical Mr. Robjohn and young Douglas.

"Take it to your office and see if anyone recognises him."

"I'll tack it up in Mr. Playfair's room with a notice reading Ten Pounds Reward."

"It might be worth ten pounds to us," Dagobert said. "That reminds me. Who pays us for all the trouble and expense we're incurring to bring Mrs. Robjohn's murderer to justice?"

"Nobody, I suppose."

"I never thought of that. How do we amateur sleuths live?"

"Your girl friends have jobs."

"It's a damn scandal, isn't it?" he said.

He returned to the scrutiny of his photograph, apparently striving to read the riddle of Mrs. Robjohn's death therein.

"It's a nasty face," he said. "Sadistic."

It was a disagreeable face, which in view of its marked resemblance to Douglas's was unexpected; for Douglas had a pleasant face. It seemed to represent the other half of Douglas's character, the sinister, shadow half. I told Dagobert about Douglas's arrival and as briefly as possible about the events of the afternoon. He made several notes. He was taking the business seriously.

I sometimes think Dagobert would become a rich man if he ever took up making money as a hobby.

"Would you write to me every week for three years if you went to Ceylon?" I asked.

"Yes, dear." He patted my hand absently, still deep in his notes.

"Would you like to take me out somewhere dancing to-night?"

He glanced up. "Why not?" he said unexpectedly.

My question had been academic; I only wanted to know whether he would *like* to, not whether he actually would. But he was already on his feet.

"Where shall we go?" he asked. "The Normandy?"

"Jimmy and Rosemary will be there. We could combine business and pleasure. Let's *not* go to the Normandy."

"What an excellent idea!" he agreed. "We've been working too hard."

We had a lovely evening. I wore my new Molyneux-type

and drenched myself in what remained of the bottle of Lanvin's Scandal Dagobert had brought me from Paris. I put on a pair of silly ear-rings which hurt the lobes of my ears, but made me feel foolish and giddy.

Dagobert looked very distinguished and rather dangerous in his tails, which if not faultless, still fitted him. Like most men he pretended that he hated crawling into a boiled shirt, but like most men he really loved to dress up.

In the restaurant Dagobert swept aside the menu and the wine list offered by the head waiter and sent for Monsieur Sorel, the owner. Actually Dagobert has very little money, but he looks rich. Monsieur Sorel came running, or rather waddling.

There ensued a discussion of a highly technical sort, the details of which I could not follow. I gathered that they agreed on the basic point that the *blanquette de veau* had best not follow the *sole bonne femme* as the sauces were too similar in colour. This depressed me as both had sounded thoroughly delicious as described by Monsieur Sorel and Dagobert both talking at once, and it meant they had to start again.

The next snag they ran into was over the *Homard Thermidor*. Having cheese in it, it meant that the *fondu* made with Gruyère, yolks of eggs and Kirsch, which they had already agreed upon as a fitting close to the meal—assuming it ever began—was out.

They approached the whole question from a fresh angle: they would choose the wines first, and the appropriate food afterwards.

This was the point at which we had our third glass of Tio Pepe. I was afraid that Monsieur Sorel was going to lose his temper; for by this time both he and Dagobert had grown passionate and were gesticulating. But I was wrong. Monsieur

Sorel was enjoying the battle as much as Dagobert was.

At least the whole thing was far removed from Mrs. Robjohn.

Sole Normande and woodcock were eventually agreed upon and Monsieur Sorel withdrew, obviously on the best of terms with Dagobert. I sighed with relief, feeling that an important barrier had been crossed.

"I'm starved," Dagobert took the words out of my mouth. "Couldn't I do with a nice plate of ham and eggs!"

Dinner, in spite of the emotional ordeal we had passed through in order to obtain it, was something to dream about. So was the bill, but that didn't come until afterwards. Not once in the course of the evening did Dagobert's latest hobby (I mean Mrs. Robjohn's murder) intrude itself. I don't think either of us even thought about it.

We left Monsieur Sorel's very much poorer than when we had entered, but richer in the things which make life worth while: optimism, glowing content, love of each other and our fellow men. We even liked the people at the night club which we next visited, which speaks highly for Monsieur Sorel's skill. I suppose they were the usual terrible, vacuous bores who frequent such places, but I loved them all, even the bald Swedish businessman who trod on my instep during the Paul Jones. It was a lovely evening and I'll not hear a word against it.

16 * The next morning was Saturday and I didn't have to go to work. Rosemary and I take alternate Saturday mornings off. Whether or not Dagobert should have gone to work I don't know. Anyway he didn't.

I slept until nearly noon and awoke feeling remarkably fit—not hearty exactly and perhaps a little vague and elfin, but with no visible ill effects of last night's entertainment.

Dagobert came down, made tea and toast for me, and announced that he had borrowed a car from somebody. We were going to drive to Epping Forest. It was one of those remarkable days which sometimes occur in December when the sun is shining and you suddenly remember that spring will come again.

Another perfect day.

The strange interlude lasted over into Sunday. We read the Sunday newspapers in front of a roaring fire and walked out after luncheon through Kensington Gardens and the Park to Wigmore Street. The spell of heavenly weather still lasted. We approached the Wigmore Hall about three and suddenly decided to attend the Concert. We didn't know what was on.

It turned out to be a piano recital by someone called Sirkorski who sounded vaguely familiar, but names like that do sound vaguely familiar. He was just finishing the "Fugue in D Major" from the "48" as we crept in and stood at the back of the hall. When the fugue was finished he paused with a kind of arrogant patience while the latecomers like ourselves sneaked self-consciously into our seats.

He waited until the coughing and programme-rustling had died down and absolute silence reigned. Then he began the "Prelude in C Sharp Minor" so quietly that you could almost hear the quietness, like some unseen presence near you on a still summer night. The effect was electrifying in its restraint, in the sense you had of immense power carefully leashed. I found myself sitting forward on the edge of my seat and not breathing very much.

This ended the first section of Sirkorski's programme. He

stood up and bowed slightly as though receiving the applause of stupid people was part of the penalty he had to pay for earning his living by public entertainment. You could see he didn't like us and the more we applauded the less he thought of our judgment.

He bowed three times only, once to the audience on his left, once straight in front of him, and finally in our direction. It was the first time we'd had a full view of his face. We both got it at the same time, and I knew suddenly that our Arcadian interlude of the past two days had come to an end.

I must have clutched Dagobert's arm for he patted me reassuringly on the knee.

"The resemblance isn't bad, is it," he remarked admiringly. "We should have worked a little less grey into the hair. Maybe he dyes it."

When Sirkorski had retired Dagobert removed a postcard-size print of the photograph from his pocket. The hypothetical alterations made in Mr. Robjohn's features of twenty-five years ago were astonishingly prophetic. It was an excellent likeness of Sirkorski.

I'm afraid I didn't really get all I should have out of the Beethoven Sonata which followed.

When the recital was finished Dagobert seized me by the arm and hurried towards the door. We found Sirkorski in the artists' room just getting into his overcoat. He was exchanging a few terse words in, I imagine, Polish with a man who might have been his manager. He turned when Dagobert approached him with a brusque: "Yes?"

"You won't know me," Dagobert said suavely, "but we are most eager to publish an article on the music of Sirkorski. This is my secretary," he explained me away. "She will take notes of the interview."

Sirkorski regarded us both without interest. He put on his black Homburg and lighted a cigarette.

"You think I am wonderful?" he prompted. "You think I am the legitimate successor to Paderewski? That I play with feeling, insight, a perfect technique? Yes?"

"No," said Dagobert.

"No?" Sirkorski repeated. He put down the gloves he had just taken up and for the first time regarded us with curiosity. "What was the matter?"

"You tell me," Dagobert said. "You made a perfect muck of the *Hammerklavier* slow movement, didn't you?"

"Yes," said Sirkorski. "But everybody clapped their heads off just the same."

"I didn't."

"Didn't you? Who did you say you were?"

"I want to write up your career," Dagobert said. "You interest me. I think you may be one of those fascinating persons—a great failure."

"I am," Sirkorski admitted unexpectedly.

"Now a few biographical details," Dagobert suggested, "for background purposes. Date and place of birth, etc., etc."

"I was born in Posen in Poland in 1892."

"You studied music where?"

"In Warsaw, Vienna—"

"And in London?"

Sirkorski nodded. "Also in London."

"That would be about when?"

"I worked at the Royal College of Music for three years after the first world war."

"Is there a Mrs. Sirkorski?"

"No."

"I mean, have you ever been married?"

"No. An artist should never be married."

"Quite. No children?"

Sirkorski shrugged. "Very likely," he said as though the subject didn't interest him. "These things happen. It is nature."

"When you were at the Royal College of Music," Dagobert asked conversationally, "did you by chance ever run into anyone called Robjohn?"

Sirkorski searched his memory for a moment and then said: "There was a Blanche Robjohn."

Though I didn't look up from my notebook I stopped writing. I could tell from the casual tone of Dagobert's voice that he too was a little stunned by this unexpected stroke of luck.

"That's the one," he said.

"Next I visited the Argentine where—"

"What was Blanche Robjohn like in those days?" Dagobert interrupted.

"Like? She was pretty. She was like a pretty woman. Possessive like a devil! In the Argentine—"

"Were you in love with Blanche Robjohn?"

"In love? What is 'in love'?"

"There you've raised a difficult point, Mr. Sirkorski."

"I made love to her, yes. To a man these things happen."

Dagobert nodded. "It is nature." He fumbled for his pipe and stuffed tobacco in it. Though the man-to-man smile did not fade I could tell that Dagobert was itching to give the frustrated genius a punch in the jaw. "Speaking of nature," he drawled, "were you aware that Miss Blanche Robjohn had a baby?"

Sirkorski remained unmoved. "There was much talk about

it," he nodded. "Interminable talk. These things drive a man mad."

"Women get excited about them too," Dagobert said dryly.

"That is what women are for—to have babies."

Dagobert struck four matches in a row trying to light his pipe. I admired the way he controlled himself. He doesn't get angry easily but he has difficulty with himself when he does.

"I was under the impression," he continued fairly smoothly, "that this Blanche Robjohn was more than a potential producer of babies. I understood she was a promising pianist."

"That was it!" Sirkorski banged the table with his fist. "It comes back to me entirely! A pianist! She thought she was a pianist, a musician. She was a butcher. She was awful. She was terrible. She understood nothing about music, only to go up and down like this." He played exaggerated arpeggios along the edge of the table, making a face while he did so. "She murdered Schumann, Chopin, even Bach."

"And you could have murdered Blanche Robjohn," Dagobert suggested.

"Yes, with pleasure. One morning I found her on my piano in my bedroom playing the 'Goldberg Variations.' The 'Goldberg Variations!' Imagine this thing! 'Why do you not murder your silly Chopin!' I shout to her, 'and leave Bach alone!' And I hit her across the ear, good and hard, so that she falls down on the floor, crying and blubbering. I taught her what she was made for. For babies, not for music."

"Did she go on taking these romantic music lessons with you for long?"

"We lived together for a year, perhaps eighteen months. I forget. I taught her never to touch the piano and that was better. Until these scenes begin, these interminable talks about babies. Then I go. To South America. Shall I tell you about South America?"

"No."

Dagobert rose. I could see he'd had about as much as he could stand. I think he was beginning to regret ever having started this muckraking into the past. In many ways Dagobert is not so tough as he thinks he is. I was afraid he was going to walk out then and there. But having started he couldn't very well stop. He sat down again.

"Was Blanche Robjohn married?"

"No. When they are married, there are husbands—more trouble. When they are not married it is the same—trouble." Sirkorski sighed, struck by the unfairness of it.

"So Robjohn was her maiden name?" Dagobert said.

"Her professional name, I think. The name of some grandmother. I forget."

"Did you ever run into any of Blanche Robjohn's friends?" Dagobert asked. What he meant was, didn't any of them attempt to give him a poke in the eye.

"Why do we talk always of Blanche Robjohn? I wish to talk about Sirkorski," said Sirkorski, thus demonstrating that he was not without some human traits. "You think she is important to my career? Psychologically?"

"Something of that sort. You must have met her friends. Did you meet a man—let me see, he would be older than either of you, about thirty-eight in 1919—a man named Playfair? Daniel Playfair?"

For the first time Sirkorski showed visible signs of emotion. He scowled and his knuckles stood out white as he grasped the edge of the table.

"You know this scoundrel?" he growled.

"Very slightly."

"Someday I find him again, and then I beat him up."

"Last time he beat you up, eh?" Dagobert queried, not without a hint of satisfaction in his voice.

"He had a stick, one of those black twisted things with sharp nobs, how do you call them? Irish blackthorns."

I nodded eagerly, though Sirkorski had not addressed me. Mr. Playfair still carried an aged Irish blackthorn and it charmed me to think that it might be the same stick which had once done such good work. The thought of my mild and gentle Mr. Playfair ever having used it for the purpose of beating up a man was startling. Startling and quite delightful.

"So when you discovered that you were about to become a father," Dagobert summed up, "and Daniel Playfair had attacked you with his blackthorn you decided to go to South America. Is that it?"

Sirkorski nodded, apparently quite satisfied with this way of putting it. "I had always in mind my freedom and my career," he said.

The fascinating thing about Sirkorski was his total lack of shame. He seemed to be quite unconscious of any possible moral issue. We had been wrong in thinking from his photograph that he was a sadist. I don't think he was consciously cruel. He simply didn't have any morals at all. This, according to Dagobert—though the argument is over my head, and I rather imagine over Dagobert's head too—this is why he couldn't play the third movement of the *Hammerklavier* properly. To interpret this moving piece of inner meditation one must have suffered as well as have caused suffering. Which sounds all right when Dagobert explains it, though I wonder if it means anything?

"Tell me more about this Daniel Playfair," Dagobert said.

"I take it he didn't approve of your friendship with Blanche Robjohn?"

"It is quite simple. He was jealous. He loved her himself. Sometimes it is like this—two men, one woman—then pouff!" He drew an eloquent finger across his throat. "It is nature."

"You ought to do something about your 'nature,'" Dagobert said.

"But Blanche loved me. How she loved me! To smother me with her love, to squeeze me, never to let me alone! Him, she did not love, this Playfair. He was the faithful friend, the poodle dog. He lacked fire, romance. I used to tell her to marry him. I would say, 'Blanche, marry this Daniel Playfair. He will make you a good husband. A woman like you who has no career, who cannot even play the piano, such a useless woman, needs a husband.' She would only cry. Always this crying!"

"It must have been tough for you."

Dagobert rose again. This time I could see he meant to escape and I rose to follow him, looking forward myself to a breath of fresh air.

"Where were you ten days ago, Mr. Sirkorski?" he asked. "I mean, during the last days of November?"

"In Paris," Sirkorski replied. "I came to England only the day before yesterday."

Dagobert looked disappointed. "I was afraid of that," he sighed.

"Now I tell you about the Argentine."

"Some other time," Dagobert said. "Let's go, Jane."

And we left Sirkorski muttering something to himself in Polish.

17 ✳

Dagobert tore the photograph of Mr. Robjohn-Sirkorski into small bits and scattered them sadly in the Wigmore Street gutter.

"The next interest I take up is going to deal with something abstract," he said. "Not nature. Not human nature anyway. I suppose one ought to check up on Sirkorski's alibi, not that he did it, damn it. Why do he and Douglas—who ought to be our two chief suspects—have to be out of the country when the murder takes place. Shall we give up the whole thing?"

"Until after tea."

"Tea? All right."

But we didn't give it up, even during tea.

"We shouldn't work like this over the week-end," Dagobert complained. "Do you mind being mentioned in a divorce case?"

"Not," I replied with dignity, "if you do the right thing by me afterwards."

"According to reliable sources Irene has started proceedings."

Irene is Dagobert's wife. They were married during the war and—well, as she has nothing to do with the story there's no need to go into all that.

We got back to safer ground—the murder.

"The popular method of attacking these problems," and I could tell by the edge of enthusiasm in his voice that he was no longer referring to the problem of Irene, "is to find out what everybody was doing on the night of the crime. Then we go through their possible motives. Let's go through the motives first. No one had any motives."

"That didn't take long. Let me pour you another cup of tea."

He held out his cup.

"Next, where everybody was between eleven o'clock on the evening of November the twenty-ninth and, say, one-thirty the next morning when the gas came on again; two and a half hours. For the sake of thoroughness we'll start with ourselves."

"We left Number 17 Mandel Square at about three minutes past eleven and walked to Holland Park Avenue," I started. "We arrived there at eleven thirty-three—I remember the time because the clock had run down and I had to reset it by your wrist watch which said eleven twenty-eight and is always five minutes slow. I went to bed immediately and tossed around until about two because I had no hot-water bottle and was frozen."

"Let's remove our names from the list of suspects," Dagobert suggested. "Next, Mrs. Hawthorne. She listened to the wireless until eleven thirty-five—something called "A Smile and a Song"—and then retired. I've checked the Smile and the Song in the *Radio Times*."

I glanced at him admiringly. "You think of everything!"

"I was having a haircut," he admitted sheepishly, "and there was nothing else in the barber's shop to read. Now we come to our star turns. Rosemary Proctor. What on earth was she doing in the office till half past eleven that night?"

"The accountants were coming the next day and she was behind with her ledgers."

"Do these late-night orgies of office activity occur frequently?"

"When I did the ledgers they happened all the time," I said. "It gives you an excuse for taking the next morning off. But," I hastened to add, "I'm not trying to defend Rosemary. Let her be your murderer by all means."

He consulted the notebook he now kept of the case. It was a confused document but he seemed to be able to make something out of it.

"Let's see," he said. "She claims to have taken a taxi back to Knightsbridge at about eleven thirty-five. Note: Interview taxi ranks in Mandel Street neighbourhood," he commented, pleased with himself. He rubbed his hands together with satisfaction. "Now we come to Major James Stewart."

"Don't shout names," I warned.

"Now we come to Major James Stewart," he repeated in a stage whisper. "According to Rosemary he left the office in a disgusting state of drunkenness and with a gardenia in his buttonhole at about eleven-fifteen. Query: Was he really drunk? Query: Did he take a taxi? If so, where did it take him? He lives somewhere, I suppose?"

"Number 2, Inigo Mews, Queens Gate," I supplied.

"How do you know?"

"Keep to the point."

"That's right," he said, pacified. "There seems to be a lot of questions. Note: Interview taxi ranks re revolting ex-Major. Now—Mr. Playfair."

"What about him?" I said, instinctively on the defensive.

"He tells you about a bridge hand he had at the Club that night. Then, when cross-questioned by you, he says he went to the Swiss film at the Academy and mutters something rather unconvincing about snow scenes and the Alps. I suggest to you that he never went near that film."

"Anyway he never went near Mandel Square!"

"That's as may be. Maintain, if possible, an open mind. Women always argue from their emotions. So," he added before I could interrupt, "do men. I said it first!" He wrote something else in his notebook. "Visit stately Playfair residence in Hampstead, interviewing servants on behalf of Gallup Survey." He looked up. "You have to travel a lot in this game. It's a good thing I gave up my job with the Gas Company."

"What about Oates?" I asked.

"I shall have to take a week off to study the ramifications of Oates's character and possible movements," he sighed. "D'you know this murder ought to be solved any year now, Jane. Next, there's Sarah. . . . According to her she stayed at home all the evening. According to her father she went out gallivanting. Could hers be the powder which Rosemary reported on Stewart's faultless tails?"

"I doubt it."

"So do I. Still there's something very satisfactory about suspects who tell whoppers. And she hated Mrs. Robjohn."

"Do you blame her?" I asked, again on the defensive; for Sarah's untruthfulness about what she did on the night of the twenty-ninth had been worrying me.

"No," said Dagobert fairly. "I don't. But she is in love with Mrs. Robjohn's son. Mrs. Robjohn had threatened to disown him if he married a member of the lower orders— meaning Sarah. If I can recognise a motive, that is a motive. . . . Who's left? Douglas and Sirkorski. Both non-starters. I wonder if I ought to buzz over to Paris for a week-end to verify Sirkorski's alibi?"

"No."

"No? Perhaps you're right. It's damn cold at this time

of year." He closed his notebook and replaced it in his pocket. "That's the lot," he said. "One of them's our man—or woman."

"What if somebody we've not mentioned did it?" I pointed out. "There are eight million people in London including Mrs. Hawthorne's other lodgers."

"Don't be depressing, Jane," he sighed. "If it's not one of the nine, I give it up."

But I could see that he had no intention of giving it up. The pertinent point I had raised did not seem to depress him at all. I wondered if his confidence that the murderer was one of the people we had discussed was due to his native optimism or whether he had more solid grounds for it. I have known Dagobert to hold out on me before.

18 ✳ There is nothing which so effectively revives one's interest in a group of all-too-familiar people as the belief that one of them is a murderer. I started for the office on Monday morning wide-eyed and eager, which is certainly not my usual Monday morning habit. Not that I was altogether satisfied with Dagobert's conviction that the murderer was someone who worked at Number 11 Mandel Street, but the possibility added—to put it mildly—a certain piquancy to the character of my co-workers.

When I arrived Oates, sitting alone in the outer office, greeted me without removing the cork-tipped Egyptian cigarette from his mouth. He did however remove his feet from the desk.

"Have a nice week-end, Miss Hamish?" he inquired, putting his book down.

It was a paper-backed novel, French, by Jean-Paul Sartre. He had pushed it casually on to the desk so I could see the title and be duly impressed. Being certain that Oates's knowledge of French was non-existent, I was. He followed my glance.

"You know your Sartre, of course," he said. "Existentialism and the rest of it."

"No. Tell me all about it."

He hadn't expected this, but he parried it neatly.

"I'll lend you the book when I've finished with it."

"Don't forget to cut the pages," I advised.

He grinned and changed the subject. "How's Bill?" he asked.

"Bill?"

"Bill Perkins." He glanced up at me studiously, his eyes half shut, veiled by long curling eyelashes. I wondered which film actor he had borrowed that insolent penetrating stare from. "You remember Bill Perkins," he murmured.

"Bill, oh yes, Bill," I nodded. "He's fine, thanks." And I made a movement to pass on towards the inner office.

"Bill wouldn't sometimes go by the name of Dagobert, I suppose?" he inquired with studied casualness. "Dagobert Brown, I mean."

"I know which Dagobert you mean," I answered tartly, trying to think what to say next.

"Old Sir Clovis Brown's third, or was it fourth, son?" he suggested.

"Fourth," I said.

"Dagobert married Irene Sackville at the beginning of the war, didn't he? I seem to remember that the affair was rather splashed in the *Tattler*."

"You would have been about nine at the time," I pointed out.

"What's happened to Irene? I wonder," he mused, inhaling his cigarette without, unfortunately, choking himself.

"Don't tell me there is anything about anyone's private life that you don't know!" I exclaimed.

"I could check up on it," he said.

"You do a lot of checking up in your spare time, don't you?"

"I get around," he nodded easily.

I paused impotently, feeling frustrated and silly. My clever move last week of allowing Oates to blackmail me no longer seemed quite so clever.

"Don't you think, just for the sake of appearances," I said, "it would be better if you stood up when you spoke to me?"

He uncrossed his legs and recrossed them the other way round. "I'll hear anyone coming," he reassured me. "I have good ears." He offered me a cigarette and when I refused continued confidently: "D'you know, Miss Hamish, for over a year you've had me completely gufoogled."

"Gufoogled?" For an awful moment I was afraid it was a term of yearning or affection.

"Gufoogled. Flummoxed. Bemused, bewildered," he explained. "I had you all wrong."

"Oh, that."

"You looked so dignified, so snooty, if you know what I mean. Mind you," he hastened to add, "you were always a good-looker. I always thought that. Only you never seemed to relax. It just shows how little any of us knows about human nature, doesn't it?"

"Absorbing as these reflections are," I said, "I wonder

if you'd mind if I ran along. I work here. You can have the day off, if that's what the conversation's all about."

"Thanks, Miss Hamish," he grinned, "but I've nothing on particularly. I'll pop into your room later when you're not too busy."

"I'll look forward to that."

"So long then, for the moment." He dismissed me graciously.

I reached my own room not quite knowing whether to burst into tears or laughter. The conversation with Oates had been so preposterous that it left me light-headed. I had no idea what I was going to do about it. The situation was so far beyond me that I felt totally reckless. For the moment I didn't even seem to care.

Sarah had already been hastily through the post and put half a dozen letters on my desk which I was supposed to deal with. As a kind of exercise in self-discipline I made myself read through them attentively, jotting down an occasional note: look out the lease of 104 Walnut Grove Avenue, confirm Mr. Titterton's appointment for Thursday.

Then I looked into Mr. Playfair's room. Mr. Playfair had not yet arrived, but Major Stewart was sitting at his desk, imagining, I suppose, what it would feel like to be Senior Partner. An impressive legal tome—a precedent book —was open on the desk before him. He looked moody and grumpy, and I therefore greeted him with my most flashy smile.

"Good morning, Jimmy." I don't know what imp of recklessness caused me to add: "Seeing whether there are any Private and Confidential letters for Mr. Playfair this morning?"

His good-looking face went a deeper colour. "I was just

brushing up on some of the cases I once studied," he explained. "Amazing how one forgets."

I came round beside him. "Anonymous letter cases?" I inquired, still impelled by my demon of recklessness.

He closed the book, but not before I had glimpsed the subject matter he had been so engrossed in.

"No. Something quite different," he said.

The something quite different, had he known it, was quite as interesting to me as it was to himself. The matter he had been brushing up on was Blackmail.

"I haven't seen Rosemary this morning," I said. "It's not like her to be so late."

"Miss Proctor just telephoned," he said. "She's not feeling well today and will not come in."

Miss Proctor! I raised a mental eyebrow. It was hard for us to keep track from day to day of what terms we were on with Jimmy. Sometimes it was Rosemary, Jane and Sarah, sometimes Miss Proctor, Miss Hamish and Miss Swinburne. Jimmy keeps his women guessing.

"How was Friday evening? Rosemary told me you were going to the Normandy," I lied.

"It was all right," he said without enthusiasm.

I might, and strictly speaking should, have taken this cue to withdraw, but I had a feeling that he wanted to say something to me. With Jimmy you could always tell when there was something on his mind. You could almost hear him taking a deep breath, like a swimmer about to plunge into cold water. I strolled casually towards the door, waiting for it.

"Oh Jane, by the way."

"Yes, Major Stewart."

"Why don't we do a show together some evening?"

This was a roundabout approach to something else which I couldn't yet see. "Why don't we?" I encouraged.

"You refused me very firmly the last time I asked you," he said. "Do you remember? I had to go by myself. I got as tight as an owl. Do you know what I did?"

"I'm dying to know."

"Mind you," he chuckled merrily, "the whole thing's a bit woolly in my mind, but my recollection is that I grabbed a taxi before the show was finished and instead of giving it my Inigo Mews address I had myself driven here to the office!"

"You must have been cold," I said.

"Cold?"

"Without any gas on."

"Wasn't there any gas?" he said airily. "That's right, that was the famous night when the gas failed, wasn't it? What a night!"

"What—as you say—a night!" I nodded.

There was a pause, slightly awkward. I knew the conversation was finished, but I lingered hopefully. After all his opening move had been to invite me to the theatre.

"Cigarette?" he asked, extending his case. He felt in his pocket, presumably for a lighter or a box of matches, but without result.

"I had a lighter once," he grumbled, "a rather neat little job, gold. It seems to have disappeared."

"Things are always disappearing around this office." This wasn't strictly true, but for some reason I was thinking of Mrs. Wolf-Heatherington's coins. "There's a box of matches in the left-hand drawer."

He found it and lighted my cigarette. "Now that I remember it," he exclaimed, "Miss Proctor was here."

I looked bewildered, as though I hadn't followed him.

"That awful night," he supplied, "when I got so horribly oiled. She was deep in the ledgers, but she probably told you all about it."

At last the purpose of this great waste of Daniel Playfair & Son's time was plain. Rosemary had told him that she had told me about his nocturnal jaunt on that fatal evening. He knew, therefore, that I knew. So he had casually related the whole thing over again, just to prove how little it mattered.

"No," I answered innocently, "I don't think Rosemary said anything about it to me."

"Didn't she?" He sounded puzzled and a little annoyed. "Still it doesn't matter. We had something of a row and I went home."

"By taxi?"

"No. I couldn't find one. I walked."

"You probably met some people on the way," I said helpfully, "who could identify you in a pinch."

"Why should I want anyone to identify me?" he asked in a puzzled tone of voice. Then, as though he had just got it, he laughed heartily. "I see what you're driving at! That alibi the idiot gas inspector said I'd want for the night of the 29th-30th of November. Why should I want an alibi for that night?"

"You tell me," I smiled gaily. "Have you seen the gas man since?"

He shook his head, and at that moment the door opened. Jimmy started visibly and stared at the door. I really think he half expected to see Dagobert standing there. But it was only Mr. Playfair.

19 ✳ With Rosemary absent that day I was rushed off my feet and almost forgot Oates's promise to pop in for a moment. Sarah, too, was in a useless, silly mood. She was expecting Douglas to take her out to luncheon.

"That woman called again about the house in Airlie Gardens," she said to me. "Mrs. What's-her-name. I can never remember it."

"Mrs. Richardson?" I suggested.

"No. Don't be so dumb! She was in every day last week, fussing. Mrs. Green—no, that isn't it. Mrs. . . . what's the matter with you this morning, Jane!"

"With *me?*" I protested mildly. "Apart from the fact that I didn't spend the week-end with a handsome tea-planter, nothing."

"He is rather a dear, isn't he, Jane. Will you be a brides-maid?"

"Yes, but I'd better telephone Mrs. White first."

"White! That's the name. You are a beast. You knew who I meant all along."

I found Mrs. White's telephone number and began to dial. Sarah was inspecting her fingernails. They were broken and of unequal length, but she had coated them with a repellent blood-red varnish which was totally out of character.

"You must practise remembering Mrs. White's name," I said to her. "Clients hate you to forget their names. Besides . . . Damn! The line's engaged!" I replaced the receiver. "Have you ever heard of Freud?"

"Have we a client named Freud?"

"No. He wrote a book—all about people who forget names."

I found Mr. Playfair's room a haven of peace after the madhouse outside. He looked up from *The Times* and smiled as though he were glad to see me. The smile became a little fixed as I told him about an appointment he'd made with a Mr. Dowling this afternoon.

"It will be about the application for a wine and spirit licence," he sighed. "You might look up the Dowling file for me sometime before this afternoon."

"I have it here, Mr. Playfair," I said, putting it down on the desk in front of him.

"Have you?" he murmured sadly. "So you have. Thank you so much, Miss Hamish."

He extricated *The Times* from under the Dowling file, which I had rather pointedly placed on top of it. It was folded back, as I had already seen, at the half-filled-in crossword puzzle.

"There's one clue here that I don't seem to get the hang of," he said. "Three words—five, three and four. If 'persiflage' is correct, the first word starts with a 'P.' I fancy it's two names, somebody and somebody."

"What's the clue?" I asked.

He adjusted his spectacles and read: "Two little dickey birds sitting on a wall."

"One named Peter, the other named Paul!" I continued triumphantly. "Peter and Paul."

"Of course! How stupid of me. I don't know what's happening to my old brain."

I left him in unhappy contemplation of the Dowling file. I'd promised to meet Dagobert at half past one, but I saw no possibility of making it. Sarah came to my rescue.

"If you really want to go out shopping at half past one," she said, "Douglas and I can eat fish paste and things here. It will save him a lot of money anyway."

"You know your man," I said. "But is that the way to lure him? You save his money afterwards. Besides, Douglas, as his mother's sole heir, is comfortably provided for."

"I hate his taking any of her money!" Sarah said with surprising venom.

"He's earned it."

"What do you mean?" she demanded quickly.

I hadn't really meant anything in particular, but Sarah had gone as white as a sheet.

"I only meant he is her son, and why shouldn't he be her heir," I answered slowly. "You'd better get him to take you out and give you a drink. You look as though you'd seen a ghost. You haven't seen a ghost by any chance?"

And I left her to think over the implications of my last remark. As a matter of fact I was thinking them over rather busily myself.

Major Stewart and Mr. Playfair went out to luncheon together at exactly one and the office was enjoying that momentary lull of peace which always follows their departure. Sarah was waiting all of a twitter in the outer office for Douglas to turn up. My door opened and Oates sidled in.

"Sorry I haven't had a moment free until now, Miss Hamish," he apologised.

"I've been reasonably busy too," I said. "Close the door behind you. I don't want everyone to hear me being blackmailed."

"Blackmailed, Miss Hamish?" He sounded hurt and disappointed in me. "I only want to do you a favour."

"Quite. How much?"

"How much what? Gee, Miss Hamish, you're a funny one. Who wants to blackmail you? I only thought you and I might, er—co-operate a little, if you follow me. Honestly, I want to help you."

"To do what?"

"To have a good time." He made an expansive gesture. "To see life."

"I've already seen it."

"To make some money."

"I'm already making six pounds ten shillings a week, Oates, on which I manage to scrape along. That is what this job is worth to me—exactly that and no more. I mention these sordid details so that you'll know where you are. I have nothing saved up, and it will be quite useless for you to try to get anything more out of me."

"Who's trying to get anything out of you?" he protested querulously.

"Aren't you?"

"Listen, Miss Hamish, couldn't we talk this thing over in a friendly way? You're a woman of the world. I'm a man of the world. We could go places together."

"What places? Gaol?"

"That's what I like about you, Miss Hamish," he grinned, making himself comfortable on the edge of my desk and toying absent-mindedly—that is, it looked absent-minded—with my handbag. "You've got a sense of humour. Gee! I hate to turn the screws on you, really I do!"

"It hurts me more than it does you," I admitted.

This mild remark also seemed to please him, for he laughed delightedly and nudged me with his elbow. "See what I mean?" he exclaimed. "Always kidding. I'd love to introduce you to some of the boys. You dress all right, too."

"Thanks, but aren't we straying from the point?"

He had my handbag open by this time and he was fumbling still absent-mindedly among its contents: my ration book and identity card, two pound notes and some loose change. He fingered my lipstick with ill-concealed contempt.

"I could get you a Guerlain lipstick," he said.

"*Rose foncé* is my colour," I supplied.

"I'll make a note of that. Could you do with half a dozen nylon stockings?"

"I am not inhuman."

He laughed again. Practically everything seemed to amuse Oates. "I don't think you are at that!" he exclaimed, sweeping me with his theatrically practised eye. I remained unmoved by the agressive male in him.

"And after I receive the Guerlain lipstick and the nylons," I inquired, "what happens next?"

"Next? Nothing."

"I can't tell you how relieved I am."

"We're just pals, that's all. By the way, what was Dagobert Brown doing the other day got up as a workman?"

"I don't know. He has a passion for fancy dress."

"He was up to something, if you ask me."

"I wonder what it could be," I said ingenuously. "Normally we have no secrets from each other."

He shook his head. "Everybody has secrets, Miss Hamish," he told me. "The most innocent-looking people have things they want to hide. Take yourself, for instance. For months I've been thinking you were like Ceasar's wife—if you'll forgive the classical allusion—above reproach. What do I find? You're running around with another woman's husband. You're human—like the rest of us. Mind you, I like you all the better for it. It makes you easier to get along with."

He didn't pat my knee, but the thought crossed his mind.

I said thoughtfully: "I wonder what poor old Mrs. Robjohn was hiding?"

He froze slightly. "Why are you always on about Mrs. Robjohn?" he demanded.

"No reason. I just took a case at random. I can't imagine that she had any very disreputable secrets in her past." I reached across and helped myself uninvited to one of the Egyptian cigarettes from the case he was fumbling in. "Unless, of course," I added carelessly, "it was something to do with the Polish pianist—you probably know his name, Sirkorski."

He drew a swift breath. "Did you know about that?"

"I get around too," I nodded.

He recovered his equanimity. "Well then," he shrugged, "you see what I mean. They've all got something to hide, even the best of them."

"The problem is how to turn this simple little fact of nature into hard cash," I suggested.

"You catch on quick, Miss Hamish."

"How do *you* do it?"

"I'm glad you asked me that, Miss Hamish. It's a problem I've given lots of thought to. The technique can be summed up in three short words: 'easy does it.'"

"I'm engrossed," I said truthfully. "Go on."

"Well, you see you don't want to rush things." He was discussing his own subject and like all experts he talked confidently and at length. "You don't want to go up to a bloke and say: 'I know you pinched a fiver out of the petty cash box, pay me to keep my mouth shut or else!' That would only put his back up, and no one would benefit. Besides, he might sock you. No. You want to sympathise with him, pretend you'd have done the same thing in his place, and then casually let slip the fact that you've accidentally left your wallet behind and borrow just enough from him to pay for a round of half pints. He'll think he's getting off easy, and what a swell bloke you are. Next time you borrow enough for, say, a round of pints. This gets him into the proper frame of mind, develops the right habits in him, if you get my meaning. The third time it can be whisky. In other words you turn the screws slowly, so it doesn't hurt. Afterwards you can borrow taxi fare, and later on perhaps you can say you're a bit short over the week-end and can he let you have a couple of quid until Monday. See the sort of thing I mean?"

I nodded. "But taking a specific example," I said. "Me, for instance. How do you start?"

He grinned, and I must confess, scored neatly on me. "I've already started," he said. "No, seriously, Miss Hamish, we're pals. With people I really like it's different. I help them, just as I'm going to help you."

He took the two pound notes from my handbag, folded them neatly and placed them in his own wallet.

"I thought you didn't get around to the 'couple of quid' stage until much later," I complained.

"Oh this!" He dismissed my objection lightly. "This isn't a loan. I'm going to invest these two pounds for you on the two-thirty this afternoon at Nottingham—Peg o' my Heart. She's about eight to one and—don't let this go any further—a dead cert. I'm doing you a favour, see?"

"Not altogether. I'm so slow."

"Two quid at eight to one makes sixteen," he explained patiently. "Chicken feed, but something to go on with, a beginning as you might say. You leave it to me, Miss Hamish."

He eased himself off my desk, clicked my handbag shut and handed it back to me. I took it gratefully. At least he had left my ration book.

"And the candy coupons are all for me?" I asked.

"Would you like a five-pound box of Swiss chocolates?"

"You mustn't spoil me," I protested.

"That's okay—anything you want, just let me know." He paused for a moment, draping himself gracefully in the door. He raised a willowy hand with two fingers intertwined. "You and I are going to be like that," he said.

And he withdrew, leaving me to visualise this delightful prospect.

20 ✳ When I related all this to Dagobert shortly afterwards he was delighted. I had vaguely hoped for a different reaction. I suppose I had hoped to hear Dagobert mutter something about breaking the insolent ruffian's neck. Instead he was charmed by the picture I drew of our office boy. He seemed to think I'd made a desirable connection, a friendship worth cultivating.

We had luncheon in a cafeteria in the Earls Court Road, where our long and absorbing conversation was only interrupted by people catching us in the back with trays, and occasionally spilling a substance called coffee over us. We had shepherd's pie and half a bottle of tomato ketchup.

I gave Dagobert a brief résumé of my morning which in retrospect had not been without its points of interest. At least Dagobert thought so. He made more notes in his notebook, wiping tomato ketchup off the page and covering it with large question marks, exclamation marks and other signs which doubtless meant something to him.

"This will all be useful to you," he said, "when you come to write it up in your book." (Parenthetically it might have been had I ever been able afterwards to decipher any of it.)

Before he gave me an account of his own morning's activities he ran through the notes he had taken from me.

"What was the name of that horse again—in the two-thirty?"

"Peg o' my Heart."

"I might venture half a crown on it for a place. And that woman who is buying the house in Airlie Gardens?"

"Mrs. White."

He printed the name. "And Miss Proctor is off for the day. The day or only this morning?"

"That probably depends," I said cattily, "on what time she made her appointment with the hairdressers."

"Let's see, Stewart says they had a row that night. Peter and Paul was the answer to the crossword clue, wasn't it?" he added. "Did you say *rose foncé* was your colour?"

"What I like about you, Dagobert," I said, "is the clear systematic way you have of putting questions, so that the simplest intelligence can see exactly how your mind's working. Does any of this really get us anywhere?"

"No," he admitted, "but it gives you an amazing feeling of insight and penetration to ask these keen, apparently disconnected questions. I asked a man this morning what brand of pipe tobacco he was smoking on the night of the 29th of November, and you should have seen the way I went up in his estimation."

"Anyway you've got me guessing," I confessed. "What have you been up to?"

"I've been having a modest half pint of mild ale with a man named Joe who smokes Digger Mixture and breeds love birds. I must tell you about love birds some day. Joe also drives a taxi."

"The rank on the other side of the High Street, opposite Mandel Street?"

"That's the one. On the night of November 29th he drove a young lady from Number 11 Mandel Street to Oratory Street, Brompton Road. A rather attractive bit of goods, according to Joe."

"I'm dying to hear Joe's description of Rosemary, but what time was it?"

"Eleven thirty-five."

"Just when she *said* she went home," I nodded. "Damn."

"After leaving her in Oratory Street, Joe drove back to Kensington. Always eager for variety he returned by way of the Cromwell Road, turned right into Marlowes Road and then through Mandel Mews into Mandel Square. This was about midnight."

"Go on."

"Don't rush me. It took me two hours to get all this." He paused to empty the remainder of the tomato ketchup over a piece of bread and to pour the coffee which he had spilt into his saucer back into his cup. I knew that something important was coming: he was being entirely too casual.

"So Joe saw the murderer that night in Mandel Square?" I suggested.

"He may have," Dagobert nodded. "This coffee's good. I wonder how they make it. . . . There was another taxi in Mandel Square when Joe drove through. It was parked in front of Number 17. Someone got out and went up to the door. From now on Joe becomes less reliable. He didn't catch sight of the fare's face. But he is certain (a) that it was a man and (b) that the man was wearing evening clothes." He lighted a cigarette and tossed the match into his coffee. "That," he concluded, "is the sum total of my morning's work. I think I'll go to the movies this afternoon."

"It might have been someone else coming home, one of the other lodgers," I said, controlling my excitement at the very startling discovery Dagobert had made.

"It might," he agreed, "but it wasn't. Mr. Peterkins, on the second floor front, was in all the evening. He had a cold and Mrs. Hawthorne took him up a cup of tea at about nine-thirty, just before she gave Mrs. Robjohn the shilling for two sixpences. Mr. Havers, the only other male member of the household, does not possess evening clothes."

"Major Stewart was wearing tails that night," I mused. "By the way, I told you, didn't I, that he couldn't find a taxi when he left the office shortly after eleven. He walked home."

Dagobert nodded. "He could have picked up one on the way and given it the wrong address again. He had rather a flair that evening for giving the wrong address. He could have said 17 Mandel Square instead of 2 Inigo Mews. He *could*."

"If I were going to murder someone I don't think I should call a taxi and give it my proposed victim's address."

"Not if you had planned to murder her. If the idea occurred to you after you'd got there—if you found the gas had conveniently failed, and you merely took advantage of the opportunity, you might. Good Lord!" He glanced at his wrist watch and jumped to his feet. "I'll miss the Mickey Mouse—I hope. Can I drop you anywhere?"

He leapt on the first bus which passed us while I walked back to the office.

"Look, Jane, what Douglas has brought us," Sarah greeted me. "A complete new tea set. That is, it was complete before we broke the sugar basin."

"Very pretty," I admired it briefly. "He must drop in some day *around tea-time*, and use it."

"I think that's a hint," Douglas grinned.

"In a way," I said. "Sarah, the Cornwall Gardens deeds are somewhere at the bottom of the pile beside the coal scuttle in Mr. Playfair's room. Send Oates round to the bank with them. He's in the front office pretending to read a French novel; he'll be glad of an excuse to stop."

It was an exhausting afternoon and by four-thirty we were glad of the tea Sarah brought round in Douglas's new tea set.

I put my cup to one side for a moment while I finished off a clause of the Airlie Gardens Assignment I was preparing for Mrs. White. Then I sat back for a moment's breathing spell, sipping my tea gratefully. My eye fell on a copy of a late edition of *The Star* which Sarah had left me with my tea-cup. The headlines stated that the Foreign Ministers were meeting again next week when it was hoped that a formula might be found. I turned to the Woman's Page, noting how it was possible to turn one winter outfit into six different outfits by the cunning disposition of a silk pocket handkerchief and a refreshing change of buttons. As I refolded the paper I glimpsed the Stop Press news out of the corner of my eye. The Racing Results. Peg o' my Heart had won the two-thirty at Nottingham at eight to one. Twice eight made sixteen. Why hadn't I let Oates blackmail me before?

The telephone rang. I lifted the receiver and said hello. It was Dagobert.

"Ever been psychoanalysed over the telephone?" he asked.

I said I hadn't.

"I want your very first association with the test words I give you," he said. "I say a word. You reply with the first thing that comes into your mind. You're not to hesitate or think. Are you ready?"

"Does this go on for very long?" I asked.

"Fortnum."

"Mason."

"Mason."

"I said that. All right, Dixon."

"Gin."

"Sherry."

"There's nothing wrong with you," he said. "Reaction all too normal. Fish."

"Queue."

"Flower."

"Scrophularia aquatica."

"I don't believe you. You hesitated."

"Wouldn't you, over a name like that?" I pointed out.

"Ham and eggs."

"You're supposed to say ham, while I reply eggs."

"Don't argue. I want the first thing that comes into your mind. Ham and eggs."

"A joke in *Punch*—something about a perplexed child asking startled parent what are ham and eggs."

"Peter and Paul."

"What was that?"

"You heard me. Now fast. Peter and Paul."

"Rob Peter to pay Paul," I said, honestly stating the first association which came into my mind.

"Rob Peter," he continued.

"Robjohn," I said. "Did it have to take all this time? Or were you merely putting me at my ease?"

"Rouge," he said.

"Red."

"White."

This time I did hesitate and I must confess my heart was fluttering. You can never tell with Dagobert; sometimes there is method in his madness.

"All right," I acknowledged, "you've made your point quite clear. My first reaction to White was Blanche. But none of this proves anything."

"It's interesting though, isn't it," he said cheerfully.

I had to admit that it was. Unlike Sarah I had read that book by Freud, not very intelligently perhaps, but enough to grasp the fact that when people forget names which they ought to remember there is a reason. And the reason is almost always because the name has a disagreeable association. Subconsciously it reminds them of something else—something which they wish to or must forget. In other words, Sarah couldn't remember Mrs. White's name because subconsciously she linked it with Blanche Robjohn. Peter and Paul eluded Mr. Playfair because in his unconscious mind there was a chain of association—through the missing link, Rob Peter—which ended with Robjohn. Both Sarah and Mr. Playfair, deep down in their subconscious minds, felt an imperious need to forget Blanche Robjohn.

"Was this all you wanted to say to me?" I asked.

"You know my Aunt Osyth?" He said.

"The vegetarian?"

"That's the one. She wants me to dine with her tonight. She's about to become a Buddhist, and I imagine she wants to talk it over with me. That means we can't forgather this evening. Have you got a good book?"

"I'll find one," I promised and rang off.

On the whole I rather looked forward to an evening alone. I should make myself a powdered-egg omelette and have a raw-carrot salad, prop a book up on the edge of my tray and have supper in front of the fire. Afterwards I would have leisure for those running repairs which one is so apt to neglect; laddered stockings, buttons which are just about to come off, the lining of my tweed suit. Then I should have a very hot bath, using some of the new bath essence I had bought for Rosemary's Christmas present—I could buy her some more tomorrow perhaps. Afterwards I should read in bed.

Spiritually fortified by these agreeable anticipations I pitched in to Mrs. White's assignment so effectively that I finished the draft by five o'clock and turned it over to Sarah to type. She said she'd do it tomorrow. I then returned to Sir John's accounts. Mr. Playfair went, Sarah departed in a flurry and I worked on with leisurely efficiency. It was delightful not feeling hurried.

I'd almost forgotten about Peg o' my Heart when Oates appeared. I greeted him with a cool self-possession which took him momentarily aback and made him forget we were now "like that."

"It's about the race this afternoon, isn't it," I said. "Do sit down for a moment while I finish these figures."

He sat down on the edge of a chair, giving his trousers a slight hitch up so as not to spoil their knife-edge crease. I observed his shoes with admiration: they were suède brogues, olive green.

"I see we won this afternoon," I said finally. "Congratulations."

He removed his wallet and tapped it affectionately. It was bulging. The feel of it seemed to restore his confidence.

"We could have a party on this," he said. "Doing anything tonight?"

"I'm afraid I am," I said sweetly.

"Okay, okay," he shrugged. "Some other time."

He strolled over to my desk and counted out sixteen pound notes. I watched fascinated by the sight of such riches. He divided the notes into two equal piles of eight pounds each. One he replaced in his wallet.

"Commission?" I asked.

"We're partners, aren't we?" he pointed out.

He divided the remaining eight pounds into two further piles of four pounds each. One of these he clipped with a paper clip and put into another compartment of his wallet.

"Expenses?" I suggested.

"Reserve capital," he explained. "Sometimes in this game you take a loss. Then you fall back on your reserve capital."

"I see," I nodded, making an instinctive motion towards the remaining four pounds.

He anticipated me. He divided them a third time. Two pounds he folded carefully and returned to his wallet.

"This is your bet for tomorrow," he said. "Pink Lady in the three o'clock at Windsor. Only five to two, but we can't afford to take chances."

"No, I can see that," I nodded. "If she wins at only five to two I'm bound to be out a packet. And have I won all that?" I added, glancing doubtfully at the two remaining pound notes.

"Sure," he said. "Why not?"

I should have grabbed them then and there, for he suddenly wavered.

"Perhaps," he reconsidered, picking them up himself, "since Pink Lady's only five to two we'd better have four quid on her. You leave it all to me, Miss Hamish. I told you we'd get along all right. I've got to run along now. But don't you worry your pretty little head about anything."

He had a further change of mind before he reached the door. Plainly he'd been having a struggle with his conscience.

"I'll tell you what I'll do," he said. "I'll only put three pounds on Pink Lady. Here's a quid for you. That'll show you what sort of bloke I am. Spend it any way you like." And he tossed a pound note lavishly on my desk. I put it hastily in my handbag before he asked me for ten shillings change.

"Have you any evening clothes, Oates?" I inquired.

"Evening clothes!" he repeated. "She asks me if I have any evening clothes! Sister, you ought to see my tails; they're cut like a dream. Or my double-breasted dinner jacket for informal occasions. It fits me like a glove. Just say the word one night and we'll step out."

I didn't say the word and he went.

After that I wrote a covering letter to Sir John Hartley with the accounts and, when I had locked up the office, posted the envelope at the bottom of the street. A lovely free evening was before me, the evening I had planned so carefully. I walked up the High Street and went to the cinema.

21 ✳ Next day just before one o'clock Mr. Playfair went out to luncheon and shortly afterwards Douglas arrived for Sarah. I covered the typewriter and started towards Rosemary's room with the idea of consulting her about food. I nearly ran into Jimmy just coming out. He looked black and angry and he made for the front door, ignoring me.

"What was the matter with the gallant Major?" I asked as I entered.

"Life would be so much simpler, Jane," Rosemary sighed, "if there were no such thing as men."

"Simpler, yes," I agreed. "Did you enjoy your day off?"

"Jane, I had the most extraordinary day! I'm dying to tell you all about it. I . . ." She broke off, blushing suddenly. "It was really rather dreadful, I suppose."

"In that case let's have all the details at once. Was it the man upstairs?"

"No. No, I haven't seen him for weeks, well, days. I had to be rather firm the last time with him. Thank heavens Sarah is out and we can talk. Jane! He was really most exciting. I suppose I was silly to say anything about it to Jimmy—what do you think?"

"Always a mistake," I agreed, lighting the gas ring under the kettle. "What did you say?"

But Rosemary was incapable of coherence. She was now examining herself critically in her handbag mirror. "Would you say the streak of white in my hair made me look naïve and unsophisticated?"

"I always imagined its intention was the opposite. Did he say that?"

She nodded thoughtfully. "Maybe I am unsophisticated, underneath it all, Jane. I've often wondered that."

"Just a lost child—looking for something. We all are. I'm looking for that can of sardines."

"You've just put it on the table," she pointed out, practical for a moment. "He used exactly the same words: a lost child—looking for something."

"Then his line is lousy," I said.

"I think he was teasing me."

At this moment I hadn't a notion what she was talking about, or I might have added: "then his line is familiar." Instead I concentrated on the sardines, waiting for her to tell her story in her own way.

"It's fun being teased, Jane. I haven't been teased for years. Most men are so intense. Do you think Jimmy's jealous? I know I ought not to have said anything; but he has no *right* to be jealous. He of all people—with all his little shopgirls! What's sauce for the goose is sauce for the gander, and besides if he feels like that he might have come round yesterday to see me himself. He knew I wasn't well."

"You look extremely well," I said.

"Anyhow he *thought* I wasn't well. I telephoned him yesterday morning to say so. I think he might at least have suggested coming round to see me, don't you? It's really *his* fault I got so involved yesterday."

To my bewilderment she was suddenly dabbing a tear in her eye with the corner of a small lace handkerchief. Rosemary's emotional life is getting too complex for me.

"I can't quite make out whether you're furious with Jimmy, or delighted with the handsome stranger," I said.

"Both," she admitted frankly. "Let's not talk about Jimmy."

"We do seem to have exhausted that subject on one occasion or another," I agreed.

"He isn't really handsome, you know." The threatening tears had vanished; all was sparkling sunshine again. "Interesting rather, and immensely vital. I think I've fallen for him —just a wee bit."

"I'm afraid you'll have to start at the beginning and introduce me," I said. "You see I haven't the faintest idea whom you're talking about. What's his name?"

Rosemary giggled happily. "I don't even know!" she gasped. "You'll think I'm a complete tart, Jane, but, well, you know how these things happen."

"At any rate I'm dying to learn," I confessed.

"I'd come back after luncheon from the hairdresser," she continued eagerly, "I meant to lie down for a while. I really had a headache. I took two Veganins, put on my house gown —the one with the ostrich feathers and the adorable ruby clasp—my fluffy pink lambskin mules, drew the curtains and lay down. Then the bell rang. I opened the door and there he stood!"

"The interesting, vital stranger?"

"Yes. He said: 'Have you a vacuum cleaner?' I said, yes. He said: 'Could I interest you in the *Encyclopaedia Britannica* on easy payments?' I said, certainly not. 'What about an electric refrigerator?' he asked. I explained that I had one. I should, of course, have closed the door in his face, but somehow I didn't, and somehow I found he had stepped inside and removed his hat. 'I'm relieved,' he said, 'to find that you have a vacuum cleaner and a refrigerator and that you don't want the *Encyclopaedia Britannica*, because I'm not selling vacuum cleaners, refrigerators or encyclopaedias.' I asked him what he was selling. The question seemed to stump him for a moment. Then he said: 'Let's see . . . I've got a rather exclusive line here in lipsticks: Guerlain, *rose foncé*.' And he actually produced one."

I spilled some of the sardine oil on the blotting paper and scraped it up with a paper knife.

"Just a second!" I interrupted. "What time did all this take place?"

"About four, I should think. What difference does it make?"

"None at all. Do go on. I'm entranced."

"Well, I bought the lipstick," she said, giggling irritatingly. "In fact, here it is." She produced it from her handbag and waved it before my narrowed eyes. "One thing led to another. You know how it is, Jane."

"I know."

"He took off his overcoat and made himself completely at home. We had tea. In fact he went into the kitchenette and made it himself."

"I'll bet he did!"

"In fact he was so informal I felt at the end of half an hour I'd known him for years."

"At the end of about half an hour," I suggested, "I suppose he excused himself and went out to a public call box to telephone."

Rosemary looked at me with surprise. "He did, as a matter of fact!" she exclaimed. "How on earth did you know?"

"They always do," I said. "It's their regular routine. They go out to telephone their wives that they're held up in town by a business appointment, or an unexpected invitation to dinner from a rich aunt."

"He didn't look married," Rosemary protested.

"They never do."

"In fact I'm sure he isn't. I asked him, and he said he was 'walking out' with a respectable but, I gather, rather dull creature who 'appeals to the intellectual side of his nature.'"

"He has an intellectual side, too?"

She laughed merrily. "Yes, but he keeps it under control. He was really great fun, Jane. I wonder if he'll turn up again this evening?"

"I very much doubt it," I said sourly. "But to continue with the sordid story . . ."

"I really don't think you altogether approve, Jane! I suppose I *did* behave shockingly."

"Did you?" I inquired coldly.

"Well, considering I'd never seen him before. But it didn't seem like that, Jane. I wish I could make you understand. He was so pleasant, so agreeable, so easy to get along with. I found myself talking to him as though we were old friends. And yet with Jimmy I still feel strange, sometimes as though I hate him. I do hate him at times."

"We decided not to discuss Jimmy," I reminded her. "What did you talk to your salesman about?"

"I practically told him the story of my life," she sighed. "He was so understanding. That's when he told me I looked naïve and unsophisticated. We went out to dinner finally."

"What do you mean—*finally?*"

"After we'd talked and talked. He took me to a place I'd never been to before. Chantel's, Sorel's, something like that. Do you know it?"

"They're famous for their *sole normande*, their woodcock and their gruyère fondu," I said, biting viciously into a sardine.

"How extraordinary!" Rosemary exclaimed. "That's exactly what we had! I must say it was simply delicious."

"It didn't choke him, by any chance?"

"Why should it? He chose it. You don't seem to like my new friend, Jane."

"I've met the kind before. And afterwards?"

"We went dancing. He dances divinely."

This was news to me. In fact I'd had a few words with him on the subject of listening to the music and not talking so much. But then of course I only appealed to the intellectual side of his nature!

"Oh, I know it was only an episode, Jane," she sighed, "and that it won't lead anywhere. But I felt so young and gay and, yes, *happy* while it lasted. I know you're laughing at me, but I'm not hard-boiled the way you are. I wish I were."

At the moment I rather wished I were, too! One's basic reactions remain disgustingly crude. Absurd as it may sound, I was quite simply jealous. I could cheerfully have scratched Dagobert's eyes out. I am ashamed of myself, but I am trying to put down the truth.

"I *was* happy, Jane," she persisted, as though I had contradicted her. "You think I'm soppy, don't you?"

"Yes."

"All right, I *am* soppy. It wasn't because of him, really. It was the way he treated me, the way he smiled at me, laughed at me, made me feel I was a young and highly desirable woman. He may only have been a technically proficient flatterer for all I know. I didn't care. I swallowed it all greedily, without giving a damn whether it was genuine or not. When I got home eventually I felt so light-headed that I did something completely mad."

"Don't tell me if it outrages your modesty," I said, half meaning it.

"No. *He'd* gone. I suddenly telephoned Jimmy."

"Good Lord! Whatever for?"

"I don't know. Just to let him know how pleased with life I was. To make him jealous, I suppose."

"And did you?"

She shook her head and I almost regretted the coldness of my question. It was going to be difficult if I started feeling sorry for Rosemary Proctor. For some reason I felt towards her the same mingled exasperation and pity I used to feel towards Mrs. Robjohn. She looked haggard and years older as she answered my question.

"No. He was cross at being wakened up. Then, when I told him what a marvellous time I'd had, he sounded almost relieved. He said he was glad I'd enjoyed myself. He didn't care, Jane." She turned away sharply. "He just . . . didn't . . . *care*."

I said bluntly: "Why don't you forget all about Major James Stewart?"

"Why?" She stifled a little hysterical laugh. "Why indeed?"

I couldn't make out whether it was genuine or merely theatrical. I don't suppose she knew herself. Rosemary's emotional world is half fact, half fancy.

"You haven't had anything to eat," I said. "And your coffee's getting cold."

"I'm not hungry, Jane, but I'll have a cigarette if you can spare one."

I produced a packet. She took one without comment and fumbled in her handbag for her lighter.

"Anyway," she said with a brave, patient smile, "I had

a grand time last night, and that's that." She continued to fumble in her handbag. "What was I looking for?" she murmured.

"Your lighter."

"Of course. Like a fool I—" She broke off, and again she stifled that little hysterical laugh. "Never mind. I've got some matches somewhere."

"Don't tell me you've lost that pet of a lighter!" I exclaimed.

There seemed to be an epidemic of lighter-losing in our office. Yesterday Jimmy had complained of the same thing. Rosemary's lighter I remembered well, because I had myself cast covetous eyes on it: a slim, oblong gold affair, inconspicuously chic. I should have been much less casual if it had been mine.

"Never mind," she repeated. "I wonder if he's having luncheon again with that little bitch from the bank . . ."

22 * Somebody seems to have said that hard work is good for a broken heart. My heart wasn't exactly broken, but there were one or two things I wanted to say to Dagobert about last night. The Aunt Osyth angle, I decided, was what hurt most—the insult to my intelligence!

Meanwhile I tried work. I drafted out two contracts and placated at least half a dozen clients. I was efficiency itself. By the time Sarah had brought tea around Dagobert was no more to me than a faintly disagreeable incident in the dim past.

Oates had interrupted the rhythm of my efficiency for a moment at about four by dropping in to say that Pink Lady had inexplicably come in fourth at Windsor. He was going to have a word or two with the bloke who had misled him.

After I had swallowed my cup of tea I took a couple of letters for signature into Mr. Playfair's room. Douglas, apparently taking advantage of my invitation to drop in for tea some day, was there, chatting aimlessly with Mr. Playfair and wasting Mr. Playfair's time, a thing which it is only too easy to do. Since the conversation with Sirkorski I had understood a little better why Mr. Playfair was so affectionately disposed towards Douglas. It was a curious thought, but had circumstances been otherwise Mr. Playfair himself might have been Douglas's father.

Rosemary, too, was there with a tricky question about a marriage settlement she was working on. Mr. Playfair had evidently pursued his usual technique for delaying his answer by asking her to have a cigarette. She glanced at me eloquently from the edge of the chair on which she sat.

I insinuated my two letters under Mr. Playfair's eye and unscrewed the cap of his fountain pen. He glanced at the letters with apparent approval. Then he said:

"I wonder, Miss Hamish, if you'd mind running down to the strong room to fetch that box of things I brought round from Mrs. Robjohn's. There are one or two trinkets which Douglas here might like to have."

I left my unsigned letters in an exposed position and descended to the strong room. I returned with Mrs. Robjohn's box a few moments later. Mr. Playfair and Douglas were discussing the future of Ceylon, and Rosemary, bored and desperate, had begun her second cigarette. My letters were still unsigned.

I put the box on Mr. Playfair's desk and he opened it. For lack of any more interesting occupation we all glanced at its contents: articles not unfamiliar to any of us, brooches, a wrist watch, rings we had all seen Mrs. Robjohn wear a dozen times.

"I don't know whether you'd like us to sell these things," Mr. Playfair began.

"I'd like to keep them all, sir," Douglas said. "You see, I want to give them to my future wife."

It was a touching thought, for which I honoured him, though I could imagine Sarah's reaction when he suggested she wear the late Mrs. Robjohn's jewellery! I wondered if he had already told Sarah that he was illegitimate. Knowing Sarah, I think it would only have endeared him to her the more.

He picked out a rather awful sapphire brooch which even Mrs. Robjohn had detested and rarely worn. He held it dreamily in the rough palm of his big hand. He was probably thinking that his poor unloved mother had often worn this object on her breast; I saw a kind of mistiness in his dark eyes. Then I began to catch it too; sentimentality is horribly contagious. Rosemary also looked a little sniffy.

"I'll take this brooch," Douglas said. "You keep the other things for the time being, if you don't mind."

Mr. Playfair picked out a slim oblong object which gleamed between his fingers. He held it out and the polished gold glinted as it caught the light.

"I would think this might be of some use to you," he suggested practically. "It appears to be some sort of cigarette lighter."

I think Rosemary and I recognised the cigarette lighter simultaneously. For as I glanced from it to her she stared from it to me. I did not need this confirmation to know that it was her missing cigarette lighter!

My own emotions in this moment are unimportant, but they are the only ones I have any first-hand knowledge of. I felt plain scared, long before I had time to think out the implications of Rosemary's lighter being found by Mr. Playfair in Mrs. Robjohn's room on the morning after her murder. I think I heard myself gasp.

I know I heard Rosemary gasp. I saw her hands clutch at Mr. Playfair's desk, her fingers straining. Then she gave a silly little cry—something between a giggle and a sob, a sound totally inadequate to express what she must have been feeling at this moment—and collapsed.

I'd seen her sway, but had been too physically petrified to come to her assistance. Douglas and Mr. Playfair stared at her in momentary helplessness. She had fainted dead away.

Mr. Playfair was the first to recover himself. Between us we got her on to the desk. I had always admired Rosemary Proctor's figure, but handling her inert body I was struck by her frailness. She was all bones.

Mr. Playfair took charge of the situation with perfect coolness. He placed leather armchair cushions under her legs and thighs so that her head would be lower than her feet. He told Douglas to open the window and to fetch Sarah. He told me to get on to Dr. Forsyte.

Then, from that omnibus drawer of his at the bottom of his desk, he produced a bottle of smelling salts. They brought her round almost immediately. She sat up, bewildered and very white, Mr. Playfair pushed her head gently but firmly between her knees, and a moment later she was reeling uncertainly to her feet. We made her sit down again.

"I can't think what came over me," she said.

"She had nothing to eat at lunchtime," I contributed.

Meanwhile Sarah, who had been sent for a taxi, reported that the taxi was at the door.

"You'll take her home, please," Mr. Playfair said to me. "If Dr. Forsyte isn't already on the way I'll have him come to Oratory Street. I don't want to see you in the office again, Miss Proctor," he smiled, "until the doctor tells me you're fit enough to come. Is that quite clear?"

"It's really nothing," Rosemary began, but at a nod from Mr. Playfair, Douglas and I supported her down to the taxi.

By the time she got there she was strong enough to walk by herself. She protested when I got in beside her; but I insisted on going home with her.

The taxi already had the address. It was also typical of Mr. Playfair's lack of absent-mindedness, when he wants, that he had given Sarah instructions to take care of the taxi fare in advance.

The last few minutes had been so full of physical activity that it was strange to sink back in the taxi seat with nothing to do. In the previous confusion I had obeyed an impulse which I now began to regret. I had surreptitiously taken possession of the gold cigarette lighter!

At the moment it was burning a hole (figuratively) in my handbag. I don't clearly know why I took it. I think I wanted to show it to Dagobert, as evidence of something or other. I could just as well, of course, have recounted the incident; and besides the lighter was now bound to be missed by either Mr. Playfair or Douglas. I decided to slip it back into Mrs. Robjohn's box the first thing in the morning.

Rosemary spoke scarcely a word during the drive to Oratory Street, only a reference or two to how stupid it had been to faint and how she hadn't done anything of the sort for years. I felt a reluctance to question her. It seemed somehow cheating to do so in her present condition. On the other hand, the opportunity was too good to let slip.

"I wonder how that lighter could have got among Mrs. Robjohn's possessions?" I began.

Rosemary looked at me with her wide, violet eyes which seemed to betray nothing but childish bewilderment. "What lighter?"

"You know the lighter I mean," I answered dryly. "I was there when you fainted, you know. I'm referring to the lighter we both stared at with such violent reactions. Only I managed not to faint."

"I don't remember any lighter," she said, putting a hand to her brow as though to ward off another attack of giddiness. "I only remember feeling terrible suddenly, as though the floor were dropping away beneath me, and then Mr. Playfair pushing my head between my knees. Don't talk any more, Jane, please. I'm all right, but I want to be quite quiet. Do you mind, please?"

I couldn't very well argue and the rest of our journey was passed in silence. When we reached her house she thanked me for coming home with her, and I had to be very firm in order to get into her flat.

I had not visited the flatlet for months—though I remembered with mingled emotions that Dagobert had! My first feeling as I glanced round was one of faint disappointment, almost of disillusion. Though in my day I had been a little sarcastic about Rosemary's "flatlet" my sarcasm has always been tinged with envy. Her flat and all that it represented—tidiness, order—has been a kind of ideal of mine, the kind of place I might one day achieve myself. It was a daydream of mine: one day I too should hang all my clothes on hangers with perfumed sachets attached to them, my shoes too would stand in neat rows on trees.

Rosemary had let me down, destroyed a cherished dream. Her bed wasn't even made! The silk stockings she had taken off last night still lay in a heap on the floor. There were sticky rings left by cocktail glasses on the once immaculate lid of the piano. Through the open kitchenette door I glimpsed dishes and frying pans, dirty and heaped up any old how. I might have been at home.

I expected a cry of protest from her about the char-woman, or at least an apology. She didn't even seem to notice the mess.

"If you want a drink," she said, "there's some gin some-where, in the kitchen probably."

I said, thank you, no, and helped her off with her coat. I hung it up in her wardrobe where the same disorder was evident.

"Your charwoman seems to have failed you," I couldn't help commenting. "Can I give you a hand straightening up the place a bit?"

"Don't bother, Jane. It isn't worth it. I'll go straight to bed anyway."

"What about Dr. Forsyte? He'll be along in a minute."

"It doesn't matter, Jane. I shan't see him anyway. I have my own doctor."

"Shall I call him for you?"

"No thanks. I will . . . I'll be all right now. Thanks for coming home with me. See you in the office tomorrow."

"I shan't go, Rosemary," I said, "until you've called your doctor. What's his number? I'll dial it for you."

More, I think, to get rid of me than anything else she gave me the number, a Wigmore number, which I dialled. She took the receiver from my hand when I got the connection.

"Dr. Robbins?" she said. "This is Rosemary Proctor. I've just come home from the office. I had a fainting fit. Yes, I passed clean out apparently. . . . If you would, I'd be most grateful. Yes, I'll lie down and wait for you."

She rang off. "The doctor will be around immediately. I'm to keep quite quiet until then. If you don't mind going, Jane . . ."

I had no alternative. I went, my mind—as they say—spinning.

23 * My head continued to spin as I walked down Knightsbridge. It should have got used to spinning during these last few days.

A tidy mind—Rosemary's, for instance (but what on earth had happened to *her* tidiness of late?)—would doubtless have tried to get some order into the morass of details through which I was struggling. She would probably have put them down in two columns: Significant, Misleading. I tried.

Misleading would be: the startling mess I found in Rosemary's flat, this Dr. Robbins whom I was not allowed to stay and meet, Oates's evening clothes, the clue Peter and Paul which Mr. Playfair had missed. The Misleading list offered entirely too many possibilities, perhaps everything I had written down to date—an appalling thought. I concentrated on the Significant Things: surely the fact that Rosemary's gold cigarette lighter had been found in Mrs. Robjohn's room just after the murder, surely the fact that Rosemary had fainted on recognising it.

Then the tall man in evening clothes whom Joe the taxi-driver had seen outside Mrs. Robjohn's house at midnight? *After* Joe had taken Rosemary safely home. The tall man in evening clothes must also be significant.

The significant list also offered entirely too many possibilities, perhaps everything I had written down to date—an even more appalling thought!

I next toyed with the fascinating theory that I'd got my two lists mixed up, that the things I'd mentally labelled Misleading were really Significant, and vice versa. This way madness lay.

But as I pursued my way towards Hyde Park Corner the natural buoyancy of a woman who has no clothes began to reassert itself. I began to notice the windows of those attractive little shops which make the walk from Knightsbridge Station to St. George's Hospital one of the most delightful in London. I paused finally to wonder why I was walking towards Piccadilly with such determination. I remembered. I had promised to meet Dagobert in the Café Royal.

I stopped in mid-career. Why should I meet Dagobert at the Café Royal at six o'clock? Why should I drag around all over the place meeting him? Who did he think he was, anyway? True, he might appeal to sex-starved spinsters like Rosemary Proctor, and waitresses in teashops seemed to like him. Very well, he could run around with his teashop waitresses, sell them vacuum cleaners, give them Guerlain lipsticks and take them to dinner at Sorel's to his heart's content.

The subject didn't interest me; the whole thing bored me extremely. I would tell him that what he did in his own spare time filled me with the most exquisite ennui, and that he was going to have a lot more spare time in future. I would yawn delicately in his face as I said it; I would scratch his eyes out! Aunt Osyth!

I decided to let him wait all evening by himself at the Café Royal. I decided to go home, have a hot bath and go to bed. I decided to change into my new bottle-green velvet and ring up some people. I went to the Café Royal.

At any rate I was three quarters of an hour late.

"I'm sorry I'm late," I said sweetly.

"Quite all right," he greeted me amiably. "I knew you would be. I've only just arrived myself."

"I hope I didn't tear you away from anything important," I said. "Such as cocktails with Aunt Osyth!"

"Aunt Osyth doesn't drink cocktails."

"And anyhow you saw her last night!" I concluded nastily.

"No," he shook his head with complete innocence, "I haven't seen her for months. What are you drinking?"

"A treble brandy—the liqueur brandy."

"Two single whiskies," Dagobert said to the waiter. "You look charming this evening, Jane. Your eyes are bright and your cheeks are flushed. You've been walking. You must do it more. It's good for you, makes you look vital and healthy."

"Naïve and unsophisticated?" I suggested.

"Just what I was going to say," he nodded.

"I bet you were! . . . Well?" I prompted.

"Well what? Oh, you mean what I've been up to. An exhausting day. And almost nothing to show for it. I did manage to pick up a rather nicely bound copy of *Barchester Towers* in Charing Cross Road, but otherwise nothing but frustration. I'm glad I have you to hold my hand."

He'd got hold of my hand somehow; I jerked it away with disgust.

"I like jealous women," he said. "Never pretend you don't care, Jane. Never turn into one of these broad-minded women. If you feel like socking me in the jaw go right ahead."

"Why should I?" I inquired coldly.

"Don't you?" He peered at me intently for a moment. "Good," he added, somewhat relieved. "I visited Inigo Mews this afternoon. There's an all-night garage opposite Number 2. Stewart did arrive home at about a quarter to twelve that night and he didn't go out again. He stayed up until nearly three with the lights all on playing Bing Crosby records."

"So he's not the tall man in evening clothes who called on Mrs. Robjohn at midnight!" I said, partly because I was getting interested again and partly because it was pleasant to have one of Dagobert's pet theories exploded.

"No. It's a pity."

Two nearly invisible whiskies arrived and Dagobert sent the waiter back for more. He reached in his pocket and produced a small object which he handed to me.

"I'd almost forgotten," he explained with a winning smile. "I chased all over London for this. It must be the last of its kind in the British Isles."

I didn't fling it back in his face. It was a Guerlain lipstick *rose foncé*, and a woman must sometimes swallow her pride. But I did point out as I put it in my handbag. "Not the last. Rosemary has one."

"Has she?" he said airily.

"And another thing—" I began.

"Couldn't we wait until the man brings us a drink?" He murmured uneasily.

"I only wanted to give you a little *friendly* advice. If you're making passes at more than one woman at once, you should vary your technique in little details. Don't give them identical presents, don't take them to the same restaurants. Treat each one as a special case, as an individual who may have different tastes. Pretend that this thing, this place is for her alone. Otherwise you give them the impression that they're only women to you—all alike. It's unflattering. Besides, it suggests that you lack imagination, delicacy, finer feelings. It suggests that you're insensitive, a bounder, a crude yokel, an oaf, a vulgar lout and a twerp!" I rose sharply. "I can't think of any other words, so I'm going."

"I adore you, Jane, when your eyes are bright and your cheeks are flushed."

"You said that ten minutes ago when I arrived," I interrupted.

"Did I? So I did. Sit down and we'll talk it over quietly."

"You mean you'll talk yourself out of it." I sat down. "Oh Dagobert, how—how could you!"

He regarded me tentatively, fairly sure of where he stood, but not wishing to put his foot into it in case. "You mean," he began, "you mean about Miss What's-her-name, at your office? Miss Proctor?" I said nothing. "Oddly enough," he pursued, "I was just going to tell you all about that."

"Rosemary told me *all about it* today," I said.

"Did she? Did she, indeed?"

"In lurid detail."

"Dear, oh dear . . . She *has* a fairly lurid imagination, as you point out." He rubbed his hands together with a great display of heartiness as the waiter reappeared. "A cold night," he said, finishing off his whisky. "After all, Jane, we mustn't forget that all's fair in . . ." He broke off, feeling the quotation to be untactful. "I mean, we've got a murder on our hands and we must leave no stone unturned."

"Rosemary is no stone."

"No," he agreed thoughtfully. "She's a very interesting young woman and I don't at all feel I wasted yesterday evening."

"I gathered you hadn't from Rosemary, but I might as well hear your version."

"Well, the idea of calling on her struck me when Aunt Osyth called up to say the dinner party was off—"

"The idea struck you," I corrected, "at luncheon yesterday when I told you Rosemary was off for the day. You saw your opportunity to get in a little dirty work and you pounced on it."

"There's no use trying to conceal anything from you, Jane," he sighed. "After all it's very dull work interviewing taxi-drivers all the time. And I feel convinced that Rosemary Proctor plays a key rôle in our mystery. I had to meet her, win her confidence, if possible."

"And what, precisely, *did* you find out?" I asked impatiently.

"Well, nothing very precise," he admitted. "But I gained a lot of fruitful impressions. Valuable hints, you know the kind of thing—clues."

"No," I said. "Name one."

This seemed to baffle him. "Well," he said. He'd been starting a lot of sentences with "Well"—a bad sign. "Well, for instance she's slightly insane about this fellow Stewart."

"I could have told you that, and spared you the expense of dinner at Sorel's."

"I mean insane in the medical sense of the word. Barmy, bats; it's getting her down. There has been more between them than you've led me to suppose."

"Such as?"

"I didn't go into details. But she talked rather a lot about women marrying men younger than themselves. Seemed to be all for it; she's thirty-six, by the way."

This *was* interesting. "How did you find out?" I asked.

"She keeps her passport in the drawer of her kitchen dresser. Which is a funny place to keep it, when you think of it. Unless she'd just recently hunted it out and stuck it there in haste. She also had a Cook's folder advertising Holidays in the South of France. Over dinner I worked around subtly to the subject of jaunts abroad. She seemed to be very determined that nothing on earth would take her abroad. The thought of foreign travel seemed especially distasteful to her. I wonder why she got so hot and bothered at the thought." He fell into reverie. "As though it was something she *had* to do, yet loathed and dreaded."

"Any other fruitful impressions?" I prompted.

"Yes. Do you remember how neat and orderly her flat used to be? How precise and meticulous she was in all her habits? She isn't any more. Something's happened to her which has caused a complete change in her personal morale. Her place reminded me vaguely of Mrs. Robjohn's. The same carelessness, the same air of confusion. Let me pursue the parallel further. These men of Rosemary's who are always pestering her, following her back from the Brompton Oratory, telephoning in the middle of the night and so on. In a few years' time they might easily turn into 'They'—the sinister figures who dogged Mrs. Robjohn's imagination. Another curious fact. Sirkorski was younger than Blanche Robjohn; Stewart is younger than Rosemary. . . . In Rosemary Proctor we have an incipient Mrs. Robjohn." He broke off. "Let's go somewhere and eat."

We walked up Regent Street and into Beak Street to a

little Spanish restaurant where they serve wine in something called *porrons*, flasks with a kind of funnel from which the wine emerges in a thin stream. Real Spanish peasants (like Dagobert) pour this directly into the mouth, thus obviating the necessity of wine glasses. The trick requires a steadier hand than I, at the moment, had.

"I'd have brought you to a grander place," Dagobert apologised, "except that one doesn't want the Sorel type of dinner two nights running."

I ignored this and removed Rosemary's gold cigarette lighter from my handbag, placing it casually beside his soup plate.

"That's your naïve little friend's cigarette lighter," I said. "Mr. Playfair found it in Mrs. Robjohn's room the morning after the murder."

I had chosen a moment when Dagobert was using the *porron* in the best Spanish-peasant manner. He squirted wine all over his shirt front.

"Don't say things like that suddenly!" he protested. "Go on."

I recounted as briefly as possible the events of the day.

He only interrupted me once, to order another *porron*. At the end I sat back and waited for his comments.

He asked: "What was Dr. Robbins' telephone number?"

I told him and he jotted it down. He consulted his notes. "Stewart left the office at about eleven-fifteen; Rosemary's taxi called for her at eleven thirty-five. That's twenty minutes unaccounted for. Did she spend those twenty minutes with her ledgers, or did she spend them nipping down to Number 17 Mandel Square where she turned on the gas, inserted the shillings and dropped her cigarette lighter? I suppose Mrs. Robjohn *would* let her in without question?"

I nodded. "Should we do anything about it? Make an arrest or something?"

"I suppose so . . ." He sounded discouraged. "Let's talk about something else. How did Pink Lady do at Windsor?"

"She lost, and Oates is going to be pretty terse with somebody about it. He's got evening clothes, by the way, and we don't know what he was doing on the night of November the twenty-ninth."

"You're talking shop again."

"Sorry."

We concentrated on something *à la Valenciana* which was largely beans, very sustaining. Going home by bus Dagobert gave me a brief résumé of Einstein's Theory of Relativity. He got very excited and gesticulated; I slipped my arm through his.

"Is it true," I asked him, "that I only appeal to the intellectual side of your nature?"

"Your brains, Jane," he said gravely, "are what chiefly worry me. That's why I try so hard to improve your mind. The rest of you is quite satisfactory. . . ."

I sighed happily. With such crumbs of assurance women comfort themselves.

24 ✳ The most startling thing that occurred in the office next day was that Rosemary turned up! She turned up precisely on time and looking as well, efficient and healthy as ever. In fact she looked considerably better

than either Sarah or me, having spent the previous evening sensibly in bed. We both felt rather bitter about it.

Apart from that, the morning was chiefly notable for a hectic rush of work. Oates was kept running to and fro from the post office and had no time to discuss future turf investments with me, which dispensation doubtless saved me a pound or two.

Again I had luncheon alone with Rosemary, and I must say in view of the discussion Dagobert and I had had about her at the Spanish restaurant I felt, at first, an acute sense of embarrassment. I asked her what Dr. Robbins had said.

"Nothing very interesting," she replied. "Not enough to eat, too many cigarettes, too many late nights. The usual guff. It's all probably quite true. I suppose I ought really to ask Mr. Playfair for a long holiday. Dr. Robbins says so anyway. . . ."

"Where would you go at this time of year?" I said. "The South of France?"

She laughed rather wildly. "A long way away! That would suit some people at least! No, I'm damned if I will!" She twisted the key in the sardine tin viciously. "And leave him to philander around to his heart's content."

"If you're referring to Jimmy," I pointed out, "he manages that quite nicely with you in England."

She was used to my speaking bluntly about Jimmy; she no longer resented it. She looked at me appealingly with a kind of hurt wonder in her pale violet eyes. Mrs. Robjohn used sometimes to look at me like that, and again I felt the same uneasy mixture of sympathy and exasperation. Perhaps Dagobert was on to something when he said that in Rosemary we had an incipient Mrs. Robjohn.

"I don't *want* to go, Jane," she said, and there was an unhappy quaver in her voice that again reminded me of Mrs.

Robjohn. "I don't want to!" Her thin shoulders slumped. "I suppose I'll have to."

"No one's forcing you."

"No." Her laugh was brief, bitter. "No one."

The telephone rang, a client asking for an appointment. I admired Rosemary's swift metamorphosis into the efficient Chief Clerk as she answered it. They were two distinct personalities, the Miss Proctor who spoke to the client over the 'phone and the Rosemary who a second previously had been on the edge of hysteria. The phenomenon is not, I believe, rare among criminals.

When she'd finished I said: "Why did you faint yesterday afternoon?"

"Dr. Robbins says, not enough to eat, too many cigarettes . . ."

"I heard that part. I mean, why did you faint when you saw your cigarette lighter among Mrs. Robjohn's possessions?"

"What lighter?" she demanded in apparent perplexity. "You were on about some lighter yesterday afternoon in the taxi."

"Your own lighter," I said patiently. "The gold one you said you'd lost, or left at home, or something. It was in that box of Mrs. Robjohn's things I brought up from the strong room, and when Mr. Playfair produced it you fainted dead away."

"Did I?" she said. "I didn't notice the lighter. Where is it now?"

I hastened on, remembering that Dagobert had the lighter. "At luncheon yesterday you were looking for it in your handbag. Remember? It wasn't there. What had you done with it?"

"Oh *that*." She dismissed the subject with a shrug of indifference. "I gave it to Mrs. Robjohn two or three days before she died. I'd forgotten. The poor old thing adored it."

I breathed carefully. So that was that! I felt a distinct sense of let-down and also a faint sense of relief. I'd practically hanged Rosemary because of that cigarette lighter.

If she were telling the truth—*if*—then the lighter had nothing to do with the business.

But I was curiously reluctant to abandon my lighter. It was my best clue to date, almost the only tangible one I had.

During the afternoon it kept intruding itself into Sir Jasper Middletown's Sur-tax Returns. Was it reasonable that Rosemary should have given it to Mrs. Robjohn and afterwards forgotten?

As I recalculated Sir Jasper's Sur-tax it came to me. At least a theory came to me: namely that Rosemary was *half* telling the truth. She *had* given her lighter away—but not to Mrs. Robjohn! Whom she had given it to was obvious, and fitted in much better with the circumstances. She'd given it to Jimmy of course! It was the "rather neat little job, gold, which seemed to have disappeared!" The epidemic of cigarette-lighter disappearances was all caused by the same lighter.

I felt delighted with my new theory and decided to test it cunningly. My technique was to be subtle, the kind of thing I could relate smugly to Dagobert this evening. It consisted of making Jimmy deny (preferably with a start of guilt) what I had made up my mind was the truth.

I found an immediate excuse for putting my plan into action, a sur-tax query. Jimmy loved us to run to him with questions instead of to Mr. Playfair as we almost invariably did.

"I wonder if you could help me out of this muddle?" I asked, entering his room diffidently.

"If I can I shall be delighted to," he smiled up at me graciously.

He could. I had chosen a point with which I knew he was quite capable of dealing. I arranged my papers and a book of tax tables on the desk in front of him and looked helpless. He put the thing right for me in a matter of seconds. I watched him, wondering how he could fail to feel the suspicion which I must have been radiating. The moment had come for my shot in the dark.

"Do you remember that little gold cigarette lighter of Rosemary's?" I asked.

He should have said with studied casualness that he didn't, or that he may have noticed it. Instead he spoiled my whole experiment by saying warmly:

"I certainly do! She gave it to me."

The dialogue wasn't supposed to have gone this way at all. He was supposed to have denied all knowledge of the incriminating object. I was at a loss how to pursue the matter. He pursued it for me.

"I've been looking all over the place for it," he said. "Has it turned up?"

"Yes."

"Good. Where?"

I dropped my bombshell. "Among Mrs. Robjohn's valuables which Mr. Playfair brought back to the strong room."

It didn't explode. "How the dickens did it get there?" he exclaimed.

"I haven't the faintest idea," I said, "unless someone left it in her room."

This time I had, at least, made him think. But he didn't seem so much worried as simply puzzled.

"I first missed it," he searched his memory, "the day before she died. To tell the truth I half-suspected Oates of having pinched it. But maybe she took it herself, absentmindedly. I'm almost certain it was on my desk that morning when she came in and told me her usual tale about the men outside following her. Next time you're in the strong room you might fetch it up for me, Jane. I'm rather fond of it."

"According to Rosemary," I said, "she gave it to Mrs. Robjohn herself."

"The devil she did!" he exclaimed irritably. "She gave it to me!"

"She may," I suggested, "have regretted her generosity, recovered it from your desk herself and then given it to Mrs. Robjohn."

"Possibly," he admitted. "But it belongs to me. She gave it to me first."

"You'd better argue about it with Rosemary."

"I will!" he said, rising. But he relapsed almost immediately into his chair, struck by the indignity of squabbling over the trinket. "It's not worth arguing about, but I do feel *morally* that it belongs to me."

My smile was meant to be ironic. "If that's the way your morals work, I suppose you do," I murmured. "Thanks for the sur-tax assistance."

I picked up my things and went. While my memory was still fresh I wrote down the above interview exactly as it happened. Racking my poor brains over it later, the only conclusion I could draw was that my pet clue was still no good. Jimmy had actually *claimed* the tell-tale lighter. In fact it wasn't "tell-tale." When I explained *where* it had been found he had expressed only a desire to get it back again. This wasn't the behaviour of a man who has carelessly left a damning piece of evidence beside the body of a woman he has just murdered.

Nevertheless I typed out a neat copy of the conversation and presented it to Dagobert that evening. I wasn't very proud of my work and Dagobert didn't seem to be very enthusiastic either. He went over it carefully and marked one sentence with a cross.

"There may be something worth following up there," he said.

I reread the indicated sentence. *"To tell the truth, I half-suspected Oates of having pinched it."*

"I'm not very keen on remarks which are preceded by the phrase 'to tell the truth,'" Dagobert said. "But in this case Stewart may have been telling the truth."

"Wait a minute," I protested feebly, "if Oates pinched it, why did Rosemary say she'd given it to Mrs. Robjohn?"

"That is an interesting question," said Dagobert.

I was glad it was interesting, but I didn't quite see how. Dagobert was of no assistance. His mind was elsewhere.

"I wish we knew," he murmured, "why Mrs. Robjohn didn't hear those shillings being dropped into the meter."

"While we're wishing," I said, still harping on the gold lighter, "I wish we knew why Rosemary fainted when she suddenly recognised the lighter."

"I don't think she did suddenly recognise the lighter," Dagobert remarked coolly.

I stopped wrestling with my mutton chop. It was the evening when we gathered together our weekly meat rations and consumed them in my flat at a sitting.

"That's what Rosemary herself says," I complained. "Whose side are you on anyway?"

"The trouble in this case is," he said, "that people sometimes tell the truth, and that confuses us. I think Rosemary was telling the truth when she told you she didn't notice the lighter. *You* were startled at the sight of the lighter, and you naturally expected Rosemary to be startled too."

He picked up his mutton chop in his fingers and nibbled it delicately.

"She *may* have been lying about giving it to Mrs. Robjohn," he continued with his mouth full. "Her mind works in devious ways. Perhaps Mrs. Robjohn really did 'adore' it and Rosemary now *wishes* she'd given it to her. There is an odd bond of sympathy between Rosemary and Mrs. Robjohn. In some ways I imagine Rosemary identifies herself with Blanche Robjohn, if you know what I mean . . . 'There but for the grace of God . . .' sort of thing. Poor Rosemary . . . I'm afraid the requisite grace may be withheld."

"You know her so much better than I do, of course!" I said, unable to let the-night-before-last alone.

"Yes," he agreed thoughtfully, "the fanciful little parallel I drew last night between Rosemary and Blanche Robjohn can now be completed. Another mutton chop?"

I shook my head. "What have you been up to today?" I asked curiously.

"I've been having tea with Dr. Robbins."

"Tea?" I don't know why I picked on the inessential part of his statement. It seemed such an odd meal for Dagobert to have with anyone.

"Yes," he said. "Dr. Robbins is a woman."

"I see."

I didn't, until he added:

"A gynecologist."

He went on munching his mutton chop deliberately while this—and its implications—sank in.

"You have now grasped why Rosemary fainted yesterday afternoon," he concluded. "She is going to have a baby."

25 ✳

The next morning in the office—Thursday— I went through the most shattering ordeal I had as yet undergone, not excepting the day when I was first blackmailed by Oates, and the moment when Rosemary had fainted. And yet, as I try to write it, it seems undramatic, pedestrian and vague. Nothing I can get my teeth into. It scarcely seems, in retrospect, worth telling.

All that happened was that Mr. Playfair sent for me. He asked me to sit down and offered me a cigarette. We discussed a bridge hand he'd had at the Club last night and we filled in a couple of crossword clues. We touched briefly on the Hartley Estate. There was little outward difference between the session and a hundred like it in the past, except for the feeling I began to have that he'd asked me in for some purpose not yet revealed.

He asked me how I thought Rosemary was. I said she appeared to be blooming. Had she not, in my opinion, been working too hard lately, coming back to the office at night, assuming too much responsibility and so on? The fainting fit worried him.

"I think she needs a good long holiday, Miss Hamish," he rumbled on. "Perhaps you could help me persuade her to take one. Several months I mean."

I agreed warmly and promised to do my best.

"I daresay you'd be willing to take on her work," he

said. "Of course we'd try to get someone to help you. That's really what I wanted to speak to you about."

But was it? He removed and polished his spectacles, replaced them and gazed at a point on the ceiling.

"I knew her father and mother," he said. "They were delightful people. I acted for them. They were killed, you know, at the same instant in a motor crash. I had to break the news to Rosemary. She was still at school. That was a year or two before she came here. Dear, oh dear, how time passes."

He was referring to the years, not the minutes during which I was neglecting the Hartley Estate. I made a vague movement to go. He continued, as though to himself:

"A family solicitor has many curious duties to perform, which they don't teach at the University. He sometimes comes across things which worry him, Miss Hamish, moral problems, questions to which there are no answers in the precedent books."

His gaze returned from the spot on the ceiling to me. I murmured something vague in agreement.

"Sometimes he has to act when no written law tells him to act," he continued, returning to the ceiling. "More often he has to refrain from action, Miss Hamish, when a literal interpretation of the law he serves bids him to act. That is sometimes even harder. To fold your hands and look away. It seems to be shirking your responsibilities, if you know what I mean."

Did I know what he meant? I wasn't sure, but my mouth felt suddenly dry.

"As you get older, Miss Hamish," he continued, smiling now vaguely in my direction, "you'll come across more and more of these occasions when you must decide not to look at certain things too closely. Perhaps what I really mean is that you must look at them even more closely, from all points of view, coming to the conclusion that your first impression may have been hasty, bigoted, too cocksure. You must develop what is commonly called tolerance, a name which lazy people admittedly employ to cloak their moral slackness, but which in its best form is merely another word for wisdom. The laws of man are quite specific on what is legal and what is illegal; but God allows many things to take place which are beyond our feeble understanding."

This kind of thing might have been embarrassing from anyone except Mr. Playfair. But he spoke so mildly, in such a conversational tone of voice that I found myself taking it in as easily as I might have listened to a description of the round of golf he had played last Saturday.

"I remember once, many years ago," he continued, "when I was chief clerk for a firm in Lincolns Inn, finding an office boy stealing half a crown from the petty cash box. I reported him to one of the Junior Partners. Nothing happened, the office boy was not removed, so I—filled with a righteous sense of duty—took the matter higher, to the Senior Partner. The boy was dismissed in disgrace. I thought I'd done my duty in pursuing the matter. What I didn't know was that the Junior Partner I had first spoken to was well aware of the boy's weakness, that he had patiently been curing him of his tendency to petty theft, and that the boy was the sole support of an elderly mother, who committed suicide, Miss Hamish, after I had had her son publicly exposed. I've never forgotten that boy's mother, Miss Hamish. For I killed her."

I don't know whether this story was true or whether Mr. Playfair had made it up on the spot, but I was sure he'd told it for my especial benefit. Had he warned me in so many words not to poke my nose into matters which I did not understand, he could not have done it more plainly.

How on earth could he guess that that was exactly what I'd been doing ever since the morning Mrs. Robjohn had been found dead! I moved uncomfortably on the edge of my chair.

"I could tell you lots of stories like that which have happened either in my own experience or in the experience of some of my colleagues, though happily few have had such tragic endings. No, Miss Hamish," he folded his hands and regarded me amiably, "it is sometimes easy to establish *what* a person did, but *why* he thus acted escapes our understanding. What the world calls a crime has sometimes been committed from the best motives and *with results* which are beneficent."

He rose and began fumbling through the papers heaped on his desk. Our conversation was evidently finished. I rose too, feeling curiously empty in the stomach.

"Sir John Hartley tells me you've done a first-rate job on the Trust," he said to me. "He seemed as pleased as punch over the telephone this morning. But I'm keeping you . . ."

"Not at all," I murmured. "We're fairly slack this morning."

"Then you must get on with your novel, Miss Hamish," he said cheerfully. "I hear you're writing one."

"Er, yes, more or less," I admitted, wondering how he knew. "There wasn't anything else, was there?"

"No, I don't think so." My hand was on the door knob when he added, apparently as an afterthought: "Oh Miss Hamish, you might put that cigarette lighter back in Mrs. Robjohn's box when you've finished with it."

I don't know what I replied, something like "Yes, of course" probably; but in the mercifully darkened corridor outside I clung for a moment to the door handle to steady myself. My heart was thumping and my hair felt as though it were standing on end.

I regained my own room and sank down in a chair. I felt scared through and through. The feeling was a little analogous to the shock children get when they discover that Father knows more about what's going on than they'd supposed.

I called up Dagobert with the object of recovering Rosemary's cigarette lighter at the first possible moment, but he wasn't there. I stuck grimly to a lease there was no particular hurry about until one o'clock. I made no effort to sort out what I had learned from my talk with Mr. Playfair, or rather his talk with me. I didn't want to sort it out. From now on I wanted only to Mind My Own Business.

I made an excuse for walking out by myself for luncheon. I had no taste for fish paste etc. with Rosemary and Sarah. In the nearest telephone booth I again telephoned Dagobert. He still wasn't there. I ate something—I don't remember what—at Ponting's Cafeteria and afterwards walked up and down the High Street looking in shop windows I already knew by heart. At two, when I telephoned Dagobert again, he still didn't answer, not that I really expected him to.

Back in the office I again tackled the lease. Oates tried to attract my attention as I passed through the outer office, but I ignored him. I heard him muttering something under his breath which sounded like: "Miss Snoots, huh?" Major Stewart, already back from luncheon, was coming out of Rosemary's room, and I scarcely spoke to him. I gained a vague impression that he and Rosemary were once again on good terms, but the subtle variations of their emotional life no longer interested me.

I shut myself gratefully in with my lease, enveloping myself in the security of such things as "Blank hereinafter called the Lessor of the one part and Blank hereinafter called the Lessee of the other part." Nice, comforting, familiar phrases.

About four o'clock Sarah burst in while I was still in the middle of it.

"Guess what's happened!" she exclaimed breathlessly.

I glanced up, shaking the lessee's covenants out of my mind. "What?" I asked mechanically.

"Babs has come back."

"Babs?"

"The Fair Maid of Purley!" Sarah explained, quoting me. "Jimmy's in a dither and Rosemary's biting her fingernails. Little Babs couldn't bear Scotland another minute without her naughty Jimmy, and there's to be a big reconciliation. Doesn't it make 'ums feel 'ick at your tummy!"

And she was gone.

I should, I suppose, have gone in to watch Rosemary biting her nails, in case her reaction to this development had any bearing on things, but I didn't. I was still Minding My Own Business. Besides, Sarah had summed up the situation exactly: it did make me feel sick at my stomach. There was no doubt in my mind that Major Stewart was the father of the baby Rosemary was going to have, and I am old-fashioned enough to think that men ought to marry the mother of their children. Babs's return made that event less likely. Damn Babs! It was a pity that Mrs. Robjohn was not still alive to write another swift anonymous letter to her. In fact I might try something in that line myself!

I felt wretched and impotent. It was all very well for Mr. Playfair to preach the virtue of inaction, of looking the other way. Why hadn't he given me that lecture a month ago? I was already too deeply involved. I may have found out practically nothing to solve the riddle of who killed Mrs. Robjohn, but I had certainly unearthed a lot of disagreeable things about the very ordinary set of people I worked with.

Sarah stuck her head in again. "Coming into Rosemary's for a cupper?" she asked. "The atmosphere's stormy."

"May I have my cupper—I mean my cup of tea—in here?"

"Okeydoke," she agreed cheerfully. "I don't blame you."

I jumped as she slammed the door behind her. I, too, needed that long holiday Mr. Playfair was talking about. I heard Sarah whistling irrepressibly in the corridor. *She*, at least, had no dark secrets. I had almost forgotten the night she went dancing—the night she said she stayed at home as usual—the night, in fact, of the murder. Damn! Was Oates, then, right when he said that everyone had something to hide?

My opinion of the human race had just hit rock bottom when the telephone rang. I answered it. It was Dagobert.

"Hello," he said, "this is Dagobert Brown. I want to speak to Miss Hamish. It's very important. Dagobert Brown is the name."

"I *had* recognised the voice," I answered. "And I rather thought you might have recognised mine."

"Is that you, Jane? This is Dagobert."

"Yes, I know. I wanted to speak to you."

"Did you? That's a coincidence." He dropped his voice to a confidential shout. "Found out anything—important, I mean?"

It struck me about now that there were telephone extensions in the outer office and in Rosemary's room. The lighter about which I wanted to speak to him would have to wait.

"I'll meet you this evening at the usual time," I said. "I'm very busy at the moment."

Before I could ring off he said urgently: "Ring me back immediately from the public telephone box across the street. My number is Mayfair 8860."

The line went dead. I held the receiver to my ear for a moment to hear if I could make out the click of other receivers being replaced on hooks. I heard nothing and finally hung up. Then I slipped on my coat and went across to the public call box.

As I felt in my handbag for two pennies I saw Oates mooching out of the front door of Number 11, with his hands in his pockets pretending to be going to the post office. He was glancing speculatively towards me, but there was nothing he could do about it. I waved to him gaily; he pretended he didn't notice and continued now purposefully towards the post office.

The number Mayfair 8860 seemed familiar as I dialled it. The girl who answered cleared up that point. "Claridges Hotel," she said. I asked for Dagobert; he must have been waiting for me for he answered immediately.

"What was the idea of making such a song and dance about who you were just now?" I asked.

"Did I?" he said innocently.

"There are extensions to my telephone."

"So there are!" he said. "Well, well, well."

"I don't get it."

"I thought," he explained, "it might stir your sleepy

old office up a bit if people thought I was taking a friendly interest in things. You know my methods."

"No, I don't," I confessed. "I want Rosemary's lighter back at once. Mr. Playfair saw me take it."

"Excellent! I always thought the old boy was less unobservant than you've depicted him. Splendid!"

"Stop sounding so pleased. It isn't splendid at all. It's horribly embarrassing. He thinks I pinched it. Why did you ring me? And what are you doing at Claridges?"

"An interesting point has arisen," he said, ignoring my second question entirely. "Did Mrs. Robjohn have a typewriter?"

"No."

"Could she use one? Did she know how to type?"

"No. I'm nearly certain she didn't."

"That's just what I thought. Do you remember that poison-pen letter Miss Barbara Jennings received on the morning it all began? The one we assumed that Mrs. Robjohn wrote?"

"Yes."

"It was typewritten."

I caught my breath. "Major Stewart," I remembered suddenly, "said it was printed handwriting."

"He said he thought it was," Dagobert corrected—accurately, as I discovered upon rereading my account of that scene between Junior Partner and the gas man. "Stewart never saw that first letter. He only saw the Private and Confidential letter on Mr. Playfair's desk next morning—the one he burnt. That second letter *was* hand-printed. Mrs. Hawthorne noticed it in Mrs. Robjohn's hand before she posted it. Stewart merely *assumed* the first letter was similarly written."

"All right," I agreed. "So what?"

"So Mrs. Robjohn was not the author of the original poison-pen letter. Rosemary was, or else Sarah . . . or, of course, you."

"I'll plunk for Rosemary," I said feebly.

"Me, too," he agreed cheerfully. "Well, good-bye. I thought you'd like to know I'm not idling away my time."

"What are you doing at Claridges?" I asked again.

"At Claridges? That's right, you know the number. Just having tea."

"Who with?"

"With whom? do you mean?"

"I mean what's her name?"

"Oh, her name? I'm glad you asked me that. I wanted you to know that I'm still keeping my mind on my work. Her name's Babs."

26 ✳ It was after six that evening when I locked up the office. Though I am frequently the last to arrive in the morning, I am nearly always the last to leave at night. It was no novelty, therefore, to glance into empty rooms before I closed the doors or to hear my footsteps echoing through empty corridors.

And yet tonight as the cold and darkness reclaimed their nocturnal reign over the premises of Number 11 Mandel Street I was oppressed by the atmosphere. It had never occurred to me before that the office had an atmosphere. I shivered slightly, though not unreasonably in view of the fact that it was mid-December and all the fires had been turned out.

My nerves were in a poor state. Dagobert's telephone call had more or less undone the good work of Mr. Playfair's lecture. I was again horribly conscious that murder had been done, and done probably by one of my co-workers in this office.

With no effort of the imagination, I could fancy that the murderer's presence still haunted these empty rooms. This was arrant nonsense, but I found myself none the less hurrying into my coat, hat and gloves, eager to get away from the place. Familiar objects—the filing cabinet, Rosemary's covered typewriter, the gaunt letter press in the outer office—were beginning to assume queer shapes. I heard creaking sounds which seemed to come from the strong room; the door of Major Stewart's room suddenly banged. It had merely been left ajar, but the sudden sound didn't do me any good. I could understand how places got the reputation of being haunted.

Nothing, of course, happened and I locked the outer door as usual, descending the bare stairs which lead down into the street. The street itself was almost deserted except for a parked car or two. One of these cars—a small four-seater of popular make—was drawn up immediately in front of Number 11. Its engine was ticking over slowly and there were three people in it. As I emerged on to the pavement beside it, the front door swung open and a man's arm groped out. A gloved hand grabbed me and a voice growled:

"Get in. And make it snappy."

I didn't scream, though I felt like it. I was glad I hadn't a second later, for I now recognised my kidnaper. It was Douglas Robjohn, in his new car which Sarah had been so excited about. He impelled me with a powerful arm into the back seat. I sank down into the darkness gasping slightly as the door slammed behind me and the car jerked forward.

The whole thing—it seems—was a huge joke, a species of rag. I love people who do this kind of thing, much as I love people who whack you unexpectedly on the back!

"It's a surprise party, Jane!" cried Sarah, who was the until now unidentified figure sitting beside Douglas in the front seat.

"Why?" I muttered, still very disgruntled.

"It's your birthday! Why didn't you tell anyone?"

They didn't hear me say: "Because my birthday's in the middle of July," because they had all begun to sing: "Happy Birthday to you! Happy Birthday to you!" the words and music of which I particularly detest. They hadn't had anything to drink, or they wouldn't have been so revoltingly jolly.

"What are *you* doing here?" I asked the third occupant of the car who sat in the back seat beside me.

"It's a surprise party," said Dagobert, as though that explained everything.

"It would have been more of a surprise," I said, "if you hadn't been part of it."

"We're going to a wonderful place on the Great West Road your friend knows about!" Sarah exclaimed, as Douglas turned into the High Street towards Hammersmith.

"The Cairo Club," Dagobert explained. "For a special birthday treat."

The Cairo Club is a peculiarly garish roadhouse, frequented by young men in sporty cars and girls with Veronica Lake hair-dos. They have the noisiest dance band for its size in the United Kingdom, a real slap-up soda fountain and brilliant neon lighting. I do not care for the Cairo Club.

"Have you three all known each other long?" I inquired.

"I'm a kind of friend of the family," Dagobert said.

"Kind of is good," I murmured.

"Yes," Sarah enlarged, "he's a friend of Dad's. They drink beer together at The Swan. Isn't it a coincidence, Jane?"

"There are no such things as coincidences," I muttered darkly.

"We only met half an hour ago," Sarah continued, not hearing my comment. "Dagobert called at Lillie Road to see Dad. Douglas was there and we suddenly decided, as it was your birthday, we'd have a surprise party."

"I'm surprised all right," I admitted. "Do we stop somewhere on the way to have a drink?"

"Let's wait until we get there," Sarah suggested, apparently forgetting that it was *my* birthday. I've often noticed how domineering the meekest woman becomes when she sits in the front seat of her own man's car. "Dagobert says they've got the most marvellous ice-cream sodas and milk shakes and things."

We drove along the Great West Road without much gaiety being contributed to the party by the Birthday Girl. We not only did not stop on the way, but when we reached the Cairo Club, Dagobert actually ordered for Sarah and me a Strawberry Malted Glory, while he and Douglas retired to a bar marked Men Only for a pint of beer.

"I think he's sweet," Sarah told me, as soon as we were alone.

"Who?"

"Dagobert, of course."

"Oh, do you," I said unenthusiastically. I was thinking

quite a few things about Dagobert myself, but not that he was sweet.

"He's told us, Jane!"

"What?"

"All about you and him!" she went on eagerly, not noticing the set expression which had come over my face. "Why don't you do it, Jane?"

"Do what?" I may have sounded a little exasperated. I was.

"Marry him, of course," she said. "He's always asking you to. You've no right to keep a man dangling like that for years. And anyway he's so devastatingly attractive. Douglas thinks so too, and Douglas is an awfully good judge of other men." She kept talking, which saved me the necessity of expressing my own views, which was probably as well. The Strawberry Malted Glory seemed to have gone to her head. "Of course I've always *known* there was *somebody* in the background, Jane. But you've been so cagey. Why haven't you ever brought him round to the office? Rosemary and I have heard his voice on the 'phone once or twice and we've discussed it till the cows come home. We've even decided what he looked like—quite wrong, of course! Imagine his knowing Dad all the time! I think he's grand. If I were you I'd snap him up at once. Naturally it's none of my business." She interrupted herself long enough to suck up through a straw some of the viscous, puce substance in her glass.

It was most unlike Sarah to talk like this to me, but women about to be married always proselytise.

"I know!" she exclaimed. "Why don't you accept him and we can have a double wedding? After Christmas some time. Oh, I forgot! I suppose we ought to wait . . ." She was evidently thinking of Mrs. Robjohn and the memory dampened her ardour for a moment. "But people don't pay much attention to mourning nowadays do they? Maybe in the spring, at Easter. Clothes are much more fun in the spring. Why don't you do it, Jane?"

The need of answering this question was avoided by the return of the "boys." Douglas and Dagobert were obviously already pals; they had both lighted pipes and were looking very manly as they strode towards us.

Sarah looked up suddenly to find them beside our table. She blushed and murmured quickly:

"Maybe I've been talking out of turn."

"I'll bet you two little women have been discussing clothes," said Dagobert with unbearable heartiness.

I glanced up venomously from the sticky, pink, gelatinous mass in the bottom of my glass. He knows how I loathe that kind of remark. That Sarah had just introduced the subject of clothes made it all the worse.

"No," I said, "we were wondering about a double wedding. I understand you're impatient to publish the banns."

He had the grace at least to look embarrassed. "Er," he stammered, "you know I am, Jane." I saw him counting hastily on his fingers. "Any time after April the tenth."

It was the first I'd heard of April the tenth; I learned later that his divorce would be through by that date.

We found a table as far as possible (a concession to me) from the band. We ordered dinner. The menu was in French and Dagobert made the waiter translate each item. We had bright-green pea soup, followed by rissoles and Choc-ice Marshmallow Nut Sundaes.

"Would you like Grapefruit Squash, Orangeade or Lemon Sunshine?" Dagobert asked me, after he had ordered beer for himself and Douglas.

The second the waiter brought the soup, Douglas and Sarah got up to dance. We remained to eat; I wanted to get the taste of the Strawberry Malted Glory out of my mouth, and there were one or two things I wanted to say to Dagobert.

"What's the idea?" I began aggressively.

"The idea? You mean this place?"

He swept the room with an admiring eye, lingering on the green Egyptian columns with their spangled lotus-leaf capitols picked out in pillar-box red and tiny hexagons of mirror glass, which supported a ceiling of startling blue in which real stars appeared to twinkle. I followed his gaze in a kind of fascination to the walls which were done in multi-coloured marble-type plaster and represented—I imagine—typical scenes of Egyptian life, sphinxlike creatures, mythological beasts, palm trees. I was sure that I recognised the Nile, except that it seemed to be full of gondolas and flowed into something which looked remarkably like the Bay of Naples with Vesuvius (or maybe it was Fujiyama) behind it.

"It makes a nice change," Dagobert concluded.

"I mean what's the idea of picking up Sarah and Douglas?"

"Oh them," he shrugged. "Background."

"Why can't you leave them alone? What have you got against them?"

"That," he said with a cryptic smile, "is what will appear as the evening wears on."

"I think that's a dirty trick."

To my surprise he sighed. "It is, rather," he admitted. "But then murdering Mrs. Robjohn was a dirty trick, too."

I moved uncomfortably. Everything always came back to that.

"They couldn't have had anything to do with it."

"I sincerely hope not." But he sounded worried.

"In the first place, Sarah was—" I hesitated, remembering that to give Sarah a helping hand I ought to be a little surer of my facts—"she was out dancing all that night," I concluded lamely.

"She got home that evening at about ten to twelve," Dagobert said. "Remember I'm a pal of her father's."

"And you use your charm to pump him about his daughter!" I exclaimed scornfully.

"I've already admitted I feel like a bum," he protested. "An amateur detective can only afford to behave like a gentleman in his spare time."

"Anyway," I pointed out, surer of my facts this time, "Douglas was a thousand miles away when it happened."

"Quite," he nodded, gasping with sudden amazement at the brilliant Nile-green liquid in his soup plate.

"Why do you say 'quite' in that smug way?" I asked suspiciously.

"Did I? I didn't notice."

I continued to stare at him thoughtfully. He was holding out on me again.

"Besides, neither of them had the faintest motive," I returned to the attack.

"I'm sorry you brought up the subject of motive," he said. "Because they are about the only people in the picture who had motives. Sarah frankly loathed Mrs. Robjohn who had threatened to disown Douglas if he married her; and Douglas himself came into a tidy sum of money on his mother's death."

He glanced up at me solicitously and beneath the table-cloth his hand found mine. I think I had gone slightly pale all of a sudden. For some reason Mr. Playfair's words had come back to me with a vague but horrible significance. "What the world calls a crime has sometimes been committed from the best motives and *with results* which are beneficent." That Mrs. Robjohn's death had resulted in Douglas and Sarah's obvious happiness certainly no one could deny.

Dagobert must have divined something of what was going on in my mind for he pressed my hand reassuringly. There was a slight twinkle in his eyes as he spoke.

"We may however be able to clear them," he said, "if they'll only come clean—*and*," he added grimly, "I think they will."

We watched the dancers for a moment without speaking. I did not withdraw my hand from his. We caught a glimpse of Sarah and Douglas, blissfully unaware of their soup growing cold on the table, the scrum around them and the blaring band.

"They *are* sweet together," I murmured.

"Shall we?" he asked.

"Why not," I said, rising for what I took to be an invitation to dance.

"I meant shall we make it April the tenth," he said. "Irene's solicitors assure me that that's the day. I thought you might be interested. Shall we also dance?"

I nodded.

"I'll take that as a 'yes' to both questions," he said quietly.

I didn't argue, and we too joined the scrum, equally unaware of it and, I think, equally blissful. Frankly I kept thinking about April the tenth, and the more I thought of it the more I liked it.

"Me, too," Dagobert suddenly murmured in my ear. "I'm so excited I can't think of anything else."

I was sniffing slightly. "Let's not be sentimental," I said. "Why not?"

"That's right," I agreed, "why not indeed?"

It was a bit of an effort after that dance to descend to earth again. We started back towards our table, but Dagobert arrested me as we saw that Sarah and Douglas had reached it first.

"You're a nice girl and I like you," he said. "There's a fully licensed bar over in that corner."

"You're so good to me," I murmured, following him hastily.

"We'll have several children," he said, "even if it means my getting steady work."

"Let's work out the details later," I suggested as we reached the bar.

He handed me a glass of whisky. "Drink this," he said. "You've survived one shock this evening on a Strawberry Malted Glory but there may be others to come."

On the dance floor they had begun something called a Spot Dance and the bar was relatively empty. We found a corner where we could almost hear each other speak. We lighted cigarettes.

"Did Babs enjoy her visit to Scotland?" I asked.

"Your mind seems to jump around in the most unregulated way, Jane. What is it that women see in your Major Stewart?"

"The usual things—only more so, if you know what I mean."

"No, I don't," he confessed. "I thought he was an awful stick, pompous, dull and uninteresting—except, of course, as a potential murderer. Why do women get in such a dither about him?"

"Because," I said, "he gets in a dither about them. He's always vividly aware that you are a woman and he lets you know it. Other men take you out and talk about, say, Einstein's Theory of Relativity. But Jimmy always talks about *you*."

"I must try that," he sighed.

"We seem to have wandered from Babs. How do you manage to meet all these people?"

"She wrote me that she would be arriving at King's Cross this afternoon. I met her train."

"Wait a minute! She wrote *you*?"

"I forgot to say I first wrote her about a week ago. I got her address by calling up her mother in Purley."

"Who on earth does Babs think you are?"

Dagobert looked a little embarrassed by the question. "As a matter of fact I'm not quite sure where I stand on that point. I gave her the impression that I am one of the Big Three—is that the right number?—at Scotland Yard. She was tremendously impressed. She read a book, she tells me, about Scotland Yard. She greatly admires us."

"She'll tell Jimmy all about it this evening," I pointed out.

"Probably," he agreed. "Anyway it's high time we gave Jimmy another jolt."

"I suppose you know what you're doing."

"No," he said. "But at least I'm doing something."

"What did she tell you?"

"Chiefly that the anonymous letter she received was

typewritten. Which eliminates Mrs. Robjohn as its author, leaving us someone in your office."

"Rosemary," I said.

"All right, Rosemary," he agreed. "Something in this business is bound to make sense."

"Rosemary wrote Babs an anonymous letter," I said. "What's that got to do with Mrs. Robjohn's getting murdered?"

"I see your point; maybe nothing. You're very discouraging, Jane, after a man's done such a hard day's work . . ." He stared into the bottom of his empty whisky glass. His mind must have been far away, for he did not seem to notice that it was empty. "Who," he asked, as though speaking to himself, "would Mrs. Robjohn reasonably have unbolted the door for and let into her room in the middle of the night?"

"Any of us three women," I said.

"Or her own son," Dagobert suggested.

"Yes, if he hadn't been somewhere in the Mediterranean."

"Or," he added, "a very old family friend."

I didn't say anything, but I felt a resistance rising in me. He was, I knew, referring to Mr. Playfair.

"And why," he changed the subject, "didn't she hear those shillings being dropped into the gas meter?"

"Since you're asking imponderable questions," I said, "who was the tall man in evening clothes who visited Number 17 Mandel Square at midnight?"

"Him?" Dagobert said. "Oh I know who he was. I'd forgotten to tell you."

27 ✳ I must cure Dagobert some day of making startling announcements in such a casual tone of voice. It is an affectation and it's hard on the nerves. It's like sneaking up behind one on tiptoe and saying boo!

"For heaven's sake do two things," I protested feebly. "Tell me who, and give me a drink."

"That is," Dagobert qualified, "I *think* I know who Joe saw stepping out of the taxi in Mandel Square at midnight that night. Will you have a drink first, or shall we go in and talk it over with him now?"

"Him? But . . ." I stopped short.

"Is *this* where you two have been hiding!" exclaimed Sarah, who, closely followed by Douglas, had run us to earth.

The entrance was so theatrical I fancied for a moment that Dagobert had stage-managed it, but that was absurd.

"It's a small world," I heard him murmur under his breath.

I was staring at Douglas as though I had seen a ghost. Indeed Douglas at that moment seemed to be furnished with supernatural qualities. I was trying to reconcile him with being "the vaguely familiar bronzed young man in a mackintosh" I had seen that morning from my office window buying a paper on the corner of the High Street, the tall man in evening clothes whom Joe had seen in Mandel Square that same evening, and the young Colonial who had disembarked from the S.S. *Van Dam* in Southampton a week after his mother's death. Dagobert was enjoying my confusion. What Sarah and Douglas thought of it I couldn't imagine.

"There's a place where you can play ping-pong," Douglas announced. "What about a game?"

"If you can take it on an empty stomach," Dagobert agreed, "I'm your man."

Sarah and I traipsed after them; they both made a great display of removing jackets. I could see from the first rally that the game wouldn't last long. With a ping-pong bat in his hand Douglas was a tiger; Dagobert hadn't a chance.

The score was 17 to 3 when Dagobert said: "Where did you and Sarah go that first night when you arrived back from Ceylon?"

"That first night," Douglas repeated, "let's see . . ."

"Not *that* first night. The other first night."

Douglas served the ball into the net. "Let's see," he repeated.

"We went to the movies," Sarah supplied quickly.

"In evening clothes?"

"No, of course not." It was still Sarah who did the talking. "Well, perhaps we did. I don't remember."

"My serve," said Dagobert, taking the ball. "D'you know I think I'm going to win this game—one way or another. No, I meant on the night of November the twenty-ninth. Ready?"

He served; Douglas hit the ball wildly in the direction of the ceiling. His face was dark, and at that moment he reminded me vividly of Sirkorski, his father. Sarah continued to do the talking.

"Douglas wasn't in England then," she said. "His ship didn't dock at Southampton until a week later. Don't you remember?"

"That's right," Dagobert said. "The S.S. *Van Dam* docked on the sixth of December to be exact. Ready? I'm serving . . . But Douglas wasn't on the S.S. *Van Dam*."

Douglas missed the ball entirely. "How d'you mean? Of course I was."

"Keep your eye on the ball," Dagobert prompted, winning another point. "You were—as far as Port Said. You took a plane on from there. Your serve."

"But that's silly!" Sarah said. "Why should he do that?"

"You tell me."

Douglas served two more into the net. It may not have been in the best sporting tradition, but this was certainly one way of winning the game.

"How do you know he did?" I asked, since no one else said anything.

"I spent the morning in Pall Mall, in the offices of the Steamship Company," Dagobert explained. "He hopped on a plane at Port Said and arrived in England on the morning of the twenty-ninth. Is that right, Douglas?"

"Yes," said Douglas, as simultaneously Sarah said: "No."

"The same day that Mrs. Robjohn was—er—gassed."

"What's that got to do with it!" Douglas snapped savagely. "Would you mind not talking about my mother?" He served a vicious ball which left Dagobert completely standing.

"I'd like not to talk about her," Dagobert conceded, "but that's why we came out here this evening. I'll make a confession. This isn't Jane's birthday."

"Of all the filthy tricks!" Sarah began. She was as white as she had been that day when I'd innocently remarked that Douglas had "earned" the money his mother had left him.

"Let me tell you what I think," said Dagobert hastily, "before you smash that ping-pong ball at my head. It's my serve again, anyway. I think you hopped on to that plane in order to see Sarah a week sooner. Right?"

"Yes," Douglas growled.

"But when next day you heard your mother was dead, why didn't you turn up at once, instead of hiding until the *Van Dam* docked a week later?" Dagobert shook his head gravely. "That was a dam' silly thing to do when you think of it." He held his bat ready to serve, waiting for Douglas's reply.

"I—I don't know." Douglas's chin jutted out aggressively.

Dagobert served. "I think I know," he said.

"How could you?" his opponent rasped. "What business is it of yours?"

Sarah again spoke. She had drawn slightly away from me, as though she didn't like me much. I must say I don't blame her. "He wanted to," she said. "But I wouldn't let him."

Dagobert turned on her. "Why not?"

"Because, because, well—I thought it would start endless questions."

"You thought there was something phoney about Mrs. Robjohn's death?"

"No. No, of course not. Why should I?"

"Then why were you afraid of questions? Why are you *still* afraid of questions?"

"We're not," Douglas stated.

"In that case," Dagobert said, serving, "let's not be so tense. Where did you go dancing that evening?"

"The Hungaria, I think it was called."

"Were you both in evening clothes?"

"Yes."

"What time did you deliver Sarah back to Lillie Road?"

"Oh, about—"

"About two," Sarah interrupted.

"I don't mean by British Double Summer Time," Dagobert murmured dryly. "No, you returned to Lillie Road just before midnight—commendably early. Your father told me. Of course you *might* have had something to do afterwards . . ."

"What the hell do you mean?" Douglas exploded.

"You know we'd get this over in a much more friendly and co-operative spirit if you two would come clean. I'm on your side—I think. Your serve."

"What do you want to know?" Sarah asked carefully.

"Let me tell you what I think happened that night, and then tell me whether I'm right or wrong. At the Hungaria, after you'd dined and danced a bit and discussed this and that you began to talk about the future, getting married and so on."

"Is there anything wrong with that?" Douglas demanded.

"Then the question of your mother came up," Dagobert continued, ignoring the interjection. "You both knew she'd be dead set against the marriage, in fact that she'd probably cut you out of her will."

"I'm quite able to support us both."

"Quite. But I'm trying to reconstruct the way your conversation went. I suggest that Sarah was keen on your getting your mother's favorable consent before you made definite plans."

"Naturally," Sarah nodded.

"I suggest that Douglas, thereupon, said he'd go around to Number 17 Mandel Square then and there—to force her consent, if necessary. I suggest he was angry and maybe a little violent about it."

Sarah's pallor seemed to confirm Dagobert's suggestion. "But he didn't go round," she said.

"Yes, he did," Dagobert contradicted her amiably. "D'you know I'm being very unfair with you two. I should have told you before that Douglas was seen getting out of a taxi at midnight in Mandel Square. My game, I believe. Shall we have another?"

"No thanks," Douglas said. "All right! I took a taxi to Mandel Square at midnight. But I—"

"Just a second," Dagobert broke in, "I want to ask you a question and I warn you it's a vitally important question. When you left Sarah in Lillie Road and took the taxi on to Mandel Square *did you borrow any small change from her?* Don't hurry to answer. Think it over."

He glanced from one to the other. Both looked slightly bewildered by the question. I looked grave but I felt equally bewildered.

"Yes, as a matter of fact I did," Douglas answered finally. "The smallest thing I had on me was a fiver, and she gave me a handful of silver so I could pay the taxi."

"Did you give it all to the taxi-driver, or was there some left over?"

"I think there were a few shillings, yes."

I saw now what Dagobert was driving at. Had Douglas the necessary shillings to put into the gas meter? But the importance of whether or not he had borrowed them from Sarah escaped me at the time.

Dagobert turned slowly to Sarah. "Sarah," he said, "you knew that Douglas was going to see his mother, that he was angry with her and that there would doubtless be a stormy session. The next morning you learned that Mrs. Robjohn was dead. You therefore advised Douglas to say nothing of his midnight visit, and to keep under cover until the ship he was supposed to be on arrived in Southampton. Is that it?"

"Yes."

"Reasonable, if stupid," he nodded. "Sarah, did you suspect foul play?"

"No!" she cried. "But I thought other people would! Besides . . ."

"There's one other thing I must say to you both before we go on," Dagobert again intervened. "After I've said it we'll have an hour off for food and self-composure. At the end of that time we shall, I trust, have four amateur detectives on this case instead of only Jane and me."

"Case?" Douglas echoed. The Sirkorski look had come into his eyes again. I felt uncomfortable at the revelation of this side of his character.

"Yes," Dagobert said quietly. "Your mother was murdered."

We had dinner. Neither Sarah nor Douglas ate a great deal. Dagobert, while he didn't force conversation upon them, managed to keep the party ticking over so that a stranger watching us would not have found us more gloomy than the average table of four.

He paid the bill and proposed that we drive back to town. "We can have a bite there later if we feel like it," he said. "Do you mind if I drive? I haven't a car and I love driving."

We drove in relative silence until Douglas himself broached the subject we were all thinking about.

"I'd better tell you exactly what happened that evening," he said. He must have been thinking it over, for he spoke simply and without hesitation. "I got out of the taxi in front of Mother's place at midnight, as you seem to know. I hadn't yet seen her and she had no idea I was already in England. I *was* angry with her. Sarah had given me a hint of the kind of cracks Mother was always taking at her. Besides she was always on about Sarah in her letters to me, insinuating rotten things and the rest of it. She knew Sarah and I were in love, and more or less engaged. I'd made up my mind to have it out with her that very night. She'd always kept me under her thumb, until I joined the Army and got away from her. I was going to let her know once and for all that I didn't give a damn for her opinion, her money or anything to do with her. When I walked up to her front door I was in a filthy temper. At that moment I could cheerfully have shaken a consent to my marriage with Sarah out of her. I didn't see any lights in her room. I assumed she must be asleep. Then, as I stood there, I began to feel a little ashamed of myself. It seemed a funny way for an only son to come back to his mother after years of absence. I began to remember how as a child she had looked after me, given me everything I wanted, stayed up all night nursing me when I was ill. I thought of her lying in that huge four-poster bed asleep, looking frail, maybe older than when I'd last seen her, maybe worried about me . . ."

He was silent for a moment. Dagobert behind the wheel seemed to be giving his full attention to the Great West Road. None of us said anything.

"Finally I turned away—or rather I began to," Douglas continued. "I decided I'd sleep on it, come back in the morning in a calmer frame of mind and tell her then about Sarah and me. Perhaps when she realised our minds were made up she'd be reconciled to the idea and give us her blessing."

"You said you *began* to turn away," Dagobert prompted.

"Yes. This is the part that worries me, if—if what you

said back in the Cairo Club is true. But how could she have been murdered? Who could possibly have wanted to kill a harmless old woman?"

"What happened?" Dagobert said sharply.

"Well, as I was about to go I thought I heard someone talking in the front room, her room, that is. The bay window of the room is only a few feet from the porch where I was standing. As I said, the window was completely black and I couldn't understand why anyone should be talking in there in the pitch dark."

"Your mother," I said, "kept the black-out curtains she had used during the war."

"Yes, Sarah told me that afterwards," he said. "But it puzzled me at the time. I thought she must be talking in her sleep or something."

"So you recognised her voice?" Dagobert asked.

"Almost certainly."

"Did you catch anything she said?"

"No. I only recognised the tone of her voice. Since she was awake I changed my mind again and decided to go in. Then I heard another voice. She was not alone."

Though I couldn't see his face I could almost hear Dagobert cautiously exhaling his breath. "And this other voice," he said carefully, "did you hear what it said?"

"No."

"Would you recognise it again?"

"I doubt it. The windows were closed, you know."

"Was it a man's voice? Or a woman's voice?"

"I'm not sure."

"You're not sure!" For a second I was afraid Dagobert was going to lose his temper, but he was sweet reason itself as he added: "But you recognised the tone of your mother's voice; you ought to be able to recall whether the second voice was male or female."

"I know I ought," Douglas said wretchedly. "But I can't."

"If you can't, you can't," Dagobert sighed. "Go on, please."

"There isn't much more. Realising she wasn't alone I once more changed my mind and walked off. I walked to the High Street and eventually hailed a passing taxi which took me back to my hotel in Bloomsbury. It was the Midlothian, if you want to check up or anything."

"So you never even went inside the house?" Dagobert said.

"No."

"That would seem to clear you of all possible suspicion," Dagobert said with sudden cheerfulness. "By the way, did you ever pay Sarah back those shillings you borrowed from her?"

28 ✳ Next morning Dagobert made breakfast for me. I heard him letting himself into my flat with the spare key and scrabbling around in the kitchen. Strictly speaking, he shouldn't possess the spare key to my flat, but his own—one flight up—is minute, and I let him keep a lot of junk—tennis rackets, skis, books, ancient leather trunks, etc., in my place.

My alarm clock had not, to my knowledge, yet gone off and I lay there thinking about what I should put on, a reverie which imperceptibly merged into planning my next summer's wardrobe.

I sat up with a start, grabbing for my dressing-gown to find Dagobert standing there with a breakfast tray. He put it down, lighted the gas fire, threw back the curtains and turned on the electric light.

"This is very thoughtful," I stifled a yawn.

"After April the tenth," he reminded me, "you'll have to make my breakfast—and of course I'll have to go to work."

He retired modestly while I flung a few things on. We had breakfast in front of the gas fire. Dagobert, I knew, had something on his mind, several things as a matter of fact. He approached the first as I handed him a cup of tea.

"Speaking of April the tenth," he began, "I rather wondered if it might not be a good idea if you gave up your job at the office a bit sooner than that date."

"How do you mean?"

"Well, you will be giving it up eventually, won't you?"

"I suppose so."

"Then why not give it up right away?" To my bewilderment he didn't look at me as he said this. "I mean, at once, today," he concluded. "I could go around with you if you liked, help you fetch away your things."

"I couldn't leave today. It's pay day," I reminded him lightly, not yet grasping that I was supposed to take this preposterous suggestion seriously.

"I mean it, Jane."

I watched him in growing amazement. "But why?" I asked.

"I don't awfully like to think of you there, that's all," he said almost diffidently. "It may be silly, but I don't."

"But that's absurd!" I began.

"I know."

"I can't just walk out on Mr. Playfair like that. Without notice. Without a word of explanation!"

"I'll telephone him and say you're unwell."

"You'll do nothing of the sort!" I stared at him blankly. "What's the matter with you? Are you losing your nerve or something?"

"I am, rather," he admitted.

I was wide awake by this time. My first shock of astonishment had given away to a kind of anger at his high-handed attempt to run my life for me. This anger had swiftly died down as I realised he was worried on my account. I spoke more gently.

"But nothing could possibly happen, Dagobert, not to me, not at the office. How could it?"

"No, of course not," he rumbled on unhappily. "Only . . ."

"Only what?"

"Only I wish you wouldn't go."

"We'll talk it over next week," I conceded. "I might leave after Christmas or at the New Year, if Mr. Playfair can find somebody else. But I must be getting ready now. Since I'm up I might as well be on time for a change."

We continued breakfast for a while in silence. We argue a lot as a rule, but there are occasions like the present one when each of us knows that further argument is futile. He knew that nothing he could say would make me consent to chuck up my job then and there.

"Where's your manuscript?" He asked suddenly.

It took me a second or two to adjust my mind. I had been living the Robjohn affair so fully these past few days that I'd almost forgotten that I was also writing it.

"It's in the office," I said. "It's quite safe. It's in the strong room, filed in the Hartley deed box."

"You'd better bring it back here," he said.

"I see what you mean," I nodded with a slightly uneasy smile. Other people besides myself visited the strong room.

"How long has Mrs. Robjohn had that four-poster bed, I wonder," he said unexpectedly.

"Oddly enough, I can tell you if you want to know," I said. "About two years."

"I see," he mused, and added: "I'll have luncheon with you."

"If I can possibly get away."

"And tea, too, if you don't mind."

"You sound as though you were afraid someone were going to poison me!" I smiled brightly, and then stopped smiling.

For again I saw what he meant.

"By this time whoever murdered Mrs. Robjohn must be doing a lot of quiet thinking, to say the least. In fact I think we may say that nearly all the characters involved have been warned." He decapitated his egg neatly. I waited for him to go on.

"Douglas and Sarah both know all they need to know," he continued. "Stewart has been uneasy ever since the time he threatened to call up the Gas Company to complain about me. If Babs told him about yesterday he'll be even more uneasy. Rosemary must be wondering why you've been on about her lighter so persistently."

"By the way, I want that lighter," I put in.

Somewhat to my astonishment he handed it over without demur. He had never thought much of my favourite clue. He continued:

"Mr. Playfair obviously suspects that something is up. And Oates normally knows what's going on; besides, I imagine he listened in to my telephone call yesterday afternoon. One of these six *is* a murderer, Jane. I wish you'd let me call up and say you're ill . . . just for a few days, if you like."

"Can't we eliminate most of them?" I said, refusing to begin the argument again about my going to the office.

"Can we?" He raised an eyebrow. "Let's try. Still reckoning the operative time between eleven o'clock and one-thirty, where was everybody? We've done this before, but let's try it again. Until eleven-fifty Sarah and Douglas were at the Hungaria or in a taxi returning to Lillie Road, witnesses—each other. At eleven-fifty Sarah arrived home—witness, her father who heard her, but *didn't see* her, get out of the taxi. Douglas was outside Mandel Square at midnight—witness, Joe."

I poured out two more cups of tea. Dagobert went on:

"Rosemary was in the office until eleven-fifteen—witness, Stewart. She took a taxi home at eleven-thirty-five—witness, Joe. Twenty minutes unaccounted for, presumably spent in the office. She was in Oratory Street at eleven-forty-five. We don't know what happened to her from that time onwards; presumably she went to bed. But she *could*—just—have hopped into another taxi and beaten Joe back to Mandel Square, or else even visited Mrs. Robjohn *after* the still unidentified person Douglas heard there at midnight."

"Stewart was in the office at eleven-fifteen—witness, Rosemary. He walked home—witness, himself. He arrived at Inigo Mews at about eleven-forty-five—witness, all-night-garage man across the way. A half an hour accounted for by a walk he *could* have done in fifteen minutes. From eleven-forty-five onwards he remained at home—witness, the all-night-garage man again.

"Sirkorski, for the record, was in Paris—witness, the newspaper *Humanité* which reviewed the concert he gave there that evening.

"Mrs. Hawthorne was in bed asleep—witness, herself.

"Mr. Playfair did not go to your Swiss film at the Academy. He was at his Club, Cockburn's in Kensington High Street."

I began to interrupt, but I lighted a cigarette instead. Obviously Dagobert would have checked up on Mr. Playfair.

"Mr. Playfair left Cockburn's at ten past eleven to walk towards the Underground—witness, one William Burns, porter at Cockburn's. He arrived in Hampstead about one in a taxi—witness Mary Forbes, his housekeeper. Nearly an hour and a half unaccounted for."

"He probably walked halfway home and then took a taxi," I suggested. "He often does that."

"It's possible," Dagobert nodded without further comment. "Oates was out for the night. I've spoken to his mother who has a tobacconist-newsagent's in the Fulham Road. He often stays out all night. He has some friends Mrs. Oates does not approve of in Charlotte Street. That's all night unaccounted for."

"That's the lot then," I said, jumping up briskly and regarding the clock with horror. In spite of the day's promising start, I was going to be as late as ever! Interesting as our conversation may have been, my job was my job and I must not lose my sense of proportion. It was strange, when you think of it, that I automatically felt my work as a law clerk at Daniel Playfair & Son to be more important than the task of running down a murderer. The mind moves in that kind of groove.

An atmosphere of gloom and tension seemed to brood

over Number 11 Mandel Street when I arrived that morning. Jimmy was saturnine and forbidding, in his Miss Hamish-Miss Proctor-Miss Swinburne mood. Rosemary was silent, thoughtful, inclined to stare at the ledgers instead of getting on with them. Sarah was fidgety, restless and apt to say silly things. Oates was never there when you wanted him to run an errand, and when he was, he kept whistling and banging doors. Mr. Playfair was hopelessly inefficient and impossible to get any work out of. Even I was not my usual cool, competent self.

I went into Mr. Playfair's room just as he was preparing to go out to luncheon. I had forgotten to tell him I'd made an appointment for him for two-thirty that afternoon. I told him and apologised. He said thank you and took up his blackthorn walking stick. He paused in the door and said:

"Old Mary Forbes, my housekeeper, you know, is immensely excited at being interviewed and questioned about my movements."

He smiled at me benevolently and went.

29 ✳ Mr. Playfair was getting almost as bad as Dagobert at dropping bombs in a mild conversational tone of voice and leaving me to pick up the scattered fragments. While I was trying to do this, Dagobert telephoned to remind me of our luncheon engagement. I explained that I couldn't possibly get away. There was a client in my room at the time and I was terse. Afterwards Rosemary, Sarah and I had a rather constrained meal together, interrupted by telephone calls and visitors, and about two, Dagobert called again.

He had nothing special to say—except to remind me of tea—and again having a client with me I was again terse.

The trouble with people like Dagobert is that one always suspects their motives. I half suspected that this unprecedented telephoning was part of a subtle war of nerves to make me throw up my job. I now know he was really worried.

Shortly after four it happened all over again; he telephoned and again I was with a client. It was that kind of day.

"I'll call you back about half past five," I said.

He gave me a number which I jotted down on my blotting pad. The client left and a few minutes later Sarah brought me in a cup of tea.

At five o'clock Mr. Playfair went. There were no clients and the office began to have its end-of-the-day feeling. I heard Jimmy across the corridor asking Rosemary if he could give her a lift home. In spite of Babs's return they were evidently on speaking terms. Rosemary looked in to say goodnight. Was it my imagination that her manner was slightly cool? Probably—for I was beginning to suffer from a guilty conscience with regard to my colleagues and to feel like a pariah.

I was about to telephone Dagobert when the door opened and Oates came in. He was wearing a loose, belted teddy-bear coat and he carried bright yellow pigskin gloves. A straw-tipped Melachrino hung from his pouting lower lip and he was hatless.

"Hello," he said, "how's tricks?"

I betrayed myself by a rapid glance at my handbag. There were six pounds ten shillings in it; Rosemary had paid us our weekly wages after luncheon that afternoon. He interpreted my glance and disparaged my alarm.

"What's six pounds ten?" he said contemptuously. "Mere—"

"Chicken feed," I supplied. "But chickens have to live."

"If we'd had a fiver of that on Cherry Brandy yesterday at Cheltenham we'd have cleaned up. I tried to contact you, but you were so busy I couldn't. We lost fifty-five pounds because of that. Cherry Brandy started at eleven to one. What are you up to these days anyhow?"

"Nothing."

I found him regarding me suspiciously from under his long silken eyelashes. "You are," he contradicted. He added with elaborate casualness: "How's Dagobert?"

"Fine, thank you."

"What's he keep ringing you up about?"

"You know how men are—persistent."

"Yeah," he said doubtfully. "What's he so persistent about?"

He had made himself comfortable on the edge of my desk. I watched his fingers toy with the catch of my handbag, opening it and closing it again absent-mindedly. I said the first thing that came into my mind.

"We've been having a little tiff—you know, a lovers' quarrel. That's why he keeps ringing me up."

"Giving him the run around, huh?" He nodded.

"That's it."

"Well, why should I get hot under the collar!" he exclaimed, proffering his cigarette case. I had no idea why, or indeed what he was talking about. "Dagobert's loss may be Albert's gain, huh?" He smiled at me challengingly.

"Who's Albert?" I asked.

"Me, of course."

I recovered myself. "Start at the beginning again," I said. "I've lost track of the conversation somewhere."

He simplified it for me. "You and your boy friend have a

bust-up, see? Maybe there's a dame in it, a popsie he's putting in his spare time with. Otherwise what's he doing at Claridges yesterday during the *thé dansant?*"

Oates *had* listened in to yesterday's telephone conversation and checked up on Claridges' number.

"Just that," I nodded. "A popsie."

"So you decide to stand him up. When he wants to have lunch with you, you tell him where to get off, the same with tea, the same with dinner, huh?"

"I hadn't yet decided about dinner."

"I'll tell you what I'll do," he announced. "I'll take you out to dinner myself." He closed my handbag with such a snap that I jumped. "See what I mean?"

I nodded dubiously. "More or less."

"You call him up and say: 'I'm most frightfully sorry and all that sort of thing but it happens that tonight I have a previous engagement.' Snooty, but dignified. Get the idea? He's as mad as hell, but tomorrow he's eating out of your hand. Meanwhile you and I have a good time. We'll go to the King of Bohemia."

I don't know what it is about Oates, but he always cheers me up. I am well aware of the fact that he is a repulsive, nasty-minded little toad who ought to be in a reformatory. There is really not one good thing I can honestly say about him, he has no redeeming trait that I've ever discovered, but the fact remains that he cheers me up.

I was seized with an unreasoning impulse to accept his invitation. Oates was, I remembered, the only key person in the Robjohn affair we didn't know about.

"What about it, Miss Hamish?" he prompted, taking my thoughtfulness for maiden shyness. "It's only a bit of fun."

"What was the name of that pub?" I asked.

"The King of Bohemia in Charlotte Street. They've got a bloke who plays the piano—with ear-rings in his ears. Look, I've forgotten about those nylons and that lipstick—I've had other things on my mind—but I'll get them for you to-morrow."

The bribery was irresistible. "I'll come," I said.

"Swell! *Très bien*. You're going to love it."

In his restless way, he had again opened my handbag and this time out came my week's wages. I watched them with wistful interest. It was probably the last I would see of them.

"I was going to invest this on Romeo in the three-thirty tomorrow," he explained, "but I'll tell you what we'll do. We'll blow it tonight instead. There's a chance Romeo won't win, anyway." He pocketed the entire six pounds ten. "Partners, eh, Ja . . . Miss Hamish?"

The Jane part would, doubtless, follow later. I began to wonder if I weren't being a fool. He may have noticed my hesitation.

"Do you want to call Dagobert?" he said. "Do the previous engagement act?"

"Perhaps I'd better."

"I'll wait for you outside," he nodded. "Always tactful, that's me." And, with my six pounds ten, he went.

I reached for the telephone and dialled the first two letters of the telephone number I had scribbled on the blotting pad. Then I hesitated. Obviously Oates had gone to the extension in the outer office. I put back the receiver with the intention of going into Mr. Playfair's room where there is a telephone without an extension.

At that moment Sarah, whom I thought had gone home, opened the door to say she was just off.

"Sarah," I said quickly, "can you wait for about five minutes and telephone Dagobert for me? Here's his number. Tell him to be in the King of Bohemia in Charlotte Street as soon after six as possible. Got it? The King of Bohemia in Charlotte Street. From six onwards."

My conspiratorial tone of voice forbade questions. "Okay," she murmured.

I gathered up my things and joined Oates in the outer office.

"Telephoned already?" he asked.

He knew quite well I hadn't. "No. I decided I'd let him just wonder where I'd gone—stew in his own juice."

"Attagirl." He held the office door open for me gallantly.

It was nearly a quarter to six as we reached Kensington High Street. It was cold, dark and miserable and already I had begun to regret my impulse. Anyway as soon as we reached the King of Bohemia I should turn Oates over to Dagobert.

"Taxi?" Oates suggested largely.

I nodded, not altogether fancying the idea of joining a bus queue in his company so near the office.

"Come to think of it a bus will get us there just as soon," he added. "Sooner, maybe."

We took our place in the queue. At any rate it was dark and no one recognised me. Nor did we have quite so long to wait as I had feared. Oates neatly jumped the queue when the first Number 73 appeared, dragging me with him, and nearly spilling a parcel-laden woman who was theoretically first in the queue into the gutter.

"Old cow," he commented briefly as he herded me up the stairs. We found seats opposite each other. He took tickets to Bond Street. "Actually we stay on to the Tottenham Court Road," he explained to me, "but they never notice at this time of day."

Between Bond Street and Tottenham Court Road I winced every time the conductor passed, wondering if the penny saved was really worth the nervous tension expended, but we reached our destination without police intervention.

Oates hesitated as we walked up Percy Street, inwardly debating, I think, whether or not to take my arm. He compromised by gallantly changing his position and walking on the outside of me. "Know this part of the world?"

"Hardly at all," I encouraged him.

"It's a bit Bohemian," he said as though he owned it. "I've practically taken a studio around the corner. We might go round and see it afterwards. That is . . . if . . ."

"How very interesting!" I exclaimed in my best Kensington manner. "I didn't know you painted."

"I don't—exactly," he admitted. "But I'm thinking of doing a bit of writing. You know, sketches, impressions, criticism. That sort of thing. Chap I know's starting a magazine called *Bang*. The idea's to shake people up a bit. That's why it's called *Bang*. I'm one of the founders."

The subject of *Bang* kept us engaged until we reached the King of Bohemia. Oates at first stated casually that he had put twenty-five pounds into the venture. By the time we'd reached the pub he'd confessed—or boasted? I wasn't sure which—that his contribution had been a hundred pounds. The editor, his pal, was a poet named Padraic O'Faolain (whom I would be crazy about) and they already had the cover design for the first issue, a rude picture which would make 'em sit up and take notice. The first issue—which was written entirely by Padraic—was devoted to showing up what a lousy country England is. Padraic wanted Oates to write for the second issue.

The King of Bohemia was packed, but I didn't see Dagobert's familiar figure among the throng. He would scarcely have had time to get there. I clutched my handbag and followed Oates towards the corner where the piano was. The man in the ear-rings was strumming "If You Were the Only Girl in the World."

"There doesn't seem to be anybody here tonight," Oates complained. "Generally I know everybody. Have something to drink?"

"Is that customary?" I asked.

"They've got genuine absinthe," he announced. "You know, the stuff all the artists in Montparnasse drink. Five bob a shot, but it does something to you."

"I need something done to me," I murmured absently, watching the door for Dagobert's entrance. I was horrified to feel Oates's nudge and to find him leering down at me.

"We're going to get on all right," he said, disappearing into the crowd around the bar.

Whether he decided he had misinterpreted my innocent remark or whether he didn't consider the prospect to be worth five bob, I don't know; but he returned with two small glasses of beer. Wedged in snugly between the piano and the public telephone, the ledge of which caught me just under the shoulder-blades, I drank the beer gratefully—that is I drank what was left of it after someone had jogged my elbow and sent most of it down the front of my coat.

"We're going to get on all right," Oates repeated. "Drink up. What'll you have?"

"Is there anything with gin in it?"

"Of course. Or would you like a double brandy—three star?"

"That sounds nice," I nodded.

He returned eventually with two more glasses of beer,

but in recompense he snaffled a seat for me on a bench beside two elderly women in respectable hats who were drinking oatmeal stout and discussing varicose veins.

It was past seven and there was still no sign of Dagobert. My interest in my escort began to flag. He had gone several times to the bar, varying his invitations with such phrases as "What about the other half? Shall we have a little tiddley?" etc., etc., but always returning with beer. He no longer even lured me on with suggestions of absinthe and double brandies. It may have been native optimism that beer alone would serve his fell purpose or he may not have considered me worth the financial risk entailed by investment in the costlier beverages. But he told me about a lot of *other* wild evenings he had spent during which champagne had flowed like water. He worked the conversation subtly round to artists' models.

"I don't see anything wrong with nudes," he stated solemnly, "not rightly looked at. After all it's only a job, like working in a solicitor's office, when you think of it."

"Don't think of it," I suggested briefly.

"Did anyone ever tell you you have lovely legs, Jane," he murmured. "They'll look all right in those nylons I'm going to get you. What about a short one, Jane—for the road?"

I nodded and he again disappeared. Oates had by this time completely ceased to amuse me. I felt bored, foolish and irritated with myself. It was nearly eight by this time and I was beginning to be annoyed with Dagobert for not coming.

When Oates came back this time he actually brought short drinks, single whiskies. The talk about nudes must have made him reckless.

"I've got the feeling that this is going to turn into one of those evenings!" he said hopefully. "I wonder if Padraic's home. I'd like you to see the studio." He went through the facial contortions of a man who gets a sudden idea. "I know what we'll do! We'll go to the studio and have supper there! It's an idea, isn't it?"

"Yes," I said, "but not a good one."

He looked downcast. The thought of a tête-à-tête supper in the studio had probably been brewing in his mind for some time. It had obvious advantages, not the least of which was the money it would save.

"As a matter of fact I've got those nylons up there," he said. The crudity of the lie nearly softened my heart towards him.

"Let's have another drink," I compromised.

"Okay—if that's the way you feel."

I got beer again this time, and for the next half hour or so he pouted, making occasional sulky references to living your own life and bourgeois morality.

By this time we were such old inhabitants that we both had seats and even a table to put our beer on. It was nine o'clock and I saw us sitting there until closing time. Obviously Dagobert had decided to ignore my message or else he hadn't got it.

I watched Oates going yet again to the bar for a half pint. He looked as depressed as I was myself. I hadn't made any progress this evening—and neither had he. I opened my hand-bag and observed that it contained at least enough for a taxi back to Holland Park Avenue. It also contained Rosemary's gold lighter which I had forgotten to return to the strong room. I removed it, toyed with it absent-mindedly, lighted a cigarette which I didn't want, and dropped the lighter beside my glass on the table.

Oates returned and took his place dutifully beside me. "We could have had fun tonight," he murmured lugubriously. "It seems a pity to have wasted the evening."

"But I'm loving it," I said a little desperately. "Seeing all these interesting people."

"What's interesting about them?" he grunted.

"That's mine!" I exclaimed suddenly, as I saw him pocket Rosemary's cigarette lighter.

I was growing used to his acquisitive instincts, but the coolness of the gesture took my breath away. He looked puzzled.

"What's yours?" he asked.

"The lighter you just put in your pocket."

He took it out again and looked at it. He looked at me and then at the lighter again. His expression remained one of genuine perplexity. Was he so used to pinching things that he no longer even noticed himself doing it?

"But this is mine," he said.

He spoke with obvious conviction; and the evening, which for me had been so dull but a moment ago, suddenly became fascinating. Once more the lighter which Dagobert despised was providing me with an absorbing interest in life.

"I just took it out of my handbag," I told him.

"I'm sure it's mine," he repeated. "I got it from—well, from a bloke I know."

"From a bloke we both know," I amended. "Major Stewart. Did he give it to you?"

Oates permitted himself a knowing smile. "Not exactly," he admitted. "I borrowed it one morning from his desk, but if I tell him I want to keep it I don't think he'll argue."

"You're so clever."

"I do all right," he said.

The peregrinations of the lighter were at last becoming plain. Rosemary had given it to Jimmy; Oates had pinched it from Jimmy's desk, just as Dagobert had suspected. The next stage of the lighter's wanderings was the interesting one. For Mr. Playfair had found it in Mrs. Robjohn's room.

I stared at Oates with the first excitment I had felt about him all evening. I saw that he was staring back at me. There was a note of interrogation in his eyes.

"I say," he began, and the knowing smile slipped slightly, "now that I think of it, this lighter's been missing for some weeks. To tell the truth I thought I'd left it around the studio somewhere and Padraic had nabbed it. You say you had it in your handbag?" He was flicking the lighter open and shut as he spoke, doing the flint no good but relieving—I fancied—his nerves. "Where did *you* find it?"

" I found it in the office," I answered quite truthfully.

"I see . . ." I thought he sounded relieved. "Tell you what, I'll give it to you." And to my astonishment he actually handed it over.

I don't know whether this was a generous impulse, or whether some vague instinct made him suddenly wish to have nothing to do with this much-travelled trinket. In either event he evidently decided not to waste his gift.

"I could give you all the gold lighters and things you wanted," he added, "if only you'd be a little more friendly."

"But I am friendly!" I said sweetly.

"You know what I mean!"

We had come back to the sulks again. It was nearly nine thirty by this time. I gave Dagobert up. On the other hand, I thought smugly, I wasn't doing so badly by myself.

"What about food somewhere?" I suggested.

"It's hardly worth it now," he said in a hurt tone of voice

which made it clear that it was all somehow my fault. "Everything decent will be off."

"We can always go to Padraic's, can't we," I said.

He recovered miraculously. "Why not?" And he added, of his own accord: "Let's have one for the road before we go."

This time he brought me absinthe!

30 ✳ I cannot bear women who walk straight into sticky situations and then complain in injured surprise that they hadn't realised what they were doing. I realised quite well what I was doing as I followed Oates along Charlotte Street.

I was going home with the person who had left that gold lighter in Mrs. Robjohn's room on the night Mrs. Robjohn had been murdered. There was now little doubt in my mind that Oates was also the unknown visitor whom Douglas had heard talking to his mother at midnight. Even the uncertainty of the visitor's sex fitted in; for through a curtained window Oates's voice might easily have been confused with a woman's. I had only to establish this fact and . . . well, I refused to think any further of what logically followed.

I thought I could even guess what had taken Oates to Number 17 Mandel Square. He had been blackmailing Mrs. Robjohn, because he knew the secret of Douglas's birth. He had been blackmailing her by the same method he had used with me, namely that of recommending horses to her and when they won collecting the proceeds.

On November the twenty-ninth Laughing Boy had come

in at twenty to one. Mrs. Robjohn had backed it. That same night I had seen on her Chinese lacquer desk a pile of new pound notes. Next morning Mr. Playfair had not found those notes. That was because Oates had in the meanwhile been there to collect them.

This was the picture I had formed of Oates's activities on the night of November the twenty-ninth, and there is now no reason to conceal the fact that the picture—as far as it went— was accurate.

He started to take my arm as we turned into Goodge Street, but decided against it. He was in an optimistic mood and doubtless felt he could afford to wait.

"What if Padraic's not at home?" I said.

"He's bound to be," he reassured me. "Besides, even if he isn't, I have a key."

And I knew that Padraic was bound *not* to be at home. It struck me more forcibly that I was behaving in a fairly stupid way. My confidence in my own ability to handle the situation was becoming a little shaky. Though Oates was ten years my junior I began to realise that youths of eighteen are frequently mature men in all the worst senses of the word. We were not on my own territory, the office, but on his. Besides he was a little intoxicated.

A prowling taxi passed us and I looked at it a little wistfully. There was really no reason why I shouldn't have hailed it. But I let it pass and immediately felt forlorn and forsaken.

We reached a street lamp which dimly illuminated a dingy alley which during the day was apparently crowded with vegetable and fruit barrows. The gaunt buildings lining it looked like deserted warehouses.

'The studio's at the top of that building," he pointed

out one of the deserted warehouses. "It doesn't look much from the outside, but it's got character."

To me its character was that of places where things happen which subsequently get reported in the *Daily Mirror*. I reminded myself that there was absolutely no necessity for me to go a step further, but I knew I was going. I had to establish once and for all that Oates was the person who had visited Mrs. Robjohn at midnight on the night of the murder. As soon as I had done that I should, I told myself, go.

I wish I could pretend that I was motivated by cool courage or even reckless bravery. I wasn't. I don't think I was motivated at all. I once dived off the highest diving board in the Southampton public swimming baths for much the same reason: because I'd told myself I would, and then had not the strength of character to change my mind.

This time as it happened I was spared the actual plunge; I only went through the harrowing emotions which preceded it. For at that moment we were joined by a man who had been trailing along after us ever since we'd emerged from the King of Bohemia.

The man was Dagobert.

"Hello," he said as he caught up with us.

"Hello," I replied. "Cutting it a bit fine, weren't you?"

"There are," he said, "twenty-three public houses in London called The King of Bohemia, some of which are in places like Hampstead."

Sarah had given him the correct public house, but she had totally forgotten that I'd said Charlotte Street. Oates was less overjoyed by Dagobert's arrival than I was. To say that I had never been so pleased to see him in my life would be a reasonable statement of fact. But Oates regarded us with sullen suspicion.

"What's the idea?" he grumbled.

"I don't think you two know each other," I put in quickly.

"I've heard so much about you." Dagobert extended a genial hand.

I introduced them formally and explained that Oates had most kindly invited me to supper. Doubtless he would extend the invitation to include Dagobert.

"That's very kind of him," Dagobert said.

"You framed this up between you," Oates growled.

"In a way," Dagobert nodded. "You see, we're working on a rather important case and we thought you might help us."

Oates's sulky mouth tightened aggressively. "You've not got anything on me," he said.

"No—not yet," Dagobert agreed cheerfully. "But we shall have, before the night's over."

Oates was unenthusiastic about his supper party as we climbed the bare stairs which led up to his studio. He muttered things about food shortages, about people who were too mean to go to restaurants, about having mislaid his key.

"If Padraic's home he won't be very keen on my barging in with a lot of odd people," he grumbled.

"Padraic O'Faolain?" Dagobert said as though the name were a household one. "He won't be home. He went to Dublin this morning to visit his aged mother."

"How do you know?" Oates took the words out of my mouth.

"I had a pint with him this morning at the Fitzroy Tavern."

"You certainly meet a lot of people," I murmured.

Oates said nothing. He was fumbling for the keyhole of

the studio door. I flicked on Rosemary's lighter to help him see, and asked Dagobert the question which must have been burning in Oates's mind.

"Did Padraic say anything interesting about Oates?"

"Not really. Only that he was a conceited little pipsqueak who had literary pretensions but was quite useful in helping to finance a scurrilous magazine which will probably get them both in jug." He seemed to recollect that Oates was actually present. "I wouldn't touch that magazine, if I were you, Oates," he advised kindly. "Though of course by the time it comes out you may be in jug anyway and it won't make any difference. . . ."

Oates had turned the key in the lock and kicked the door rather violently open. He switched on the light and I saw that his face was purple.

"I could tell you a few things about O'Faolain too," he blustered. Then the savagery went from his face and I saw suddenly the overgrown, movie-fed youth of eighteen, and like the sap that I am, I began to feel a little sorry for him. "Did Padraic really say that?" he faltered. "I could show you some stuff I've done . . ."

"Professional jealousy," Dagobert soothed hastily. "You know what minor poets are like. But I'd get out of that magazine proposition if I were you."

"I'm already out," Oates stated firmly. "If only I can get that money back again."

"You can always make more the same way," Dagobert reassured him airily. Oates looked at me with an expression of injury. I nodded contritely.

"Yes, I told Dagobert about your wonderful scheme for getting rich," I admitted.

He nibbled his thick lower lip thoughtfully. "If that's

why you're here," he said, coming rapidly to a decision and removing his wallet, "you can take back your money and scram." He began to count out the six pounds ten he had taken from my handbag. I was appalled to see Dagobert wave it aside.

"Keep your money."

"*My* money," I corrected.

"You may need it," Dagobert concluded generously.

Oates glanced at me uncomfortably. "Then what do you want?" he said, repocketing my six pounds ten.

"At the moment, something to eat. Good Lord! What's this?" Dagobert broke off as he saw a large half-finished canvas on an easel in the middle of the room. It was a picture of a lumpy nude lying on a bed of oysters. From her navel grew a Chinese pagoda and her twelve toes were drawn to represent dollar signs.

"It came with the studio," Oates said and added aggressively: "I happen to like it."

Fifteen minutes later, when Oates and I re-emerged from the kitchen with tinned spaghetti on toast and a bottle of Algerian Burgundy, Dagobert was still lost in contemplation of the nude. He had found a palette and brush somewhere and was intently engaged in adding a superb Guardsman's moustache in chrome yellow to the portrait.

"I could get fond of painting," he said, and I realised with horror that he meant it. He continued to address me and to ignore our reluctant host's presence. "O'Faolain did say something else not uninteresting about Oates. He said he spent the night of November the twenty-ninth here, but that he didn't come in until after one. That would have given him plenty of time."

"Time for what?" Oates said.

Dagobert began to add an ear-ring to the nude's left ear. "Yes, Jane," he said. "I think we might work on the assumption that it was Oates whom Douglas heard talking to Mrs. Robjohn at midnight that night."

"I'm sure of it," I nodded, laying the table before the gas fire and arranging a wicker armchair to face the tiger-skin-covered divan. "He was the one who left the gold cigarette lighter in Mrs. Robjohn's room. He'd pinched it that morning from Stewart's desk. But leave your picture till later. Your spaghetti's getting cold. Careful, Oates," I added, bringing him into the conversation, "you'll drop that bottle!"

"Look here!" Oates spluttered, "what's your game, you two? What are you getting at?"

"He went round to collect the money she'd won that afternoon on Laughing Boy," Dagobert mused, coming across to the table and taking the wicker chair I indicated. "That would be the pile of new pound notes you saw on the desk. . . . The spaghetti looks good." He glanced up at Oates. "Did you give points for it?"

"What I want to know is—" Oates began furiously.

I interrupted. "Yes, but why did he go so late at night?"

"I gather from O'Faolain that he was at the Dogs earlier and had had a bad evening. Possibly he wanted to lay his hands on some ready cash at once," Dagobert suggested.

"Hey, will you two listen to me!" Oates's voice had risen to a querulous whine. He sounded as though he were going to burst into tears. I removed the wine bottle from his hand and glanced at Dagobert.

"Do you notice the voice?" I said. "Douglas could easily have mistaken it for a woman's."

Dagobert considered. "Rather epicene," he agreed.

"What's that? Will you talk English?" Oates cried in despair.

"Yes," I nodded. "What is epicene?"

"His voice," Dagobert explained, indicating Oates with his fork. "So he was at Mrs. Robjohn's the night she died. That's Fact Number One."

"What do you mean that's Fact Number One! I wasn't near the place, and even if I was . . ."

"Sit down, Oates," I urged, gently pushing him on to the divan and putting his plate before him. "Fact Number Two is that he was there at midnight, talking in an epicene voice."

Dagobert agreed, emptied his wine glass and refilled it. "Why don't we have such good spaghetti as this at home?" he said.

"All right, what if I did go round to Mandel Square!" Oates shouted suddenly. "She was a friend of mine, see? I dropped in on business maybe. Maybe I did leave my cigarette lighter there. I went round before I went to the Dogs. Before you two dropped in on her. Since you're being so smart, *you* were there after me!"

"Does he always talk so much?" Dagobert asked me.

"He's flushed with strong beer," I explained. "Be a good boy and eat your lovely spaghetti, Oates. It's a rather interesting point, Dagobert, that he seems to know we visited Mrs. Robjohn that evening. He could only know that if she told him herself. In other words if he called on her after we'd gone home at eleven."

"I don't know what I'd do without you, Jane," Dagobert said. "Let me pour you some more of this delicious Algerian Burgundy."

"Don't you two ever stop talking?" Oates whimpered.

"So he was the last person to have seen Mrs. Robjohn alive," I suggested.

Dagobert nodded. "That's Fact Number Three," he said. "I rather like putting down facts in numerical order; it gives one a sense of precision. . . . Fact Number Four is that he collects old coins. Mrs. Oates of the Fulham Road showed me his collection this afternoon."

"Wait a minute," Oates began.

I inwardly echoed Oates's sentiments. This time Dagobert was going too fast for me too. I couldn't, for the moment, see where what he called Fact Number Four fitted in. In a vague way I remembered his interest in Mrs. Wolf-Heatherington's missing coin collection, the disappearance of which was still an unsolved mystery. But remembering that Mr. Playfair considered the missing coins to be of no value their loss had nearly slipped my mind. Dagobert's insinuation was that Oates himself had stolen them from Mr. Playfair's desk to add to his own collection, a reasonable assumption. I concealed my bewilderment as I leaned over my spaghetti.

"Were there any William the Fourth shillings in his collection?" I asked, remembering that a William the Fourth shilling had formed the chief attraction of Mrs. Wolf-Heatherington's stolen coins.

"No. His collection was less interesting for what it contained, than for what it did not contain."

I tried to look intelligent. "I see," I said.

"Wait a minute! What's the big idea of snooping around my mother! If you're insinuating I pinched any of those coins . . ."

Dagobert leaned across and removed the wine bottle from his hand. "Thanks," he said, filling his own and my glasses and putting the bottle down beside the gas fire. "We have the four facts then," he continued, talking with his mouth full of spaghetti, "but they don't necessarily *prove* that Oates murdered Mrs. Robjohn."

"Murdered!" Oates gasped. I saw him clutch the edge of the table, start to clamber to his feet, then relax as though the source of energy within him had suddenly been switched off. "Murdered?" he whispered again, as though to himself.

He stared from Dagobert to me with a groggy expression. His big ears were scarlet but his long thin face was ashen. I watched the scarlet creep from his ears and invade his face.

"No," I replied gravely to Dagobert, "it doesn't necessarily prove it."

Oates recovered. "You can't do this to me!" he screamed. "You're making it all up! You're trying to scare me. That's it, you're trying to scare me. Well, you can't. I know that game myself. You know damn well Mrs. Robjohn wasn't murdered. You saw the Coroner's report, didn't you? Accidental death—that's what it said. What if I was the last person to see her alive? She died accidental!"

"Accidentally," I corrected. "He's excited, Dagobert. Do forgive him." I glanced towards the telephone. "Shall I dial Scotland Yard now, or wait until we finish supper?"

"You're bluffing," Oates blubbered. "You can't prove *anything*."

"Can you?" I asked Dagobert.

"There wouldn't be just a bit more of this delicious spaghetti?" he said.

"Of course he can't prove anything!" The snivel in Oates's voice was slowly reinforced with a sneer; his heart-shaped mouth moved convulsively and uncertainly between the two. "I know his kind. Smart alecks! They can't prove anything. They try to frame a fellow and then turn on the screws. To hell with you!"

Dagobert paused, his fork halfway to his mouth, and regarded Oates with mild wonder. Oates relapsed on to the divan.

"You heard me!" he muttered defiantly, but not so defiantly.

Dagobert recovered the wine bottle and refilled his glass, sadly noting we had reached the dregs. "We were discussing Mrs. Robjohn's murder," he said. "You remember, Jane, how we first realised that she was murdered. We knew that she had put only one shilling in her gas meter that night—because she only had one shilling to put in—and yet that the gas was still on at eleven o'clock the next morning. This meant that someone after eleven o'clock—in other words, after the gas had failed—put in at least four or five extra shillings, switching on the gas tap again at the same time. These were the shillings which killed Mrs. Robjohn and the person who put them in the meter therefore wilfully murdered her."

I nodded. This was all quite familiar to me, but possibly it was not being repeated solely for my benefit. I observed that Oates, after a movement or two as though to interrupt, followed Dagobert with rapt attention.

"The question was therefore quite simply: who put in the shillings?" he went on, pushing back his empty plate.

"Theoretically it might have been anyone in London. I knew, however, that it was someone who either worked in or had easy access to your office. You will remember that I emptied Mrs. Robjohn's gas meter myself."

He tilted back his chair; the squeaking wickerwork made both Oates and me jump. He jingled some change in his pocket, produced a shilling and thoughtfully tossed it up, caught it again and slapped it on to the table. I glanced at it stupidly. It merely looked like any other shilling to me, but I thought I heard Oates take a quick breath.

"Yes," Dagobert said. "That is one of the shillings I took from the meter. I've been holding this one out on you, Jane. It's William the Fourth, in mint condition." He flipped it across to Oates. "You can add it to your collection."

Oates merely stared at it. He had gone silent on us lately.

"One of the coins stolen from Mr. Playfair's desk?" I suggested mechanically.

"William the Fourth shillings are not in general circulation. What do you think!"

"I think we ought to dial the police at once," I answered grimly.

Dagobert glanced from me to the shilling and then to Oates. Oates was still staring at the coin as though it had hypnotised him. Unexpectedly Dagobert rose.

"Since we've finished up the wine," he said, "I think we ought to go out and have one before the pubs close."

Dagobert's behaviour is not always clear to me, but I am adept at acting as though it were. I saw he actually meant to go. I found my handbag and coat, glanced questioningly at the William the Fourth shilling still lying on the table before Oates and prepared dutifully to follow. But it seemed an odd moment to leave.

"Coming with us, Oates?" Dagobert called from the studio door.

"What's that? Going?" Oates came to with an effort. "Hell no! I'm not coming. Why should I?" He relapsed immediately into his ugly brooding sullenness. We seemed to have lost our interest for Oates.

I felt a sense of unreality as we reached the vegetable-strewn alley outside. To me our behaviour was totally inexplicable. As far as I could see we had left the person who was almost certainly Mrs. Robjohn's murderer scot free. And with him we had left that coin, our chief piece of evidence against him.

Dagobert took my arm. He held it tight and possessively. "Don't ever do that to me again!" he murmured roughly.

I knew what he meant, and I didn't propose to. Afterwards he confessed that those hours during which he had searched every King of Bohemia in London for me were the worst he had ever spent.

"Shouldn't we go to the police at once?" I broke the silence finally as we walked towards the Tottenham Court Road.

He shook his head. "From now on we can let the mystery solve itself. In fact I think it's solved."

I frowned, not getting it. "Oates?"

"What do you think?"

"I think Oates," I said slowly.

"Whether Oates killed Mrs. Robjohn himself or whether it was someone else," Dagobert said, "he *knows* who did it."

31 * The story of Mrs. Robjohn's death—as far as either Dagobert or I personally played any part in it—is practically told by the time we turned into the Tottenham Court Road and walked towards the tube station. That is to say it went on from this point to its conclu-

sion by its own momentum, without further pushing by us.

It is not quite the story I set out to tell that morning when I gaily borrowed Sarah's typewriter. I should have preferred a more cunning and complex method of doing in my victim—something with a poisonous insect which is only found on the upper reaches of the Amazon, for instance—instead of an unromantic gas tap which anybody could have turned on. I should have liked my murderer to have turned out to be someone totally startling—like Padraic, or Sir John Hartley—instead of . . . Well, as there is still something to come which surprised me at least, I'll put it all down in proper order.

The pedestrian fact remains that murderers are usually persons who have some fairly ordinary reason for wishing to dispose of people, and therefore turn out to be obvious.

But I must get on and, as briefly as possible, clear up a few things. In the first place there is Dagobert's reason for walking out on Oates, leaving behind him an invaluable clue and, possibly, a murderer.

Dagobert was not, as he explained to me, a policeman. He could not go up, tap the murderer on the shoulder and say: "I want you." Though he believed he knew exactly who it was, there were certain things he couldn't account for—for instance, why it was that Mrs. Robjohn had presumably not heard the shillings being dropped into the meter.

There was another weak link in the chain of hypothetical events he had reconstructed. Though he was certain Oates had stolen the coins from Mr. Playfair's drawer he was equally certain Oates had not himself put them into the gas meter.

Dagobert believed that someone had caught Oates stealing the coins, someone in the office who probably intended to return them to their proper place, but didn't. This person was the murderer. He—or she—later had found himself—or herself—unexpectedly in a position to kill Mrs. Robjohn, had needed shillings for the purpose, and had used the first to come to hand: namely those recovered from Oates, still jingling in his pocket—or in her handbag—as the case might be.

Dagobert's plan was simple. That's why he told me the mystery would from this point solve itself. For Oates, knowing that murder had been done and how it had been done, would remember *who* had taken the stolen shillings from him. Though Oates might not be a murderer he was certainly an enthusiastic blackmailer. He would blackmail the murderer into confession, self-betrayal or perhaps suicide.

That was Dagobert's plan of action, or rather inaction. I may say it worked perfectly, with one flaw. . . .

The next day was Saturday, my turn for the office, Rosemary's morning off. I was wide awake at seven and glad to get up; I had derived little benefit from my six and a half hours in bed. I dressed and made a pot of tea, rather hoping that Dagobert would come down and share it. He didn't, and I finally climbed the stairs and tapped at his door. When he didn't answer I opened the door. His bed had been slept in, but he wasn't there.

I returned to my flat and drank half a dozen cups of tea while I went through the motions of reading the newspaper. It was still not eight o'clock. At the risk of spoiling the charwoman, I washed up my breakfast things, emptied my hot-water bottle and made my bed.

Then I went to the office. I walked all the way but I was still there half an hour before anyone else arrived. The office charwoman was just finishing and we exchanged a few remarks about how soon Christmas would now be. I took off my things, opened a letter or two and tried to adjust my mind to the routine of the day.

Then I remembered my manuscript which Dagobert yesterday advised me to bring home. I found the key—under the 1903 volume of the *Law Reports*—and descended to the strong room. I removed the Hartley deed box where the day before yesterday I had put the manuscript. It wasn't there. I rummaged around the strong room for several minutes, less in the hope of finding it than to give myself something physical to do.

The story of the Robjohn affair—much as you have read it up to the point where Rosemary fainted—had been stolen. My emotions were mixed. The horror of an author who visualises weeks of labour lost was tinged with a deeper horror.

While I was there I mechanically replaced the gold cigarette lighter in Mrs. Robjohn's box. I felt it had played its part for good and all. I went up to the office feeling weak. Sarah had arrived in the meanwhile.

"What's the matter with you?" she exclaimed, referring I imagine to my early arrival rather than to the pallor of my face. "I'm sorry about last night," she went on. "I couldn't for the life of me remember what street you said the King of Bohemia was in. It was Charlotte Street, wasn't it? Funny, I remembered quite clearly this morning."

"Never mind. Dagobert found me. Who went down to the strong room yesterday?"

"Everybody, I should think. They always do. Why?"

"No reason."

Jimmy pushed open the front door and entered as though he owned the place. Though there is no set rule about it, he and Mr. Playfair usually arrange between themselves which of the two comes in on Saturday mornings, and when Jimmy is in charge he is always every inch the future head of the firm. He chose to be gracious this morning.

"Good morning, girls," he said with his most engaging smile. He removed his black hat, his perfectly cut blue overcoat, his grey suede gloves and hung up his neatly rolled umbrella. "Have we anything of special importance this morning, Jane?"

He looked surprised and a little disappointed when I said no.

"If anything crops up you'll know where to find me," he said and, with another charming smile, disappeared into his room.

"We'll know where to find him!" Sarah echoed. "Does he think we're going to look in the filing cabinet for him!"

The next arrival was rather unexpected. It was Rosemary.

"It's your Saturday off," I reminded her.

"I know," she said. "I—I thought I'd drop in to get a couple of things and say good-bye to everybody. Mr. Playfair insists I need a holiday. I'm going to the South of France, as a matter of fact."

"Some people have all the luck," Sarah commented. Knowing a little more about the object of Rosemary's holiday I was less envious. "You do look a little washed-out," Sarah continued. "If you want to say good-bye to 'everybody' he's in there." She nodded towards Jimmy's door.

At that moment Jimmy's door opened and Jimmy himself looked out. "Where's Oates?" he asked.

"Not turned up yet," Sarah said. "Shall I give him the works when he arrives?"

"You might send him in to me, Miss Swinburne, if you

will be so kind," he answered with dignity, and observing Rosemary added: "Good morning, Miss Proctor."

I saw Rosemary bite her lips and I felt glad when Jimmy's door closed again.

"Do you want to come into my room for a second, Jane," Rosemary said, "and help me look for a few things?"

"I can take a hint," said Sarah cheerfully, and strolled down the corridor towards the outer office, her hands on her hips, her red-gold hair glinting in the sombre light, whistling.

"He's going to marry Babs," Rosemary told me as soon as we were alone in her room. "It's wonderful for him, isn't it! Sir Ben's going to settle tons of money on her and they're going to have a stately home—in Purley. Sir Ben thinks he's getting 'a real proper gentleman' for a son-in-law. Aren't you delighted, Jane!"

"You're lucky to be out of it," I said roughly.

She put a frail hand through her thick chestnut hair. I fancied the streak of white had widened slightly during these past few days. Her smooth rather pretty face looked even older than the thirty-six years her passport said she was.

"I suppose so," she agreed with me finally. "I suppose Mrs. Robjohn was lucky to be out of that Polish pianist too, but . . ." She didn't finish the sentence.

It was the first time Rosemary had ever referred to Sir-korski. I knew of course that she had been more intimate with Mrs. Robjohn than the rest of us, but I didn't know how much of Mrs. Robjohn's past she was familiar with.

"You know about Sirkorski then," I murmured.

"Yes. . . . She used to tell me a lot about her—" she forced a smile, "her purple past. It was rather like mine, in a sort of way. The odd part is I even used to play the piano a little . . ." She laughed briefly. "Not that *he* stopped me playing the piano. He can't tell one piece of music from another! But there were similarities." The smile went suddenly from her lips and she stared up at me with deep-sunk, haunted eyes. "Jane! Am *I* going to turn into another Mrs. Robjohn?"

"No, of course not," I said quickly.

"I am, you know." She looked away from me, and her voice was once again even, toneless, *horribly* reminiscent of Mrs. Robjohn's voice. I conceived in that moment an undying hatred towards Sirkorski and Major James Stewart both. "Not of course that an *Englishman*," she gave the word a bitter twist, "often goes so far as to strike a woman—that is, not *very* often."

"When did Stewart do that?" I asked harshly.

"Don't pay any attention to me, Jane. I'm in a silly mood."

"That night he came into the office late—when you were doing your ledgers?" I demanded with sudden insight.

"He may have. I don't really remember. I probably asked for it. We screamed at each other rather a lot that evening. I kept saying . . . well, something. And he kept saying . . . it wasn't his fault, or even if it was how did he know for *sure* that it was."

I wondered if she were just talking mechanically—as Mrs. Robjohn had often done—or whether she realised I knew what it was all about. I still don't know. But from the disjointed fragments of her speech I could picture that grim argument on that grim night: Rosemary telling Jimmy she was going to have his baby, and Jimmy suggesting that it might be someone else's for all he knew—or cared! As I have already said, I didn't feel very charitable towards our Major James Stewart just then.

"You'll enjoy the South of France at this time of year," I said lamely. "You'll meet a lot of cheerful people probably."

"It doesn't matter, really, does it? I mean one is getting older, plainer, and I imagine one doesn't care so much any more. Ultimately one dies. . . . Mrs. Robjohn died. She died peacefully in her sleep. I hope I die as peacefully as she died. She was really very lucky. Don't you think she was lucky, Jáne?"

I said: "Yes, of course," not feeling quite certain whether I wished the conversation to proceed on these lines or not.

"It was a merciful thing," she whispered. "A *good* thing."

I heard a man's footsteps in the corridor outside, a firm footstep which I didn't place for a moment.

"That's a client," I said, glad of the excuse to end this conversation.

"I must hurry," Rosemary said. "My train doesn't go until tonight, but I've a thousand things to do. Will you say good-bye for me to the others?"

"I will. Never mind your desk. I'll clear up everything for you." I wanted to get her out of the office as quickly as possible. "You push off without a word to anyone—that's always the best way. Write to me, if you feel like it. And remember, nothing matters as much as all that . . ." And I escaped.

The client was Douglas. He had wandered up the corridor to Mr. Playfair's empty room and was looking through the door.

"Sarah's around somewhere," I said. "Haven't you found her?"

"I was looking for Mr. Playfair."

"I doubt if he'll be in this morning. Major Stewart is

with us and usually only one of them comes in on Saturday morning."

"But he telephoned me about an hour ago," Douglas said, looking, I noted, remarkably grim and Sirkorski-like. "He said he wanted to see me especially . . . I can't think what for."

"Better wait in his room," I said briefly.

I wandered restlessly towards the outer office where Sarah was sharpening pencils.

"Douglas is here," I said.

"I know," she nodded. "He swept past as though he'd never seen me before. What's the matter with him?"

He was her fiancé, not mine, and I didn't venture an opinion. "Has Oates turned up yet?" I asked.

She shook her head and glanced at her wrist watch. It was a handsome platinum and diamond affair, a recent gift from Douglas. I went back towards my room, feeling less and less like routine work. I was, in fact, feeling edgy and nervous.

Then I heard Mr. Playfair's step on the stairs. A moment later I saw his familiar gaunt figure as he stepped into the outer office. From this distance I could not see his face clearly, but I gained an impression of tiredness. Then I saw he wasn't alone. Dagobert was with him.

I watched them both approach me along the dusty corridor.

"Good morning, Miss Hamish," Mr. Playfair said with absent-minded courtesy.

Dagobert greeted me in much the same tone of voice.

"Are there any clients in the office?" Mr. Playfair asked.

I shook my head. "Douglas Robjohn is waiting in your office," I said.

"Good," he nodded. From this distance I saw that my first impression of Mr. Playfair had been correct. His face was drawn and haggard. "Would you be so kind, Miss Hamish, as to ask the others to step into my office for a moment?"

"It's Rosemary's day off," I began a little incoherently. "But she's dropped in to fetch away some of her personal belongings."

Mr. Playfair glanced inquiringly towards Dagobert. Dagobert's nod was just perceptible.

"Ask her if you will if she'd please mind joining us," Mr. Playfair said.

He turned and preceded Dagobert into his own room. I said nothing to Dagobert, nor did he more than exchange a meaningless glance with me. But I could guess why he was here. I delivered Mr. Playfair's message to Major Stewart, Sarah and Rosemary, without pausing to observe how each took this somewhat unusual request. I then tapped on Mr. Playfair's door and entered.

The action was so familiar that I was filled with a sense of unreality at finding Dagobert there, sitting in the leather armchair reserved for clients beside Mr. Playfair's desk. Mr. Playfair was seated in his usual place behind the desk, but instead of the familiar *Times* crossword he had his dispatch case open in front of him. Douglas was leaning, dark and watchful, beside the fireplace, toying with that awful sapphire brooch of his mother's.

"They'll all be here immediately," I said. "Except Oates —who hasn't turned up yet."

"That's awkward," Mr. Playfair murmured. "I suppose we ought to wait for him . . ." He turned questioningly towards Dagobert.

I looked at Dagobert at the same time. Dagobert's facial

expression had undergone no outward change, but I knew him better than Mr. Playfair did, and I knew that my announcement of Oates's absence worried him.

"Do you mind if I use your telephone, sir?" he said.

Mr. Playfair pushed the instrument towards him.

"There's another one in my room, first door on the left," I supplied, noting his hesitation.

Dagobert said thanks and excused himself. Meanwhile Mr. Playfair took a pile of papers out of his dispatch case. He gathered them carefully together and handed the pile to me.

"Most interesting, Miss Hamish," he commented dryly. And then with the first touch of light I had yet seen in his old eyes he added: "There are one or two points I'd like to argue with you about, but I was never for a moment bored."

The pile of paper which I clutched stupidly in my hand was my own manuscript which an hour ago I had vainly searched for in the strong room.

By this time the others were filing into the room and I had no time to re-assort my thoughts. Rosemary came in first and without a word took the seat Mr. Playfair indicated. Then Jimmy arrived and tactfully took up his position as far as possible from Rosemary.

"Something important is it, sir?" he asked Mr. Playfair.

"Yes."

Finally Sarah came in, looking a little awed suddenly at the number of people in the room.

"Did you want me, too?" she asked dubiously.

"Sit down, please." Mr. Playfair indicated the chair beside Rosemary.

There was a moment's restlessness, tinged with embarrassment on my part—and I think on Mr. Playfair's too. I felt horribly responsible for this fantastic assembly. I kept wondering what would happen if an ordinary client suddenly came in.

Dagobert returned from the telephone in my room.

"Shall we go on without Oates?" Mr. Playfair asked.

Dagobert nodded. Something about the way he nodded made my stomach turn over. "Oates won't be turning up," he said shortly.

32 * Mr. Playfair had risen with the idea, I imagine, of giving Dagobert his chair behind the desk. But Dagobert had no intention of presiding over this gathering. He took his place modestly in the corner beside me. He looked white and chastened.

"Never again!" he whispered softly to me. "This is Dagobert's Last Case."

Jimmy and Rosemary had both recognised Dagobert simultaneously, one as the fantastic gas man who had stretched out that afternoon on Mrs. Robjohn's four-poster bed and made preposterous suggestions about anonymous letters, and the other as the winning young vacuum-cleaner salesman who had taken her out for the evening. Both started, but quickly relapsed into watchful waiting.

Mr. Playfair was the one I felt sorry for. He obviously hated it. He polished and repolished his spectacles, sat down, stood up, sat down again. I thought he was going to dither, but he came with breath-taking abruptness to the point.

"It's about Mrs. Robjohn," he said.

No one said anything.

"It seems she was murdered," he added.

And still no one said anything. If only someone had protested, made sounds of astonishment or disbelief it would have been easier. But no one even moved. Mr. Playfair again polished his spectacles and glanced at some notes he had removed from his dispatch case.

"It seems that someone connected with this office may have been responsible," he went on. "I am not a police officer —in fact I am in the same position as the rest of you—but it occurred to me that we might like to clarify our positions before the police take over. I'm going to ask you a few of the questions which the police themselves are bound eventually to ask. You need not answer them if you don't want to."

He consulted his notes and I noticed even from the distance at which I stood that they were in Dagobert's handwriting.

"The questions are not very systematic," he explained with a frown, "but they may give you some idea of the sort of things you'll be asked to explain. In the first place, Major Stewart." We all followed his glance towards Jimmy, half relieved to have someone specific to concentrate on. "On the morning Mrs. Robjohn was found dead you apparently burned a letter addressed to me and marked Private and Confidential. Why did you do that?"

Jimmy had gone white. I saw him inwardly debating whether or not to deny the whole thing, and I felt for him. He decided to come clean.

"I believed that the letter contained slanderous remarks about myself," he said finally.

"You believed it was written by Mrs. Robjohn?"

"Yes."

"Did you read it?"

"No."

"Have you any reason to suspect that Mrs. Robjohn would write me a slanderous letter about you?"

"Yes."

"What reason?"

"She had written a similar letter the day before and sent it to my fiancée, Miss Barbara Jennings."

"I see." Mr. Playfair's attention reverted to the notes in front of him.

Jimmy mentally stepped down, like a schoolboy who isn't quite sure whether he's given the right answers or not. When Mr. Playfair looked up again it was towards Rosemary. Again we all followed his gaze.

"That letter which Major Stewart tells us his fiancée received," he said. "Do you know anything about it?"

"I heard something about it," Rosemary faltered. "That is, I happened to pick up the receiver in my room when Major Stewart and Miss Jennings were discussing it over the telephone."

"I suggest, Miss Proctor," Mr. Playfair said quietly, "that you wrote that letter yourself."

I had glanced at Jimmy when this was said and I saw the match with which he was about to light a cigarette snap between his fingers. To him at least Mr. Playfair's suggestion was evidently revolutionary.

Rosemary put a hand to her forehead. "I'm not feeling very well," she said vaguely.

"Did you write that letter, Miss Proctor?" Mr. Playfair asked.

He seemed to have forgotten his statement that we need not answer his questions. Rosemary bowed her head.

"Yes," she said.

"On the night Mrs. Robjohn died you were here in this office till eleven-thirty-five when you took a taxi home. Is that correct?"

"Yes."

"Had you left the office—for any reason—during the half hour before eleven-thirty-five?"

"No."

"I see." And once again Mr. Playfair's attention returned to Dagobert's notes.

He looked more tired than ever and for a moment I thought he was going to refuse to go on. He looked up towards Dagobert vaguely beseechingly, I thought. Dagobert gave him a brief flicker of encouragement, and it occurred to me that this scene might not have been unrehearsed between them. Mr. Playfair's gaze wandered from Dagobert to the ceiling, alighting finally on Sarah.

"On that night, Miss Swinburne, I understand that Mr. Robjohn took you home in a taxi from the Hungaria. Your father, I believe, heard the taxi stop outside your door and heard you say goodnight. This was at ten to twelve."

"Yes, Mr. Playfair," Sarah answered, and I saw that she, too, was looking scared. The truth is we were all looking scared.

"You gave Mr. Robjohn some change, some silver coins?"

"Yes, for the taxi."

"And after you had said goodnight to each other what did you do then?"

"I—I don't understand."

"Where did you go then?"

"Why, I—I went into the house, I suppose. Naturally . . ."

"You didn't get back into the taxi again?" Mr. Playfair prompted.

This time three of us started: Sarah, Douglas and the third was myself. Dagobert gave my hand a salutary squeeze and I relapsed into immobility.

"But why should she?" Douglas intervened.

"That wasn't my question," Mr. Playfair remarked. "I asked *if* she got back into the taxi again. Did you, Miss Swinburne?"

"She refuses to answer that question," Douglas scowled.

"She needn't answer it," Mr. Playfair said mildly. "I'm just trying to give you a foretaste of the things the police will want to know. Perhaps you will answer a couple of questions, Robjohn? At midnight you were seen standing on the steps of Number 17 Mandel Square. A taxi was parked at the kerb before the house."

"I've already explained all that to Brown," Douglas glowered aggressively towards Dagobert and me. We seemed to have gone down suddenly in his estimation. Looking at him I wished I could stop thinking of Sirkorski. Their resemblance confused my judgment.

"Quite," Mr. Playfair took over quietly. "Your intention was, I gather, to call on your mother?"

"Yes," Douglas admitted sullenly.

"And you kept the taxi waiting?" Mr. Playfair gazed at the young man over the rims of his spectacles. "Why? To drive you home afterwards?"

"Yes, I suppose so. Why not?"

"And yet only a moment later, finding someone with your mother—it was Oates, by the way—you say you walked towards the Kensington High Street and eventually found a taxi there. Why didn't you take the one you'd told to wait?"

"I changed my mind. I wanted to walk."

Mr. Playfair frowned and drew triangles on his blotting pad. "I'm not trying to antagonise you, Douglas," he said, slipping unconsciously into the use of the younger man's Christian name. "I don't really like doing this at all, but I must warn you—" he glanced up and around at each of us in turn—"I must warn all of you . . . unless you have a *supreme* reason for hiding the truth, don't try to hide it. *If Miss Swinburne was in that taxi* which was waiting at the kerb while you stood on the steps of Number 17 Mandel Square the police will find out. And you'll have to explain it to them."

In the silence which followed my eyes were upon Mr. Playfair himself. Though outwardly calm, almost relaxed, I could see that something inside him was on the verge of snapping. For him, I believe, the tension was worse even than for the rest of us. He was fond of several of the people in this room, and I realised suddenly that he too had no clear idea of where these questions were leading.

Sarah broke the silence. "I *was* in that taxi," she said in a small, hushed voice.

Mr. Playfair sat back. I saw his left hand grope mechanically as though feeling for something on his desk, some pills Dr. Forsyte had recently recommended. I poured out a glass of water from the jug on the bookcase and gave it to him. He murmured "thank you" as he swallowed the pills and sipped from the tumbler. He turned his chair towards Sarah and Douglas.

"Did you both go in to see Mrs. Robjohn?" he said.

Neither answered. Mr. Playfair continued to watch them. I wondered which of the three was going to give in first.

"You told Brown, Douglas," Mr. Playfair prompted

gently, "that, standing outside your mother's door, you visualised her lying in her four-poster bed. . . . She didn't have that bed when you were last in England."

"Yes," Sarah whispered suddenly. "We did go in."

Mr. Playfair swivelled his chair back again towards our corner of the room. He was ashen grey. "That's what you wanted to know, isn't it, Brown?" he said to Dagobert. "Will you carry on, please?"

Dagobert recovered himself reluctantly from his leaning position against the bookcase. He spoke more quickly and less confidently than Mr. Playfair had spoken, and he seemed to enjoy his task as little.

"Perhaps I'd better explain that Mrs. Robjohn was killed by someone who put four or five shillings into her gas meter that night after the gas had failed. One of the shillings was a William the Fourth shilling and easily identified. It was taken from Mr. Playfair's desk here in this room earlier the same day. The problem was always how the murderer put the coins into the meter without Mrs. Robjohn's hearing. The answer is that there were *two* people with Mrs. Robjohn when the shillings were put in: one person who talked to her while the other put in the shillings. The person talking to her doubtless knew nothing of the murderer's intentions."

Dagobert paused. I saw Sarah and Douglas rather studiously not looking at each other. It must have been a bad moment for them both. Each may have been thinking that the other had inserted the fatal coins—and one of them may have been right!

"You say you have this William the Fourth shilling," Jimmy Stewart said.

Dagobert hadn't said he *had* it, but he made a vaguely affirmative sound.

"Then all we have to do is find out who stole it from Mr. Playfair's desk," Jimmy concluded.

"You have grasped the position perfectly, Major Stewart," Dagobert nodded gravely. "We have only to find out who had the fatal shilling."

"If you ask me," Sarah intervened a little stridently, "Oates is the only one in the office who would have pinched those coins."

Dagobert again nodded. "Oates did pinch them," he said.

"Then aren't we wasting our time going on without him?" Jimmy suggested.

"No, because someone caught Oates pinching them and relieved him of the coins."

"How do you know that?"

"I don't," Dagobert said. "I'm guessing. But someone in this room knows I'm guessing right." No one challenged the statement and Dagobert continued more conversationally. "Let's return to the point that there were two people with Mrs. Robjohn when the murder took place, one of whom was quite innocent of the fact that her death was being planned. The trouble is we all seem to have gone *in pairs* to visit Mrs. Robjohn that night. Jane and I went there about half past nine. Sarah and Douglas visited her after midnight—just after Douglas had seen Oates come away. Why didn't you tell me, Douglas, that it was Oates, instead of saying you didn't know whether it was a man or woman?"

"I didn't see him," Douglas supplied ungraciously. "When I heard him coming towards the front door I jumped back into the taxi. We drove around Mandel Square and when we came back to the door he wasn't in sight."

"As Mr. Playfair has already warned you the police will check up on the accuracy of that statement," Dagobert re-

marked. He turned his back on Douglas and faced Mr. Playfair. "I'm afraid I'll have to ask you a couple of questions, sir."

Mr. Playfair came to, as though he had not been following the conversation, and nodded for Dagobert to proceed.

"On the night in question you left your Club, Cockburn's
in Kensington High Street, at about ten past eleven. You told
the club porter that you were going to walk to the Underground. Did you take the Underground?"

"No. I decided to walk part of the way home. I walked as
far as Piccadilly where I found a taxi to take me back to Hampstead."

"So you passed the top of Mandel Street."

"I did."

"That would be at what time?"

"At eleven thirty."

"You noticed the time exactly?"

"I glanced at my watch."

"For any particular reason?"

"Yes . . ." He was staring at his blotting pad and answering Dagobert's questions as though in a trance. "I thought
it was late for any of my people to be entering the office."

"Who was entering the office?"

"Look, Brown," Mr. Playfair glanced up anxiously, "perhaps we'd better leave this to the police . . . No, go ahead.
It's kinder. I saw Miss Proctor coming up the street. She went
into the office."

"Up the street? You mean from the direction of Mandel
Square?"

"Yes."

Dagobert turned slowly to Rosemary. "Miss Proctor stated
a while ago that she never left the office."

Rosemary stared up at him hypnotised. I wondered for

a second if she were going to faint; I think she would have liked to. "I . . . I . . ." she began.

I thought Mr. Playfair was going to intervene, but he relapsed into his chair with resignation. It was Jimmy who came unexpectedly to her rescue.

"She may have stepped out for a breath of air," he suggested. Like the rest of us he was staring hard at her.

Dagobert raised his voice for the first time. "She was coming back from Mrs. Robjohn's!" he snapped. I wondered if the emphasis he put on the words meant he was uncertain of himself, or whether it meant the climax had come.

"You can't prove that," Jimmy replied. And still acting as Rosemary's self-appointed defender he repeated: "He can't prove it, Rosemary. Remember he can't prove it!" He had come across to her and laid a protective hand on her shoulder. He faced Dagobert. "Besides, we're straying from the point," he insisted. "The key to your case is that coin. Where is it? Produce it! Who has it?"

He appealed to all of us, as though we were a jury of some sort and he a clever barrister who had floored his opponent. I can't think why I chose to open my stupid mouth, but I was appalled to hear myself saying:

"Oates has it."

"Oates," Dagobert corrected me, "*had* it."

I don't know why Dagobert's words should have produced such a ghastly silence. Even Rosemary who had begun to whimper went deathly still. I saw a kind of sneer start on Jimmy's face, but it stopped there, half completed. Dagobert took advantage of the silence to complete his remark.

"The coin was recovered from Oates late last night—by Mrs. Robjohn's murderer. Probably it is in your pocket, Major Stewart."

Later I personally bought Douglas a double brandy in gratitude for his behaviour during the next few seconds. Your man of action has his big moments and this was Douglas's. I think poor Dagobert would probably have been throttled had it not been for Douglas. Dagobert explains that he was coolness itself, and quite capable of handling the situation. But the facts are that Jimmy—who had never really loved Dagobert—leapt savagely towards him and that there was a paperknife in his hand. More important, Douglas at the same time threw himself at Jimmy and the two struggled wildly on the threadbare, but heretofore respectable, carpet of Mr. Playfair's sanctum. Douglas had obviously not enjoyed himself so much since his early Commando days.

"Clients!" I cried suddenly, hearing footsteps outside in the corridor. Such is my long office training that I think I was nearly as horrified by the vision of clients finding the premises of Daniel Playfair & Sons in this state of confusion as I was by the struggle on the floor. "Clients!" I repeated hysterically.

Dagobert permitted himself the ghost of a grin. "With those feet?" he said.

There was a knock on the door. Dagobert helped Douglas to put a panting and livid Jimmy on his feet again. Mr. Playfair nodded to Sarah who opened the door.

It was a triumph for Dagobert's skill in detection. My "clients" were in fact two heavily built plain-clothes policemen; but then, of course, Dagobert had been expecting them.

"Which of you is Mr. Stewart?" one of the newcomers asked. We all pointed him out and Stewart nodded.

"I am Detective-Inspector Watkins of Scotland Yard," he said. "You are James Stewart."

"Yes."

"I am going to arrest you on a charge of murder."

Stewart cut him short. "There's not a scrap of evidence that I had anything to do with Mrs. Robjohn's death!"

Detective-Inspector Watkins looked puzzled. "You are charged," he said, "for that you did on the twentieth of December 1948 feloniously, wilfully and of your malice aforethought kill and murder Albert Oates. . . ."

We closed the office early that Saturday morning, much to the displeasure of Mrs. White who arrived to protest about the Assignment of her Lease just as we were all leaving. Mr. Playfair drove off with Rosemary in a taxi. He was extremely gentle and kind to her; I think—though naturally he won't admit it—that there was a time when he thought Rosemary herself had done it, as a kind of mercy killing.

It was a long time before Dagobert recovered from Oates's death. It was that which made him vow he'd never play the amateur detective again, that and something he calls "sub-realist" painting which he has recently taken up with some enthusiasm.

Actually Dagobert's plan had *seemed* reasonable enough. What he had done was this: on the night we'd left Oates with the William the Fourth shilling (which parenthetically *did* turn up in Jimmy's possession) Dagobert had posted his pal Joe, the taxi-driver, with instructions to follow Oates wherever he went. Oates would—Dagobert thought—go to Inigo Mews to turn the screws.

Instead Oates telephoned, and Jimmy came to the studio. Jimmy stayed, Joe reported, for twenty minutes, emerging alone at about half past three. Joe, whose taxi rank is at the top of Mandel Street, knows all of us at Number 11 by sight, and he had clearly recognised Jimmy by the light of the street lamp outside Oates's studio. He waited, as Dagobert had told him to do, until morning. At about eight a charwoman arrived to do the studio and Joe adjourned to a nearby café for a cup of tea. Returning to his post half an hour later he found the place swarming with police. Upon inquiry he found that Oates had been shot. Joe remembered now the sound of a shot during Stewart's visit, a sound which he had dismissed at the time as a car back-firing in the next street. He immediately gave what information he had to the police who at once went to Inigo Mews. There, under a pile of Jimmy's shirts, they actually found the army revolver with which Oates had been shot. The case was too cut and dried even to make more than a perfunctory newspaper story.

We have a new partner at Number 11, an energetic young man with go-ahead ideas. He has, I gather, put a lot of money into the firm, and has ambitions. He sees us as a smart, up-to-date firm dealing chiefly with high-class divorces and company promotion. He will doubtless make a lot of money, but I rather think he will soon have a new staff. Sarah can't stand the new level of efficiency demanded; I must confess I myself don't much like it being politely but firmly noticed whenever I arrive half an hour late in the morning. And I know Mr. Playfair isn't at all happy with the new pickled-oak panelling in his room and the brand-new shiny red leather armchairs. He keeps studying estate agents' letters about small villas near Bexhill and Hastings and talking about the golf courses in that vicinity. I expect him to announce his retirement any day now. I shall announce mine at the same time.

I had a long and rambling letter from Rosemary the other day, postmarked Cannes. She refers briefly to poor Jimmy of whom at one time, she says, she was quite fond. "In some ways," she confesses, "I feel terribly guilty about what happened last winter." (*Last* winter! What does she think we're

having now? It's all very well to refer in this off-hand way to
winter when you're writing from Cannes!)

I shouldn't have let Jimmy think poor Mrs. Robjohn
wrote that anonymous letter, (she goes on). That night
when he came to the office and we had such a row, he
rushed off swearing he'd have it out with Mrs. Robjohn
immediately and make the old devil mind her own business. I was really quite frightened, Jane, and so I followed him. We had our row all over again in front of
Mrs. Robjohn. She took my part, of course, and said
she'd be around in the office tomorrow to congratulate
us both publicly on our forthcoming marriage. That
would certainly have finished Jimmy's hopes of the
alluring Babs and Sir Ben's even more alluring millions.
But to my surprise, he piped down suddenly and took
it like a lamb. He must have suddenly got the idea about
the gas, for I remember now he disappeared into the alcove for rather a long time while Mrs. Robjohn and I
talked about men. Even now it seems incredible that he
should do such a thing—I didn't think he had the guts.
But then I suppose it seemed easy. He always liked
"things" that were easy! It's rather ironic—when you
think of it—that he should have burned that Private
and Confidential letter to Mr. Playfair. Mrs. Robjohn
told me all about it while Jimmy was in the alcove. It
was about the milk bottles left on her front steps!!!

Poor Jimmy—he was such a fool. Thinking back, it
struck me that he was a bit funny that night when we
parted outside Number 17 Mandel Square. But then
men are funny, so I didn't pay much attention, until
weeks afterwards when you kept asking me about my
lighter. I remembered I'd given it to Jimmy and I supposed he must have left it at Mrs. Robjohn's that night.
Since we'd decided not to mention our visit of that

night, I told you I'd given it to Mrs. Robjohn so that you wouldn't keep asking questions about it. But doesn't it all seem stupid now?

You're quite right; nothing is all that important. Another thing which had me silly with worry was what Dr. Robbins thought was going to happen. Nothing of the sort, Jane. A complete false alarm!!! I wish you were here. It's really terrific fun and all the Paris *couturieres* are showing the most sickeningly lovely Spring and Summer models. I'm flirting with a black crepe dress by Dior with one shoulder strap and caught-up drapery to show your ankle, though I feel faint whenever I think how much it's going to cost. There's an Argentinian who's just arrived at the hotel with the perfect name of Ruy Lopez de las Vegas O'Brien and he has ash-blond hair. I *think* I scent trouble in the offing! Last night when he came into the cocktail bar . . .

She goes on for several pages in this way. Naturally I am eaten by envy and furious with her.

Anyway Dagobert has already made arrangements for us to go abroad in the spring. He's taking me down to Lillywhite's tomorrow to choose a pair of good, sensible walking shoes.

THE PERENNIAL LIBRARY MYSTERY SERIES

Delano Ames

FOR OLD CRIME'S SAKE   P 629, $2.84

MURDER, MAESTRO, PLEASE   P 630, $2.84
"If there is a more engaging couple in modern fiction than Jane and Dagobert Brown, we have not met them."   —*Scotsman*

E. C. Bentley

TRENT'S LAST CASE   P 440, $2.50
"One of the three best detective stories ever written."
         —Agatha Christie

TRENT'S OWN CASE   P 516, $2.25
"I won't waste time saying that the plot is sound and the detection satisfying. Trent has not altered a scrap and reappears with all his old humor and charm."   —Dorothy L. Sayers

Gavin Black

A DRAGON FOR CHRISTMAS   P 473, $1.95
"Potent excitement!"   —*New York Herald Tribune*

THE EYES AROUND ME   P 485, $1.95
"I stayed up until all hours last night reading *The Eyes Around Me*, which is something I do not do very often, but I was so intrigued by the ingeniousness of Mr. Black's plotting and the witty way in which he spins his mystery. I can only say that I enjoyed the book enormously."
         —F. van Wyck Mason

YOU WANT TO DIE, JOHNNY?   P 472, $1.95
"Gavin Black doesn't just develop a pressure plot in suspense, he adds uninfected wit, character, charm, and sharp knowledge of the Far East to make rereading as keen as the first race-through."   —*Book Week*

Nicholas Blake

THE CORPSE IN THE SNOWMAN   P 427, $1.95
"If there is a distinction between the novel and the detective story (which we do not admit), then this book deserves a high place in both categories."   —*The New York Times*

THE DREADFUL HOLLOW   P 493, $1.95
"Pace unhurried, characters excellent, reasoning solid."
           —*San Francisco Chronicle*

END OF CHAPTER   P 397, $1.95
". . . admirably solid . . . an adroit formal detective puzzle backed up
by firm characterization and a knowing picture of London publishing."
           —*The New York Times*

HEAD OF A TRAVELER   P 398, $2.25
"Another grade A detective story of the right old jigsaw persuasion."
           —*New York Herald Tribune Book Review*

MINUTE FOR MURDER   P 419, $1.95
"An outstanding mystery novel. Mr. Blake's writing is a delight in
itself."   —*The New York Times*

THE MORNING AFTER DEATH   P 520, $1.95
"One of Blake's best."   —Rex Warner

A PENKNIFE IN MY HEART   P 521, $2.25
"Style brilliant . . . and suspenseful."   —*San Francisco Chronicle*

THE PRIVATE WOUND   P 531, $2.25
[Blake's] best novel in a dozen years . . . . An intensely penetrating study
of sexual passion. . . . A powerful story of murder and its aftermath."
           —Anthony Boucher, *The New York Times*

A QUESTION OF PROOF   P 494, $1.95
"The characters in this story are unusually well drawn, and the suspense
is well sustained."   —*The New York Times*

THE SAD VARIETY   P 495, $2.25
"It is a stunner. I read it instead of eating, instead of sleeping."
           —Dorothy Salisbury Davis

THERE'S TROUBLE BREWING   P 569, $3.37
"Nigel Strangeways is a puzzling mixture of simplicity and penetration,
but all the more real for that."   —*The Times Literary Supplement*

THOU SHELL OF DEATH   P 428, $1.95
"It has all the virtues of culture, intelligence and sensibility that the most
exacting connoisseur could ask of detective fiction."
           —*The Times* [London] *Literary Supplement*

THE WIDOW'S CRUISE   P 399, $2.25
"A stirring suspense. . . . The thrilling tale leaves nothing to be desired."
                                        —*Springfield Republican*

THE WORM OF DEATH   P 400, $2.25
"It [The Worm of Death] is one of Blake's very best—and his best is
better than almost anyone's."   —Louis Untermeyer

John & Emery Bonett

A BANNER FOR PEGASUS   P 554, $2.40
"A gem! Beautifully plotted and set. . . . Not only is the murder adroit
and deserved, and the detection competent, but the love story is charming."   —Jacques Barzun and Wendell Hertig Taylor

DEAD LION   P 563, $2.40
"A clever plot, authentic background and interesting characters highly
recommended this one."   —*New Republic*

Christianna Brand

GREEN FOR DANGER   P 551, $2.50
"You have to reach for the greatest of Great Names (Christie, Carr,
Queen . . .) to find Brand's rivals in the devious subtleties of the trade."
                                        —Anthony Boucher

TOUR DE FORCE   P 572, $2.40
"Complete with traps for the over-ingenious, a double-reverse surprise
ending and a key clue planted so fairly and obviously that you completely
overlook it. If that's your idea of perfect entertainment, then seize at once
upon *Tour de Force.*"   —Anthony Boucher, *The New York Times*

James Byrom

OR BE HE DEAD   P 585, $2.84
"A very original tale . . . Well written and steadily entertaining."
  —Jacques Barzun & Wendell Hertig Taylor, *A Catalogue of Crime*

Marjorie Carleton

VANISHED   P 559, $2.40
"Exceptional . . . a minor triumph."
  —Jacques Barzun and Wendell Hertig Taylor, *A Catalogue of Crime*

George Harmon Coxe

MURDER WITH PICTURES   P 527, $2.25
"[Coxe] has hit the bull's-eye with his first shot."
                                          —*The New York Times*

Edmund Crispin

BURIED FOR PLEASURE   P 506, $2.50
"Absolute and unalloyed delight."
                        —Anthony Boucher, *The New York Times*

Lionel Davidson

THE MENORAH MEN   P 592, $2.84
"Of his fellow thriller writers, only John Le Carré shows the same
instinct for the viscera."   —*Chicago Tribune*

NIGHT OF WENCESLAS   P 595, $2.84
"A most ingenious thriller, so enriched with style, wit, and a sense of
serious comedy that it all but transcends its kind."
                                              —*The New Yorker*

THE ROSE OF TIBET   P 593, $2.84
"I hadn't realized how much I missed the genuine Adventure story
. . . until I read *The Rose of Tibet*."   —Graham Greene

D. M. Devine

MY BROTHER'S KILLER   P 558, $2.40
"A most enjoyable crime story which I enjoyed reading down to the last
moment."   —Agatha Christie

Kenneth Fearing

THE BIG CLOCK   P 500, $1.95
"It will be some time before chill-hungry clients meet again so rare a
compound of irony, satire, and icy-fingered narrative. *The Big Clock* is
. . . a psychothriller you won't put down."   —*Weekly Book Review*

Andrew Garve

THE ASHES OF LODA   P 430, $1.50
"Garve . . . embellishes a fine fast adventure story with a more credible
picture of the U.S.S.R. than is offered in most thrillers."
                                —*The New York Times Book Review*

THE CUCKOO LINE AFFAIR   P 451, $1.95
". . . an agreeable and ingenious piece of work."   —*The New Yorker*

A HERO FOR LEANDA   P 429, $1.50
"One can trust Mr. Garve to put a fresh twist to any situation, and the
ending is really a lovely surprise."   —*The Manchester Guardian*

MURDER THROUGH THE LOOKING GLASS   P 449, $1.95
". . . refreshingly out-of-the-way and enjoyable . . . highly recommended
to all comers."   —*Saturday Review*

NO TEARS FOR HILDA   P 441, $1.95
"It starts fine and finishes finer. I got behind on breathing watching Max
get not only his man but his woman, too."   —Rex Stout

THE RIDDLE OF SAMSON   P 450, $1.95
"The story is an excellent one, the people are quite likable, and the
writing is superior."   —*Springfield Republican*

Michael Gilbert

BLOOD AND JUDGMENT   P 446, $1.95
"Gilbert readers need scarcely be told that the characters all come alive
at first sight, and that his surpassing talent for narration enhances any
plot. . . . Don't miss."   —*San Francisco Chronicle*

THE BODY OF A GIRL   P 459, $1.95
"Does what a good mystery should do: open up into all kinds of ramifications, with untold menace behind the action. At the end, there is a
bang-up climax, and it is a pleasure to see how skilfully Gilbert wraps
everything up."   —*The New York Times Book Review*

THE DANGER WITHIN   P 448, $1.95
"Michael Gilbert has nicely combined some elements of the straight
detective story with plenty of action, suspense, and adventure, to produce a superior thriller."   —*Saturday Review*

FEAR TO TREAD   P 458, $1.95
"Merits serious consideration as a work of art."
                                        —*The New York Times*

Joe Gores

HAMMETT   P 631, $2.84
"Joe Gores at his very best. Terse, powerful writing—with the master,
Dashiell Hammett, as the protagonist in a novel I think he would have
been proud to call his own."   —Robert Ludlum

C. W. Grafton

BEYOND A REASONABLE DOUBT   P 519, $1.95
"A very ingenious tale of murder . . . a brilliant and gripping narrative."
—Jacques Barzun and Wendell Hertig Taylor

Edward Grierson

THE SECOND MAN   P 528, $2.25
"One of the best trial-testimony books to have come along in quite a while."   —*The New Yorker*

Cyril Hare

DEATH IS NO SPORTSMAN   P 555, $2.40
"You will be thrilled because it succeeds in placing an ingenious story in a new and refreshing setting. . . . The identity of the murderer is really a surprise."   —*Daily Mirror*

DEATH WALKS THE WOODS   P 556, $2.40
"Here is a fine formal detective story, with a technically brilliant solution demanding the attention of all connoisseurs of construction."
—Anthony Boucher, *The New York Times Book Review*

AN ENGLISH MURDER   P 455, $2.50
"By a long shot, the best crime story I have read for a long time. Everything is traditional, but originality does not suffer. The setting is perfect. Full marks to Mr. Hare."   —*Irish Press*

TENANT FOR DEATH   P 570, $2.84
"The way in which an air of probability is combined both with clear, terse narrative and with a good deal of subtle suburban atmosphere, proves the extreme skill of the writer."   —*The Spectator*

TRAGEDY AT LAW   P 522, $2.25
"An extremely urbane and well-written detective story."
—*The New York Times*

UNTIMELY DEATH   P 514, $2.25
"The English detective story at its quiet best, meticulously underplayed, rich in perceivings of the droll human animal and ready at the last with a neat surprise which has been there all the while had we but wits to see it."   —*New York Herald Tribune Book Review*

THE WIND BLOWS DEATH   P 589, $2.84
"A plot compounded of musical knowledge, a Dickens allusion, and a subtle point in law is related with delightfully unobtrusive wit, warmth, and style."   —*The New York Times*

WITH A BARE BODKIN P 523, $2.25
"One of the best detective stories published for a long time."
—*The Spectator*

Robert Harling

THE ENORMOUS SHADOW P 545, $2.50
"In some ways the best spy story of the modern period.... The writing
is terse and vivid ... the ending full of action ... altogether first-rate."
—Jacques Barzun and Wendell Hertig Taylor, *A Catalogue of Crime*

Matthew Head

THE CABINDA AFFAIR P 541, $2.25
"An absorbing whodunit and a distinguished novel of atmosphere."
—Anthony Boucher, *The New York Times*

THE CONGO VENUS P 597, $2.84
"Terrific. The dialogue is just plain wonderful."
—*The Boston Globe*

MURDER AT THE FLEA CLUB P 542, $2.50
"The true delight is in Head's style, its limpid ease combined with humor
and an awesome precision of phrase." —*San Francisco Chronicle*

M. V. Heberden

ENGAGED TO MURDER P 533, $2.25
"Smooth plotting." —*The New York Times*

James Hilton

WAS IT MURDER? P 501, $1.95
"The story is well planned and well written."
—*The New York Times*

P. M. Hubbard

HIGH TIDE P 571, $2.40
"A smooth elaboration of mounting horror and danger."
—*Library Journal*

Elspeth Huxley

THE AFRICAN POISON MURDERS   P 540, $2.25

"Obscure venom, manical mutilations, deadly bush fire, thrilling climax compose major opus.... Top-flight."

       —Saturday Review of Literature

MURDER ON SAFARI   P 587, $2.84

"Right now we'd call Mrs. Huxley a dangerous rival to Agatha Christie."   *—Books*

Francis Iles

BEFORE THE FACT   P 517, $2.50

"Not many 'serious' novelists have produced character studies to compare with Iles's internally terrifying portrait of the murderer in *Before the Fact,* his masterpiece and a work truly deserving the appellation of unique and beyond price."   *—Howard Haycraft*

MALICE AFORETHOUGHT   P 532, $1.95

"It is a long time since I have read anything so good as *Malice Aforethought,* with its cynical humour, acute criminology, plausible detail and rapid movement. It makes you hug yourself with pleasure."

       —H. C. Harwood, Saturday Review

Michael Innes

DEATH BY WATER   P 574, $2.40

"The amount of ironic social criticism and deft characterization of scenes and people would serve another author for six books."

       —Jacques Barzun and Wendell Hertig Taylor

HARE SITTING UP   P 590, $2.84

"There is hardly anyone (in mysteries or mainstream) more exquisitely literate, allusive and Jamesian—and hardly anyone with a firmer sense of melodramatic plot or a more vigorous gift of storytelling."

       —Anthony Boucher, The New York Times

THE LONG FAREWELL   P 575, $2.40

"A model of the deft, classic detective story, told in the most wittily diverting prose."   *—The New York Times*

THE MAN FROM THE SEA   P 591, $2.84

"The pace is brisk, the adventures exciting and excitingly told, and above all he keeps to the very end the interesting ambiguity of the man from the sea."   *—New Statesman*

Thomas Sterling

THE EVIL OF THE DAY   P 529, $2.50

"Prose as witty and subtle as it is sharp and clear...characters unconventionally conceived and richly bodied forth .... In short, a novel to be treasured."   —Anthony Boucher, *The New York Times*

Julian Symons

THE BELTING INHERITANCE   P 468, $1.95

"A superb whodunit in the best tradition of the detective story."   —August Derleth, *Madison Capital Times*

BLAND BEGINNING   P 469, $1.95

"Mr. Symons displays a deft storytelling skill, a quiet and literate wit, a nice feeling for character, and detectival ingenuity of a high order."   —Anthony Boucher, *The New York Times*

BOGUE'S FORTUNE   P 481, $1.95

"There's a touch of the old sardonic humour, and more than a touch of style."   —*The Spectator*

THE BROKEN PENNY   P 480, $1.95

"The most exciting, astonishing and believable spy story to appear in years.   —Anthony Boucher, *The New York Times Book Review*

THE COLOR OF MURDER   P 461, $1.95

"A singularly unostentatious and memorably brilliant detective story."   —*New York Herald Tribune Book Review*

Dorothy Stockbridge Tillet
(John Stephen Strange)

THE MAN WHO KILLED FORTESCUE   P 536, $2.25

"Better than average."   —*Saturday Review of Literature*

Simon Troy

THE ROAD TO RHUINE   P 583, $2.84

"Unusual and agreeably told."   —*San Francisco Chronicle*

SWIFT TO ITS CLOSE   P 546, $2.40

"A nicely literate British mystery . . . the atmosphere and the plot are exceptionally well wrought, the dialogue excellent."   —*Best Sellers*

Henry Wade

THE DUKE OF YORK'S STEPS P 588, $2.84
"A classic of the golden age."
  —Jacques Barzun & Wendell Hertig Taylor, *A Catalogue of Crime*

A DYING FALL P 543, $2.50
"One of those expert British suspense jobs . . . it crackles with undercurrents of blackmail, violent passion and murder. Topnotch in its class."
  —*Time*

THE HANGING CAPTAIN P 548, $2.50
"This is a detective story for connoisseurs, for those who value clear thinking and good writing above mere ingenuity and easy thrills."
  —*Times Literary Supplement*

Hillary Waugh

LAST SEEN WEARING . . . P 552, $2.40
"A brilliant tour de force." —Julian Symons

THE MISSING MAN P 553, $2.40
"The quiet detailed police work of Chief Fred C. Fellows, Stockford, Conn., is at its best in *The Missing Man* . . . one of the Chief's toughest cases and one of the best handled."
  —Anthony Boucher, *The New York Times Book Review*

Henry Kitchell Webster

WHO IS THE NEXT? P 539, $2.25
"A double murder, private-plane piloting, a neat impersonation, and a delicate courtship are adroitly combined by a writer who knows how to use the language." —Jacques Barzun and Wendell Hertig Taylor

Anna Mary Wells

MURDERER'S CHOICE P 534, $2.50
"Good writing, ample action, and excellent character work."
  —*Saturday Review of Literature*

A TALENT FOR MURDER P 535, $2.25
"The discovery of the villain is a decided shock." —*Books*

Edward Young

THE FIFTH PASSENGER P 544, $2.25
"Clever and adroit . . . excellent thriller . . ." —*Library Journal*

**If you enjoyed this book you'll want to know about
THE PERENNIAL LIBRARY MYSTERY SERIES**

Buy them at your local bookstore or use this coupon for ordering:

Qty	P number	Price

postage and handling charge $1.00
_____ book(s) @ $0.25

TOTAL

Prices contained in this coupon are Harper & Row invoice prices only.
They are subject to change without notice, and in no way reflect the prices at
which these books may be sold by other suppliers.

**HARPER & ROW, Mail Order Dept. #PMS, 10 East 53rd St., New
York, N.Y. 10022.**
Please send me the books I have checked above. I am enclosing $_____
which includes a postage and handling charge of $1.00 for the first book and
25¢ for each additional book. Send check or money order. No cash or
C.O.D.s please

Name_____

Address_____

City_____ State_____ Zip_____
Please allow 4 weeks for delivery. USA only. This offer expires 12/31/83.
Please add applicable sales tax.